"I'm no angel," Jenna said firmly. "I'm just a woman who wants to help her sister."

Margo hugged Jenna tightly. "You are a good person. My daughter is lucky to have you in her life."

Margo kept hugging her and thanking her while it occurred to Jenna that, although they'd never be friends, she wouldn't be able to think of Margo in quite the same way again. Jenna's body slowly relaxed and she patted the other woman on the back, realizing that in this, at least, they were allies.

"Clay was right to bring you to Memphis."

The declaration reverberated through Jenna. "You mean Clay intended all along for me to help Darcy?"

"Of course. Clay's not the kind of man who stands by and does nothing when he has the means to make a difference."

The means to an end, Jenna thought.

"Are you okay, Jenna? You look pale."

"I'm fine," she lied. She had to find Clay. Jenna no longer wanted to surprise him, as she'd planned when she set out from Little Rock this morning.

She wanted the truth.

Dear Reader,

Carrie Fisher gave me the idea for *The Other Woman's Son*. Yes, the Carrie Fisher who was Princess Leia in the *Star Wars* movies. She was being interviewed about how her father, Eddie Fisher, famously left her mother, Debbie Reynolds, for Elizabeth Taylor.

In the next breath she talked about her affection for her half sister Joely Fisher. Joely is the daughter of another of Eddie Fisher's wives, but the account got me thinking about the havoc the other woman can wreak on a family.

Thus Clay Dillon and Darcy Wright were born, characters who in my book are the other woman's children. Jenna Wright, the heroine of the story, is the daughter of the woman scorned. Add Darcy's pressing need for a kidney donor and things get more complicated than a Hollywood actress's family tree.

Another character in my story is the setting. Two summers ago I was one of a skeleton group of parents who accompanied our sons to a national basketball tournament in Memphis. While my son's team was winning the eighty-four-team tournament, I was falling in love—with the city.

I hope a little bit of that love comes through in the story. Not only for Memphis, but for the precious gift of family.

All my best,

Darlene

THE OTHER WOMAN'S SON

Darlene Gardner

HARLEQUIN®

TORONTO • NEW YORK • LONDON
AMSTERDAM • PARIS • SYDNEY • HAMBURG
STOCKHOLM • ATHENS • TOKYO • MILAN • MADRID
PRAGUE • WARSAW • BUDAPEST • AUCKLAND

ISBN-13: 978-0-373-78176-8
ISBN-10: 0-373-78176-8

THE OTHER WOMAN'S SON

This is a work of fiction. Names, characters, places and incidents are either the product of the author's imagination or are used fictitiously, and any resemblance to actual persons, living or dead, business establishments, events or locales is entirely coincidental.

This edition published by arrangement with Harlequin Books S.A.

® and TM are trademarks of the publisher. Trademarks indicated with ® are registered in the United States Patent and Trademark Office, the Canadian Trade Marks Office and in other countries.

www.eHarlequin.com

Printed in U.S.A.

ABOUT THE AUTHOR

While working as a newspaper sportswriter, Darlene Gardner realized she'd rather make up quotes than rely on an athlete to say something interesting. So she quit her job and concentrated on a fiction career that landed her at Harlequin/Silhouette Books, where she wrote for Harlequin Temptation, Harlequin Duets and Silhouette Intimate Moments before finding a home at Harlequin Superromance.

Please visit Darlene on the Web at www.darlenegardner.com.

Books by Darlene Gardner

HARLEQUIN SUPERROMANCE

Don't miss any of our special offers. Write to us at the following address for information on our newest releases.

Harlequin Reader Service
U.S.: 3010 Walden Ave., P.O. Box 1325, Buffalo, NY 14269
Canadian: P.O. Box 609, Fort Erie, Ont. L2A 5X3

To Ebony Brown, for graciously answering my
questions about dialysis and kidney failure.
I couldn't have asked for a better source
and you couldn't be a more worthy advocate.
Any mistakes, of course, are mine.

And to my buddies in basketball,
Marian Covino and Beth Marson,
because we'll always have Memphis.

PROLOGUE

JENNA WRIGHT BOPPED down the stairs to the beat of a song she'd heard that funny man John Belushi singing in the movie she'd watched last night with her big brother.

"Gimme some lovin'," she sang, then sang it again, those being the only words she remembered.

She hit the ground floor running, her small bare feet slapping against the kitchen tile. Maybe she could talk Mom into getting her a black hat and black sunglasses like the cool guys in the Blues Brothers movie wore.

"Gimme some…"

She skidded to a stop beside the wall phone, the words dying on her lips. Mom had been talking on the phone when Jenna got the idea to put on her bathing suit and cool off with the water sprinkler in the backyard. Even though the window air-conditioning units were running, the house still felt hot.

Where was Mom?

Jenna scratched her head, feeling her sloppy ponytail get even messier. Mom wouldn't like it if Jenna didn't ask permission. Mom didn't like much since they moved from the big house in Memphis to this tiny one in Little Rock.

But Jenna so wanted to get wet. Maybe then some of the kids on the street would come over and she'd have friends like she used to in Memphis.

She was about to yell for Mom when she heard a sob. Then another. And another.

Jenna's heart jumped like the frog she'd seen down by the creek when her brother Jeff took her for a walk. She followed the sounds to the family room and froze.

Mom sat in a chair, her face in her hands, her body sort of shaking. Jeff must have heard Mom first, because he was moving toward her. He looked real sad, like he had on the day they'd left Memphis.

"Are you okay, Mom?" he asked.

Mom's head jerked up. She wiped at the tears on her cheeks and smiled, but not her happy smile. The smile she'd used when the kid next door asked where Jenna's daddy was.

"I'm fine, Jeff."

Jenna was only eight, but she could see that

Mom wasn't fine. Jeff must have known it, too, because he put a hand on Mom's still-shaking shoulder. Jenna felt so scared she thought she might throw up.

"Was that Dad on the phone?" Jeff asked. A pretty dumb question. Whenever Dad called, Mom usually yelled, mostly about "that woman."

Mom rubbed her head like it hurt, then shook it. "No, honey." Her voice was all slow and tired like. "It was your Grandma Wright. She called about your Dad and Margo."

Jenna grew even more still. They didn't talk about Margo. Ever. If Dad hadn't met her, they'd still be living with him in the big house in Memphis and Mom wouldn't cry so much.

Mom squeezed her eyes tight but tears still ran down her face. "They had a baby girl. Darcy."

Jenna's mouth dropped open. She knew that Margo had a son about her age, but Jenna couldn't picture her with a baby. Jenna had only seen Margo once, in front of a restaurant back when Mom and Dad were still married. Margo didn't look like a mom. She looked like a model in a magazine.

"Grandma wanted to tell you Dad won't be coming to visit this weekend after all," Mom said.

Jenna's stomach felt like it dropped to the floor and splattered. Since they moved to Little Rock,

Dad had only been to see them once. Jenna didn't remember exactly when that was but it had been cold enough that she'd been wearing her red winter jacket.

And now Dad wasn't coming to visit because of the baby who was making Mom cry.

Maybe Dad loved the baby more than he loved her and Jeff. Jenna got a yucky feeling behind her eyes and blinked hard a couple times to try to get rid of it.

"I'm going upstairs for a little while." Mom squeezed Jeff's hand, then got slowly out of the chair.

Mom took the other way out of the family room, away from where Jenna still stood. But the house was so small that Jenna heard Mom sobbing again on the stairs. Jeff left the house, the screen door leading to the cement back porch banging shut.

Jenna blinked some more, then followed him outside. Jeff would make things better. He always did.

She found him sitting in the shade on the cracked top step, staring at the water spraying from the sprinkler. He barely glanced at Jenna when she sat down beside him.

"I heard you and Mom talking," she said.

"Then you know about the baby." His voice

sounded funny, like he was trying not to cry, too. Her heart jumped again, like that frog was trapped inside her. Jeff had just turned thirteen. She hadn't heard him cry in forever.

"Uh-huh," she said. "Mom said they named her Darcy."

"A dumb name for a dumb baby," Jeff spat out.

They sat in silence, watching the water soak the brown grass. The grass even smelled dry. Jenna heard birds singing, dogs barking and, in the distance, what sounded like a baby crying.

Jenna liked babies. Maybe it wasn't so bad that Margo and Dad had one. Their baby would be real tiny so of course Dad had to stay with it in Memphis this weekend. That didn't mean he wouldn't come to visit Jenna and Jeff other times.

He might even bring the baby. Before they'd left Memphis, Jenna's best friend Rachel's dad had a baby girl with his new wife. Rachel lived with her mom but told Jenna the baby was her sister.

"Jeff," Jenna asked softly, "is baby Darcy our sister?"

He whirled on her, his face all scrunched up and fierce looking. "No!"

"But if she's Dad's baby, wouldn't she be our—"

"No," Jeff snapped. "And don't you ever say that again."

That horrible feeling behind Jenna's eyes returned. "But why?"

"Didn't you hear Mom crying? Dad left her for Margo. He left us for Margo, too."

"But he still loves—"

"If he loved us, he'd come visit. He loves Margo and the baby now. And Margo's son, too."

Jenna tried to stop her tears from coming, but her eyes still got as wet as the grass. She no longer felt like singing a Blues Brothers tune or playing in the sprinkler.

Long moments passed before Jeff awkwardly patted her thigh. "Aw, don't cry, Jenna. Mom and me are all the family you need."

For the first time Jenna could remember, Jeff hadn't made her feel better. That could be because he was crying, too.

CHAPTER ONE

Twenty-two years later

CLAY DILLON COVERED his sister Darcy's much smaller hand with his, hoping the dread flowing through his veins like icy river water hadn't chilled his skin.

She glanced at him with wide blue eyes, and he tried to convey with his expression that they'd get through this crisis no matter what the news.

Their mother Margo sat rigidly on the opposite side of Darcy, her pink lipstick standing out starkly on a face that had gone pale despite her expertly applied makeup.

If the patient consultation room hadn't been rather richly redecorated and the slim, somber man behind the gleaming mahogany desk hadn't lost three-quarters of his hair, time would seem as if it had rewound.

Dr. Phillip McIntyre tapped his chin, a habitual gesture Clay recognized from the last time the family had dealt with him. It meant the doctor was having difficulty putting his thoughts into exactly the right words.

"I'm sorry to have to inform you of this, but the biopsy confirmed our suspicions." His somber voice contrasted vividly with the Memphis sun streaming through the blinds. "The kidney is indeed failing."

Clay's stomach plunged like a skydiver realizing that his parachute wouldn't open. The diagnosis, though, came as no surprise. The creatinine levels in Darcy's blood had been rising, an early indication her kidney wasn't filtering out waste products the way it was supposed to.

The doctor's compassionate gaze zeroed in on Darcy, who'd inherited their mother's heart-shaped face and blond good looks. Except now Clay let himself notice that her complexion appeared sallow and her skin puffy. Clay tightened his hand on hers. Blood seemed to rush to his head, clogging his ears, making it seem like Dr. McIntrye's voice came from a distance.

"Darcy, we need to put you back on the transplant list."

A voice in Clay's mind screamed at the injustice, but he schooled his features and said nothing. Neither did Darcy, whose right hand sheltered the spot where the doctor had extracted a sample of tissue from her kidney to be biopsied.

"But she was doing so well." The anguished protest erupted from their mother. "And you said the kidney could last for decades."

Dr. McIntyre pushed the glasses up his nose and tapped his chin some more. The sunlight shone on him through the skinny slats of the blinds, casting his face in both light and shadow. "I said that although there have been cases of cadaver kidneys lasting for decades, those instances were isolated. We hoped the kidney Darcy received would last longer than five years, but that isn't a terrible result for a cadaver organ."

Had it really been five years?

The ordeal actually began even longer ago than that. Darcy had been only ten or eleven when the family's new pediatrician discovered that a previously undiagnosed strep infection had damaged Darcy's kidneys. Still, it had come as a shock to learn that Darcy had end-stage organ failure at age sixteen.

The shock precipitated a nightmare that Clay remembered as vividly as if it had happened yesterday.

Four-hour dialysis sessions three times a week that purified his sister's blood but drained her of energy. The dawning realization that she needed a transplant. The agonizing wait for a cadaver organ. Then the anxiety-filled predawn trip to the transplant center when a matching kidney finally became available.

The transplant had been successful, and the nightmare ended. Until today, when it started again.

"You'll have to go back on dialysis until a donor organ becomes available. The sooner, the better," Dr. McIntyre told Darcy. "Let's see. Monday's Memorial Day. So I'd suggest you start the treatments Tuesday."

Today was Friday. A muscle in Darcy's jaw tensed, but other than that she exhibited no outward sign of the disappointment that must be raging inside her. Her silence worried Clay more than an outburst would have done. Even at her sickest, Darcy was the most unremittingly cheerful person Clay knew.

"How long do you think it will be before my daughter can have another transplant?" Their mother's voice shook, and Clay wished he'd sat between the two females so he could hold both of their hands.

The doctor gazed at the open file on his desk and shuffled papers before raising his eyes and peering over the top of his rimless glasses. "I can't seem to find the information here, so refresh my memory on how long the wait was last time."

"Nine months," their mother answered immediately.

Nine *interminable* months, Clay thought.

Darcy had barely recovered from one dialysis session when it came time for another. She'd fallen hopelessly behind in her classes, eventually being forced to repeat her junior year of high school.

"Ah, yes," Dr. McIntyre said. "I remember Darcy was extremely lucky to get that kidney. Unfortunately, we can't count on something like that happening this time. You do recall the problems associated with the blood type. Type-O blood means she can only receive a donated organ from another individual with type-O blood. But since type-O is the universal donor, those cadaver kidneys can and do go to sicker patients of other blood types. Added to that, Darcy has an uncommon tissue type that makes it even tougher to find a match."

"Give us a ballpark estimate of the wait time," Clay said.

"Ballpark, I'd say two to four years if we're lucky, but it could be even longer."

Clay fought to keep himself from recoiling, which wouldn't help his silent sister. Even two to four months on dialysis was too long.

"You do know, of course, that matching

kidneys from living donors tend to last significantly longer and function better than cadaver
kidneys," Dr. McIntyre said. "But I recall that
several members of your family have already
been tested."

Clay had volunteered first, armed with the
knowledge that blood relatives presented the best
chance for a match. He'd quickly learned about
the importance of tissue typing, the blood tests
comparing six specific antigens between the potential donor and recipient. None of Clay's
mirrored Darcy's, and further testing determined
him to be a poor match.

"Everybody was tested but nobody was a
suitable donor," their mother replied.

"Then we have no choice than to proceed with
the plan of action I've outlined." The doctor began
to explain about the transplant team being assem-
bled to work on Darcy's case, but Clay no longer
listened.

No choice.

In Clay's experience, there was always a
choice.

When the bar he owned in downtown Memphis
had come up for sale, the first loan officer he
visited had informed him no bank would lend
him the money for a down payment. So he'd
traded in his new Mustang for an old clunker, sold

his condo to cash in what little equity he'd accrued and visited every bank in the city until one put together a loan package.

No choice.

That simply wasn't true.

His mother misspoke when she claimed everybody in the family had been tested. Clay could think of two notable exceptions, although Clay himself was no relation to either Jenna or Jeff Wright.

He was surprised he even remembered the names of his stepfather's children from his first wife. His mother had married Donald Wright when Clay was eight years old, making Darcy his half sister. It had always troubled him that Darcy's two other half siblings, who were around his age, had never bothered to meet her.

Clay had strongly suggested those half siblings be tested the last time Darcy needed a transplant, but his stepfather shot down the notion after discovering a cadaver kidney was an option. Donald claimed his first wife, and her children by extension, harbored a grudge the size of the state of Tennessee.

Donald couldn't veto the idea anymore: He'd died two years ago after a sudden heart attack.

Clay knew little about his late stepfather's oldest two children except that they'd been so far estranged from their father they hadn't bothered to attend his funeral. That wouldn't stop Clay.

No choice.

Clay would see about that.

JUST SAY NO.

Great advice, if you could bring yourself to say it.

Jenna Wright hadn't managed it, which was why on Friday night she found herself passing under the larger-than-life bird painted over the entrance to the Blue Mockingbird Saloon in downtown Little Rock.

She could have legitimately claimed she didn't have the time. For the past nine years she'd worked for Morgan and Roe, a full-service public accounting firm specializing in assisting private corporations and high net-worth individuals.

If not for her job and the personal financial statement it had been imperative she finish for an important client, she wouldn't be arriving with only—she glanced at her watch—two minutes to spare.

Yes, she should have said no.

Even though she hadn't really wanted to.

She consciously slowed her pace once inside the bar, as though she hadn't just dashed from the third floor of a nearby parking garage after fighting heavy Friday-night traffic.

Customers filled the Blue Mockingbird, the

happy hour crowd having not yet headed for the door. Some of them milled about, drinks in hand, laughing and talking. Others, like the raucous group of men with two half-full pitchers of beer, jammed tables.

The crowd surrounded her, but nobody seemed to pay attention to her entrance except the petite woman who met her at the foot of the stage clutching an acoustic guitar. She was dressed in a clinging ebony pant outfit that accentuated her long, black hair.

"I've never been so happy to see someone in my entire life." Only Corrine Sweetland could make over-the-top relief seem charming.

Jenna and Corrine had instantly hit it off as University of Arkansas freshmen when they'd both been members of the Jazz Club. Although Jenna dropped out of the club to concentrate on her accounting classes and Corrine left college before her sophomore year, they'd remained friends.

Corrine had waged a constant struggle to eke out a living throughout the ensuing decade, playing the guitar and singing backup vocals for a succession of rhythm-and-blues and jazz bands that never hit it big.

Jenna enjoyed attending Corinne's gigs whenever her busy schedule permitted, but had never gone back on stage herself, keeping to her long-ago decision to give up singing.

Jenna still wasn't exactly sure how Corrine had talked her into performing at the Blue Mockingbird. At first Jenna had listened sympathetically as a panicked Corrine relayed how she'd made arrangements for the gig before her latest band had splintered. Jenna had agreed that Corrine, as band manager, ran the risk of getting a reputation for not fulfilling commitments if she couldn't figure out a solution this time.

Before Jenna knew it, she was the lead singer for a temporary rhythm-and-blues duo called Two Gals. Corrine was the guitarist and back-up vocalist.

"You might not be glad I'm here after I start singing," Jenna told Corrine, glancing over her shoulder at the noisy happy-hour crowd. She felt her heart speed up, like the sticks of a drummer playing eighth notes. "The audience might not be, either."

Corrine pinned her with the huge hazel eyes that stood out against her pale skin even when she wasn't accentuating her lashes with coal-black mascara. "I've heard you sing. Trust me, they'll love you." She made a face. "As long as you don't croak the first song," Corinne teased.

"I warmed up my voice in the car on the drive

over." Jenna nodded at a nearby wall clock, which showed the time as seven o'clock. The owner of the Blue Mockingbird had insisted on an early start time to provide the happy-hour crowd a reason to stick around once the prices went up. "So we can start anytime."

"Anytime after you lose the jacket."

Jenna tugged the lapels of the cream-colored fitted blazer she wore with chocolate-hued slacks. "What's wrong with my jacket?"

"You look like you're heading to the office."

"I just came from there," Jenna said even as she shrugged out of the jacket and laid it on a nearby table. "How's this?"

"Undo the top two buttons of your shirt and roll up your sleeves." Corrine surveyed her critically. "Not bad. But before our next performance, girl-friend, we're going shopping. You got it, so we should flaunt it."

"I'd rather leave the flaunting to you."

"I've got no problem with that. We're perform-ers, Jenna. We're supposed to flaunt it." Corrine executed a shimmy with her shoulders, then smiled encouragingly. "Let's do this."

The time of reckoning upon her, Jenna posi-tioned herself behind one of two microphones on the stage. She grabbed it and gazed out into the maze of people. The sprawling bar featured dozens of tables, banks of big-screen televisions on two of the walls, a circular bar in the center of the main room and a billiards room off to her right. The stage seemed almost like an afterthought.

"Good evening and welcome to the Blue Mockingbird. I'm Jenna Wright, and this is Corrine Sweetland. Together, we're Two Gals."

Nothing. None of the patrons indicated they'd heard her. Panic seized Jenna, causing her lungs to feel like something was sitting on them. How could she have let Corrine talk her into this? She hadn't sung in public since college. A spot under her eye twitched, the way it did when she was nervous.

Her gaze darted to Corrine. Her friend nodded, her expression encouraging. *You can do this,* she mouthed. Jenna inhaled deeply, exhaled slowly and faced the disinterested crowd. She'd intended to explain their repertoire included blues, jazz and soul and that most of the songs were new renditions of old favorites. But nobody was listening.

"Our first song," she spoke into the microphone, "is 'Today I Sing the Blues.'"

Corrine strummed her guitar, and the bluesy beat seemed to penetrate Jenna's skin and sink into her. Singing had come easily to Jenna from the time she was a small child and the church choir director noticed her big voice.

Others had noticed, too, eventually leading to invitations from various bands to join them. She'd been confident enough in her voice back in high school that she'd been a natural performer, but doubts crept up on her now.

She drew in another deep breath to guard against the shaky, uncontrolled sounds nerves caused, then determinedly launched into the song, a mournful ballad about the loser in a love affair.

Despite the precaution, she felt her neck muscles contract and her blood pressure elevate. Signs that her voice was about to start trembling unless she did something quick. An old trick came back to her, and she swung her gaze wildly around the bar, searching for friendly faces.

A blonde with a spiky haircut who would have fit in at a punk-rock concert set down her glass and swayed to the music, a contented smile curving her lips. Jenna's shoulders relaxed.

A craggy-faced man with deep lines bracketing his eyes and mouth nodded as she sang about walking the darkest avenue. Jenna's blood pressure fell back to its normal level.

She lowered the pitch of her voice to wring

out the full effect from the song, probing the crowd for somebody else to provide unwitting encouragement.

Her gaze collided with a pair of dark eyes attached to one of the most interesting faces she'd ever seen. She wouldn't label the man handsome, exactly. But high cheekbones, heavy brows, a long nose, a sensuous mouth and eyes she could tell were coal-black even from this distance made it impossible to look away.

Not until she tripped over a lyric she'd practiced a dozen times did she muster the will to wrench her gaze to the opposite side of the room.

Who was he?

Somebody distracting her from the song, an internal voice warned. A grave error for a singer. If she didn't feel the music, how could she expect the audience to?

Avoiding the man's gaze, she finished the song, heartened by the applause. Now that she and Corrine had captured the audience's attention, she recited the spiel she'd originally intended to open with.

"Now that we know each other better, what do you say we get down to earth with some…" She paused, lowering her voice a full octave. "…'Downhearted Blues.'"

Despite her resolve not to look at him, a quarter

of the way through the song her gaze swung to the dark-haired man. And found his eyes locked on her.

She couldn't say for certain why she'd picked him out of the crowd. Even though he was sitting down, she could tell he was a tall man. She preferred men who were less physically imposing and not so…intense.

She didn't need to look at him again to know he still regarded her with that same single-minded concentration. She drew energy from that knowledge, pouring it into her music, infusing it into her voice. By the end of the set, she'd thoroughly captured the crowd's attention.

"This is great. Did you hear the groan when you announced the break?" Corrine asked when they stepped off the stage.

"I did," Jenna said.

"Keep it short. I like the idea of striking when the crowd is hot for us."

The adrenaline that had fueled Jenna through the performance dropped off, and she collapsed into a chair beside the wooden table nearest the stage. Corrine sat down next to her.

"You knocked them dead." Corrine reached for her hand, briefly squeezing it. "But next time, take pity on my nerves and show up on time."

"I couldn't help it. I warned you it's tough to

get out of the office Friday nights. I have a job, remember?"

"Don't shoot the messenger, but I have to say this. Singing should be your job."

"Singing's a guilty pleasure," Jenna said. "Accounting pays the bills."

To bolster her position, Jenna could have pointed out the struggles Corrine endured to be a musician: Low pay, irregular bookings and zero job security. Before Corrine had married personal trainer Maurice Sweetland, her friend had worked on and off as a waitress to supplement her income.

"So you keep saying," Corrine said, but her attention wasn't on Jenna.

Following Corrine's gaze, Jenna spotted the dark-haired man navigating the labyrinth of tables. She guessed his age at about thirty, his weight at maybe two hundred pounds, his height at six feet two. *Too tall,* she thought. His lean, hard body hinted that he worked out with weights. There was nothing soft about him except, perhaps, the texture of his thick hair, the ends of which nearly reached his collar. *Too long.* He wore jeans and a collarless, short-sleeved knit shirt in a deep shade of brown that hugged his chest. *Too casual.*

It quickly became clear that the man was

headed for their table. Jenna's heart took a leap worthy of Dwyane Wade, her oldest nephew's favorite NBA player.

"Do you know that guy?" she asked Corrine.

"Never seen him before. But even us married ladies can enjoy the view. Besides, you're the one he's coming for."

He stopped shy of the table, standing there for long seconds, drinking her in with those midnight eyes that complemented brown hair so dark it verged on black. Jenna's cheeks grew warm, a puzzling response. She never reacted this way to a man, especially to a man who was so not her type.

"At the risk of telling you something you've heard before, you, lady, can really wail." He delivered the line in an understated southern accent with a charming half grin that softened the angular planes of his face.

"She has heard it," Corrine interjected with a friendly smile. "From me. About thirty seconds ago."

"Then you're as smart as you are talented." The man smiled back at Corrine. "You play a mean guitar."

He wants something, Jenna thought. She shifted in her seat, uncomfortable with the suspicion it might be her. She dated semiregularly, but usually she met the men through work or friends. She didn't let herself get picked up in a bar.

"We appreciate the compliments." Corrine included Jenna in her reply. "You know, with a tenor like yours, you can probably wail yourself."

His half grin become full fledged. "You'd be the one wailing if you heard me sing. In pain, I'm afraid. I'm Clay Dillon."

The name seemed vaguely familiar but Jenna would remember if she had ever encountered this man before. She was closer to him than Corrine so she was the one to whom he offered his hand.

"Jenna Wright." She fought off her reluctance to touch him and shook. His skin was warm, his touch firm, the feeling it elicited uncomfortable. He might not be her type, but he'd managed to get her to notice him. "And this is Corrine Sweetland."

He let go of Jenna's hand, turning to shake Corrine's. "It's a pleasure to meet you both. You ladies mind if I join you?"

"If it's okay with Jenna, it's fine by me," Corrine said, obviously charmed.

When her friend stated it that way, Jenna could hardly refuse his company without seeming rude. "Sure."

He settled into his seat with long-limbed grace,

aiming his dark gaze at Jenna. "I confess I have an ulterior motive for coming over here."

"Oh?" Jenna had already made up her mind to refuse should he proposition her, but her pulse rate still rocketed. "And what is that?"

"I'd like to hire Two Gals to play at my bar in Memphis."

CLAY KEPT HIS EYES fastened on Jenna Wright, refusing to feel guilty for not telling her they shared a half sister.

He could see nothing of Darcy in her, except a certain gentleness in her expression he might be imagining because he wanted it to be there.

She seemed to have gone through pains to play down her appearance. She'd rolled up the sleeves of a fawn-colored blouse more suited for the office than the stage. She hadn't bothered to play up her appealing features with makeup, which rendered them ordinary from a distance. And she wore her auburn hair in a conservative shoulder-length cut instead of long and loose.

He'd been watching the entrance so had noticed her arrival but hadn't pegged her as the singer until she took the stage. The transformation from inconspicuous to vibrant had been amazing, as though a different woman lived inside this button-down version.

Tracking her down had been surprisingly easy. He'd pumped his stepfather's former law partner for information, yielding no clues about Jeff Wright but discovering his sister Jenna worked as an accountant at a firm called Morgan and Roe in Little Rock.

After the friendly secretary at Jenna's office blabbed that Jenna would be singing tonight at the Blue Mockingbird, Clay had hopped in his car for the two-hour trip from Memphis to Little Rock. He'd turned over various ways to approach her as he drove but ruled them all out when she started to sing.

He would have disagreed the end justified the means before Darcy became ill, but he no longer believed that. Since Jenna hadn't recognized his name, fate was on his side.

"I guarantee the offer's on the level," he said. "My bar is called Peyton's Place."

Corrine's expression brightened. "Like that TV soap opera from the sixties? My mom used to talk about that."

Clay didn't bother to correct her, finding it smarter not to reveal the true inspiration for the name. "I bought the bar a year ago. Recently, I decided live entertainment would help business."

Recently, as in about an hour ago.

Jenna's eyes seemed to narrow, but Clay could

be imagining her skepticism. Despite everything, his conscience panged.

"I've grown up listening to rhythm and blues. I can recognize talent, and you ladies have it," he continued. "I couldn't walk away tonight without making you an offer."

A heavy dose of truth ran through his proposal. Jenna and Corrine had a rare chemistry, made extraordinary by the raw, sensual power of Jenna's voice. Persuading the duo to perform at Peyton's Place could help the bottom line—even if assuring Jenna had regular contact with the half sister she might come to love was his main objective.

Corrine placed her elbows on the table, as though readying herself to get down to business. A very good sign. "So where in Memphis is this bar of yours?"

"Beale Street." The legendary *Home of the Blues,* Beale Street was the second most-visited street in the south, trailing only Bourbon Street in New Orleans. Musicians made reputations there. "It's on the very end of the section of street blocked off to traffic, but it's still a great location."

"Anywhere on Beale's a great location," Corrine declared.

"How long are you under contract to the Blue Mockingbird?" Clay asked.

"Only until the end of the long weekend,"

Corrine said. "The owner might want to extend our gig, but we're free to entertain other offers."

"Wait, Corrine." Jenna placed a hand on the table. Clay noticed she'd painted her fingernails bright red, an interesting quirk in such a conservatively dressed woman. "Aren't you forgetting something?"

Corrine looked beseechingly at Jenna, something unspoken passing between the two women. "What's wrong with listening to what Clay has to say? C'mon, Jenna. This is Beale Street."

Jenna hesitated, then conceded, "I guess it can't hurt to just listen."

Sensing resistance, Clay named a figure higher than what good sense dictated for an establishment that had just started to turn a profit. "If that's not more than the Blue Mockingbird is paying, I'll top their offer. I'll also commit to a six-week engagement. How does Wednesday through Saturday nights sound?"

"Impossible." Jenna emphasized her response with a shake of her head. "I should have told you right away I can't perform in Memphis. I have a job here in Little Rock."

A job that would blow Clay's plan apart. His heart seemed to slam to a stop.

"Jenna's an accountant." Corrine sighed, as though sharing that bit of information pained her.

Jenna straightened her spine, and her mouth tightened. "That's right. I am an accountant. Singing's a hobby."

"You're talented enough to sing full-time," Clay said.

"And give up my job security? No, thanks. I wouldn't be singing at all if Corrine hadn't been obligated to the Blue Mockingbird. Once this job's over, I'm through singing. I certainly can't run off to Memphis for half the week."

Clay deliberately misunderstood the thrust of her argument. "What if the performances are only on Friday and Saturday nights? The bands on Beale don't get going until about nine, so you could leave Little Rock after work Fridays."

"It'd be fun, Jenna," Corrine interjected. "We can drive down to Memphis together. You're the one who always says we don't hang out enough."

Sensing Jenna's reluctance to disappoint her friend, Clay jumped in. "I'll sweeten the pot by paying for your weekend hotel stay." An expense he really couldn't afford.

"We can't turn that down, Jenna." Corrine had definitely gotten into his corner. "I know you feel strongly about the singing being temporary, but it's only six weeks. That's no time at all."

The jukebox stopped playing, signaling the time had come for Two Gals to begin its second set. The bar crowd generated an impressive amount of noise, but silence resonated at the table.

"What do you say, Jenna?" Clay prodded.

Jenna gazed back and forth from Clay to Corrine, who practically vibrated while she waited for her friend's answer. The silence stretched into what seemed like an eternity. "I suppose we can give it a try."

"Awesome." Corrine clapped her hands.

Clay tried to hide his overwhelming relief. "I'll have a contract drawn up, but for now a handshake will do. Corrine, you're the deal maker, right?"

"Right." Corrine eagerly stuck out her hand.

Clay clasped Corrine's hand but watched Jenna. She appeared wary, as though she didn't entirely trust him. She shouldn't, considering his whopper of an ulterior motive.

He shook off the image of himself as a fraud, preferring to think of himself as a loving brother trying to provide Darcy with a chance at a normal life.

Jenna would surely offer to get tested once she knew and loved Darcy. If the tests determined Jenna could be Darcy's kidney donor, Clay would console himself that the end really did justify his means.

CHAPTER TWO

"DON'T WORRY ABOUT ME. I'll be fine."

After her declaration, Darcy Wright deliberately raised the edges of her lips. The way she'd trained herself since learning four days ago that she needed a second kidney transplant.

Darcy's mother, standing in front of her dressed in a trendy tennis outfit, expected that sort of blind optimism. So did her brother Clay. Besides, if Darcy let the happy mask she'd worn during the Memorial Day weekend slip, she might not be able to put it back on.

"This doesn't feel right, Darcy. I shouldn't be playing tennis at the country club while you're getting your first dialysis treatment."

"I appreciate that, Mom. I really do. But I've gone through dialysis before. I know what to expect. And it's not like I'll be there all alone. Kenny's coming with me."

After breaking the news to her boyfriend of six months that her kidney was failing, Darcy had let her stiff upper lip quiver and asked him to keep her company at her initial session. He'd been as sweet as the sugar-coated chewy candy she used to snack on years ago, before doctors instructed her to carefully monitor her diet.

"I adore Kenny. You know that. But I'm your mother. I should be there, too."

Not if Darcy could help it. She'd learned from experience that her mother had an even harder time watching Darcy go through dialysis than Darcy did experiencing it.

"I don't need both you and Kenny there. Honest," Darcy said. "I already had to get special permission for Kenny. The people at the center would flip if I tried to bring both of you into dialysis."

Her mother shifted her weight from one foot to the other, and Darcy absently noticed her tennis shoes featured pink Nike swooshes. "Are you sure?"

"Definitely." Darcy boosted the corners of her mouth higher. "I'd hate for you to miss your Tuesday tennis match because of me, especially because you're looking so good."

"In this old thing?" Her mother swept a hand over the hot pink lycra top she'd paired with a navy blue and pink skirt that showed off her excellent figure. She'd tied her shoulder-length blond hair in a ponytail that showed off the pretty face she pampered with skin-care products. "I'm dying to get a new outfit but so far I've resisted."

"That one looks great." Darcy hoped it had finally gotten through to her mother that the household cash flow had died with Darcy's father. They could still afford the house and Darcy's college tuition, but not much else. Certainly not a country club membership. Her mother was going as a guest.

"I suppose I should head out then." Her mother's reluctance showed through in every word.

"Have fun."

"I'll try. But I'll be thinking about you every single minute." She kissed Darcy on the cheek, the light scent of her perfume lingering even after she left the house.

Darcy didn't allow her face to relax until the engine of the Jaguar her father had paid off before he died roared to life. She blew out a breath and massaged the muscles that had held up her smile.

Constantly reassuring her mother and brother that everything would be okay could be exhausting. Kenny, at least, didn't hover. They hadn't seen each other since she'd filled him in on her situation Friday night.

He'd gone through with plans to leave Saturday

morning with some college buddies for a three-day canoeing trip. She hadn't dreamed of asking him to cancel but wouldn't have minded a phone call to see how she was doing.

Shoving the thought aside, she moved over the terrazzo floors through the house that her mother had hired a top interior designer to decorate in a southwestern motif. Fabric-covered sofas, leather accent chairs and throw rugs artfully scattered on the floor reflected the red, tan and brown colors of the desert. Original landscapes by local artists hung from the walls but the most stunning view was that of the Mississippi River through the bank of large windows lining the back side of the house.

The home sat along a mile-long sidewalk situated on a bluff above a gently curving street running along the mighty river, but it was reachable by car only from the front side.

The window above the hammered copper sink in the kitchen afforded a view of the road. Darcy poured herself a half glass of ice water from the dispenser in the refrigerator door, then sipped it while she watched for Kenny Coleman's Mustang. Since dialysis patients had to limit their fluid intake, the cool water sliding down her throat felt like a luxury.

She tried to mentally talk herself out of being

disappointed that Kenny hadn't called. Instead, she'd think about how his presence would help her avoid worrying about the future while she was hooked up to the dialysis machine.

Fifteen minutes after he was supposed to arrive, Kenny's red Mustang convertible finally swung into the driveway. Even from inside the house, Darcy could hear rock music blaring from the car stereo.

She gathered up her backpack and went quickly out the door, striving to convey an eagerness to get the treatment over with. She was loath to let anyone, even Kenny, know how much she dreaded it.

He met her halfway up the driveway, looking like a college coed's dream in sunglasses, khaki shorts, a University of Tennessee T-shirt and flip-flops. The sun had kissed the ends of his brown hair, and his tanned skin glowed with health and vitality.

"Hey, gorgeous."

That was Kenny, Darcy thought. The king of charm, able to sound sincere even though Darcy realized she'd probably never looked worse.

"Hey, Kenny."

He leaned down to close the eight-inch gap in their heights and kissed her on the mouth, the contact brief and almost chaste. She got a whiff of a peppermint breath mint before he took the backpack dangling from her hand. "Ready to go?"

She summoned her smile. "Ready as I'll ever be."

He opened the passenger door, dumping the backpack in the backseat before stepping aside to let her in and closing the door. Like a true gentleman. That had been one of the things that attracted her to him in the first place.

They'd met at the University of Tennessee after she brushed too close to a display of texts at the campus bookstore. The stack had toppled, raining tomes onto the floor. Kenny helped her pick them up, making her laugh by apologizing for not noticing disaster was imminent. He'd carried her purchases to the cash register, claiming the only thing he'd accept as thanks was a date. They'd been together ever since.

A bonus in dating Kenny was that he lived not even ten miles away, which would enable them to see each other as often as they liked now that the spring semester was over.

"How'd the canoe trip go?" she asked after he slowed the Mustang to a crawl to give a sanitation truck room to pass on the narrow road.

"It was a blast." He turned the radio down

slightly. "You've met Harv, right? Tall, skinny guy with long sideburns and a soul patch. He told us he'd been on the river plenty of times. First thing he does is steer the damn thing straight into a huge rock. We hit so hard, I fell off my seat.

"Then he hangs us up on some smaller rocks and has the bright idea to get out of the canoe to jostle us loose. So me and the canoe are drifting downstream and Harv's swimming as fast as he can behind to catch up. Jake and B.B. were laughing so hard they couldn't row."

Kenny kept up a lively commentary the entire drive to the transplant center, which featured its own dialysis facilities. He didn't seem to notice Darcy had to make an effort to laugh. She was almost glad when they pulled up to the center, because she didn't think she could fake it much longer.

Bypassing the parking lot, he pulled up to the horseshoe-shaped curb in front of the building and put the Mustang into Park. Darcy's muscles froze, rebelling at the prospect of walking into the building alone.

"You don't have to let me off here." She kept her voice light. "From what I remember, everybody's pretty understanding if you show up a few minutes past appointment time. So I can walk with you from the parking lot."

"About that…" His voice trailed off, then started up again. "B.B's starting his new job Wednesday. He didn't get a chance to move his stuff into his new apartment yet because of the canoe trip. So I kind of told him I'd help him. You don't mind, do you?"

Her throat constricted, preventing speech. She managed to move her head, but she wasn't sure in what direction.

"Didn't think you would." His voice got louder, more cheerful. "It's not like I can do anything when you're on that machine but sit there."

His dark sunglasses rendered it impossible for her to read his eyes and figure out how he'd arrived at that stunningly bad conclusion.

"But—" she began.

"So what time should I pick you up?" He tapped the clock on the dashboard, which showed a few minutes past ten o'clock. "How about one-thirty? If that's not good, call me on my cell."

She nodded wordlessly and got stiffly out of the car, as though she were a robot somebody had programmed to move. She barely acknowledged the short beep of the horn as he drove away.

Her lower lip trembled so much that she caught it with her upper teeth to still it. She'd counted on Kenny to help get her through this first treatment, but now she had to face it alone.

She put one foot in front of the other, drawing inexorably closer to the center. A handsome older man who looked like Kenny might in twenty years opened the door for her. She tried to smile when she stated her thanks, but couldn't.

The faint smell of antiseptic that she associated with the center hit her like a blast from a fan when she stepped into the lobby. Her steps slowed. She couldn't do this. Not by herself.

She blindly whirled back toward the exit, nearly plowing into a tall, solidly built man. He reached out his arms, placing them on her shoulders to steady her.

"You all right, Darcy?"

She blinked until the moisture that had started to gather in her eyes cleared and the man's face came into view. Clay, her brother, a deep V of concern drawing his dark brows together.

"What are you doing here?" she blurted out.

"What kind of question is that to ask your big brother? I'm here to keep you company." The smile he wore looked even less genuine than the ones she usually pasted on. His gaze flickered over the lobby. "Where's Mom?"

"You know how she gets in places like this. I convinced her not to come because Kenny would be with me."

"Then where's Kenny?"

Darcy swallowed, unable to tell him how Kenny had bolted. "He'll be by to pick me up."

His expression hardened, and she got the strong impression he'd heard what she hadn't said. "No need for that. I'll still be here when you're finished."

Relief flooded through her like water cascading over a broken dam. But she couldn't ask Clay to spend four hours holding her hand, not when he already did so much for her.

"You don't have to stay, you know. I'll be just fine," she said, her tone less convincing than she would have liked. "I understand you have a business to run."

"My business can wait." Flinging an arm around her shoulders, he steered her toward the elevator.

Her heart felt somewhat lighter, the prospect of four hours hooked up to a machine not as daunting. But she was well aware that the treatment marked the beginning of a long, difficult journey.

If Clay realized that, why hadn't Kenny?

TOO GOOD TO BE TRUE.

Her brother Jeff's words echoed in Jenna's mind that Friday as she and Corrine stepped into the hotel elevator from the floor where they were sharing a deluxe double room during their first weekend in Memphis. Clay Dillon had made good on his word, putting them up at the Peabody, one of downtown Memphis's classiest and best-known hotels.

Corrine was strangely silent, giving Jenna time to reflect on her brother Jeff's reaction to the Memphis gig. She'd told him the news earlier that afternoon when she phoned his brokerage firm to cancel their weekend dinner plans.

"Something about this sounds too good to be true," he'd said. "What do you know about the guy who owns the bar, anyway?"

"I know he thinks I can sing."

"Of course you can sing, but you haven't performed in years. You said yourself you were rusty. So why you?"

"He hired me and Corrine, Jeff, not just me."

Even as she responded, Jenna feared her answer was misleading. From the moment her eyes had met Clay Dillon's, she'd gotten the impression it was about her.

"I have a call on another line so I've got to go." He sounded rushed, the same way he always did. "But do me a favor and check him out. People aren't always what they seem."

Excellent advice. Too bad he'd issued it too late to take him up on it. She should have thought to check out the tall, dark and mysterious Clay Dillon herself, of course, but she'd been swamped at work.

"Do we know for certain Clay Dillon is legitimate?" she asked Corrine as the elevator car descended to the lobby floor.

Corrine shifted her guitar case from one shoulder to the other and released an audible sigh. "Could you stop already?"

"Stop what?"

"Making me feel guilty for dragging you into this. My career hasn't exactly played out like I imagined it would. And, well, chances like this don't come around very often. I appreciate you coming on board."

"I know that, Corrine. I agreed so you could get the exposure you deserve." Jenna ignored the internal voice that suggested the pleasure she got from performing had something to do with it, too. "I'm simply asking how closely you checked out Clay Dillon."

"I took a trip to Memphis to see Peyton's Place before I sealed the deal."

"That's checking out the bar, not the man."

"The man owns the bar. The bar's on Beale Street." Corrine had reported the bar was "cozy," which probably meant it was tiny. "What are you so worried about? Clay put us up at the Peabody, just like he said he would."

The Peabody was a Memphis institution, as much a tourist attraction as a hotel courtesy of the ducks that marched to and from the sculpted fountain in the Grand Lobby twice daily to a John Philip Sousa tune. On a red carpet, no less.

Corrine had talked excitedly of witnessing the duck parade after learning where they'd be staying, but hadn't even complained they'd arrived too late for the show.

Come to think of it, Corrine had been subdued all day.

The elevator opened to the Grand Lobby, the focal point of which was an expansive bar area featuring the sculpted fountain where the mallard ducks spent their days before retiring to a rooftop cage. Stately columns, plush furniture, a stained-glass ceiling and deco-style lights added to the drama of the Lobby Bar, where patrons with drinks in hand were thanking God it was Friday.

As they walked through the richly appointed space, Jenna touched her friend's arm. "You okay, Corrine?"

"Sure." Her brittle smile didn't reach her eyes, but Jenna knew Corrine well enough to realize she wouldn't talk about what was bothering her until she was good and ready.

The Peabody was on Union Avenue in the heart of downtown Memphis, just a few blocks from the segment of Beale Street closed to traffic every evening. Summer hadn't yet officially arrived, but the June night was balmy, the air settling heavily over the city and dampening Jenna's brow by the time they arrived on Beale. They walked the long way, so they could take in the atmosphere.

Shops, restaurants and clubs lined the street, with neon lights proclaiming the names of establishments and live music drifting from doorways. The party crowd didn't stick to the sidewalks, straying into the middle of the street. Some held huge plastic cups of ale they'd bought at the sidewalk counter advertising Big Ass Beer.

An Elvis impersonator in a sequined outfit and blue suede shoes belted out a song on a street corner, his tip jar in front of him. A massive man with a parrot perched on his shoulder strolled in front of them. Conversation, nearby traffic noise and music blended together, bombarding the senses.

"Wow. It's crowded," Jenna said.

A large, noisy group of twentysomethings passed by, nearly separating them. Corrine hooked an elbow through Jenna's. "It's always packed on weekends. But why don't you know that? You grew up here."

"Mom, Jeff and I moved to Little Rock when I was seven." Jenna didn't have to tell Corrine how traumatic the move had been for all of them. Her friend already knew Jenna's heartbroken mother had left Memphis after a younger, prettier woman had broken up her marriage. "I haven't been back to Memphis in years."

Jenna vividly remembered her last visit eight years ago when her boss signed her up for a financial analysis seminar. The seminar had ended unexpectedly early, which Jenna took as a sign to call the father she hadn't seen in years.

She remembered her fingers shaking when she dialed his office number and her voice trembling when she asked if he was free. He pronounced it wonderful to hear from her and arranged to meet her for a drink at a downtown bar.

After a single martini and some awkward silences, he apologized for having dinner plans and left. Her father had lived six more years, but that was the last time Jenna talked to him. She hadn't been back to Memphis until today.

"I'm glad you're here with me." Corrine nudged her elbow, a quintessential Corrine gesture. The closer they got to Peyton's Place, the more whatever had been bothering her friend took a backseat to her excitement.

They continued walking along the four-block section of street, the crowd thinning exponentially until Clay Dillon's bar came into view. The building had a brick facade with bay windows flanking the doorway, over which green neon letters spelled out Peyton's Place.

The interior of the establishment was long and narrow, with a bar featuring green rails and corrugated steel running half the length of one mirrored wall. Photos of jazz and blues legends hung on the opposite wall above a series of green vinyl booths. A smattering of tables filled the space between bar and booths. Fans and lights on chains hung from a ceiling that had been painted the same shade of green found in the green-and-black checkered linoleum floor.

At first it seemed as though the raised stage was at the very rear of the place, but Jenna spotted a corridor lined with more booths that probably led to the kitchen and restrooms. She couldn't decide whether Peyton's Place really was bigger than it looked or only seemed that way because it couldn't have been more than one-quarter full.

"Let me guess. You two are Two Gals." A petite woman with long, curly red hair and the tattoo of a butterfly on her upper arm approached them, gesturing at Corrine's guitar case. "I'm Vicky. Clay asked me to tell you to get started whenever you're ready."

"Where is Clay anyway?" Corrine asked.

"He went to pick up a friend of his he just hired

to tend the bar." Vicky shook her head and muttered, "As though giving the guy a job when he knows nothing about mixing drinks wasn't doing enough."

"Why'd he hire him then?" Jenna asked.

"The guy needs the paycheck. But, geez Louise. We need a bartender who knows what he's doing." She made a face, perhaps realizing she'd said too much. "Anyway, Clay'll be here soon."

Jenna followed Corrine onto the stage, then excused herself to find a restroom while Corrine tuned her guitar. Only two stalls occupied the small space, both of which were empty, so she began her vocal warm-ups. She used the same ones she'd learned as a child, hissing like a snake and buzzing like a bee. She was midhiss when she emerged from the restroom.

"I hope you're not directing that hiss at me." Clay Dillon suddenly appeared in front of her, heading the opposite way down the narrow hallway leading to the restrooms.

She'd been sitting when they met so hadn't realized how tall he was, probably a good six inches taller than her five-eight. *Too tall,* she thought. He was dressed similarly to the other night, in jeans and a collarless shirt, this one in black. The shirt wasn't so tight that it showed off the definition in his chest, but she noticed how powerfully built he was all the same. *Too muscular.*

"No, of course not," she said. "I was just warming up my voice."

"I'm looking forward to it. Once word gets around about how good you are, we'll start filling up this place." His smile crinkled the corners of his eyes, and she felt silly for suspecting him of God only knew what. He was a bar owner trying to increase business, and she was a means to that end. "How's the Peabody? The room okay?"

"The room's beautiful." She itched to get back to the stage, but guilt over her previous mistrust of him caused her to prolong the conversation. "I hear you have a new bartender."

"Oh, yeah. Nick. He's a friend from high school who just got married. He and his wife had a baby a month ago."

The new wife and baby vividly explained why his friend needed a job. She couldn't help admiring Clay for providing one, even if his friend did lack experience.

"I should be getting back to the stage," she said. "It's almost time for us to start."

"Of course."

She moved to pass him but the hallway was so narrow that her body brushed his. Their eyes met, and awareness washed over her, as surprising as it was acute. She took a breath and caught his scent, a pleasant blend of soap, shampoo and warm male skin.

"Sorry," he said, continuing past her as though nothing out of the ordinary had happened.

She moved to the stage without looking back, telling herself she'd imagined the moment. She drew her share of male interest, but she was hardly a femme fatale who knocked men dead with her stunning looks. And he certainly hadn't done anything to indicate he'd hired her for anything more than professional reasons.

Clay Dillon, by all indications, was a stand-up guy who gave jobs to friends in need and thought Two Gals could improve his bar's bottom line.

Jenna disregarded her lingering suspicion about the gig being too good to be true. In a very short time her temporary singing career would come to a screeching halt. She intended to enjoy her good fortune before it did.

CLAY STOOD BEHIND THE BAR, his arms crossed over his chest. The rich texture of Jenna's voice washed over him as she sang an Aretha Franklin song. Her dark slacks and button-down shirt were only slightly less casual than the clothes she'd worn in Little Rock. She again seemed like a different woman on stage than off: more spontaneous, less guarded and lit by an inner passion he couldn't detect while talking to her.

He felt the unwelcome pull of attraction, but pushed it aside. It could only lead to complications in a situation already complex enough. She finished the song, acknowledged the applause from the light crowd, then sipped a glass of water while Corrine took center stage with an instrumental version of a Ray Charles song.

"Clay, did you hear a word I said?"

Vicky Smith, the best waitress in Memphis, stared up at him from across the bar, her elbows perched on the wooden surface. She stood about five feet nothing, but what she lacked in height she made up for in personality.

"You need a couple drafts?" he guessed.

"Not right now, I don't. All my customers have what they need." Her gaze challenged him to try again.

"You were complaining about Seth?"

"That doesn't prove you were listening," she rejoined. "I always complain about Seth."

"I was listening. You said he accused you of having an affair."

"He always does that, too, the big jerk. He's gentle as can be with me but swears he'll tear apart the guy I'm sleeping with. As though I'd fool around with one guy while dating another. You know I'm not that kind of woman, right?" She didn't wait for a response. "Then why doesn't he?"

"He's got a jealousy problem."

"You think?"

"I know." With difficulty he tore his attention from the stage and focused his full attention on Vicky. "Guys like Seth, they don't change, Vick. If he's this jealous now, it'll only get worse if you marry him."

"If? You're saying I should rethink the engagement?"

Hell, yeah, except he would have used the word "break" instead of "rethink." This was a conclusion Vicky needed to reach on her own. "I'm saying I want you to be happy. Since you started dating this guy, I haven't seen a whole lot of smiles from you."

She closed her eyes briefly. When she opened them, he saw resignation. "I knew there was a reason I go to you with my problems. Sometimes you're pretty smart."

"Sometimes? Mensa would be lucky to have me," he teased.

"I said sometimes, and I meant sometimes. You hired Nick, didn't you?" She nodded toward the new bartender, who consulted a book while mixing what looked to be a gin and tonic. "By the way, you should go for it."

He brought his gaze back to Vicky. "Go for what?"

"The singer. You can't take your eyes off her."

Had it been that obvious? "That's because she's talented."

She snorted. "Yeah, right."

Vicky left to tend to her tables. Clay wondered how the waitress would react if he confided the primary reason for his interest in Jenna, not that he was free to do so. Darcy had begged him not to tell anyone at the bar about her kidney problems.

No matter. He'd done what he needed to get Jenna to Memphis. His next step was bringing Darcy to Peyton's Place so the half sisters could finally meet, which could happen tonight because he'd suggested Darcy stop by with her boyfriend to hear the duo.

"Hey, Clay." Darcy appeared at the bar as though his thoughts had conjured her up. But, no. If he imagined his sister, her smile would be genuine. She usually appeared lit from an inner glow, but her essence seemed dimmed today.

"Hey, Darcy. Can I get you something?"

"What I'd really love is a big old glass of wine," she said wryly, "but I suppose tonic water will have to do. Half a glass, please."

"Coming right up," he said.

As he filled the glass part way and topped it with a lemon, he mentally reviewed what he knew of her dialysis routine. The physically taxing treatments took her out of commission for the rest of the day, but she usually bounced back on off days. She'd settled on Tuesdays, Thursdays and Saturdays for the treatments, so today was an off day. Still, if her rate of kidney failure had increased...

"Are you feeling okay?" he asked as he handed her the tonic water.

"Shh." She brought a finger to her rosebud lips and raised the light-colored eyebrows that marked her as a true blonde. "If your employees hear you, they'll ask me how I'm feeling every single time they see me, the same as you do."

He couldn't argue her point. Most of the people who worked for him knew Darcy, either from when she'd helped out at the bar last summer or her impromptu visits.

He was careful to keep his voice down. "I wouldn't keep asking if you promised to tell me when you don't feel well."

"I feel fine today," she said.

It didn't escape his notice that she'd qualified her statement with "today" and that she hadn't made any promises. "Then what's wrong?"

"Am I that transparent?" She rolled her eyes, seemingly more at herself than him. "It's Kenny."

"Is he parking the car?"

"I don't know where he is. We were supposed to hang out, but he cancelled on me at the last minute."

Clay felt his back muscles tense. First Kenny let Darcy down on her first day of dialysis and now this. "Did he say why?"

"He thinks he might be coming down with something."

Clay hadn't forgiven the younger man for not realizing how much Darcy needed his support during her first dialysis treatment, but he couldn't fault Kenny for canceling tonight's date. Not when kidney disease compromised his sister's immune system.

"You can't afford to get a cold, Darcy," Clay said.

"I can't live in a bubble, either." If another female had answered him that way, she would have sounded snappish. But Darcy managed to convey her point with wry good cheer. "I didn't feel like staying in, so I called a couple girlfriends but they already had plans. So here I am."

"I'm glad you're here." He reached across the bar and patted her on the cheek. "As long as you don't stay out too late."

This time she very definitely directed her eye roll at him. On stage, Corrine's impressive guitar work on the instrumental piece concluded, Jenna grabbed for the microphone.

"How 'bout I give you something to talk about?" she asked, then launched into the Bonnie Raitt song of the same name, interjecting the lyrics with a country twang. Corrine expertly accompanied her on slide guitar, but it was Jenna's throaty voice that filled every corner of the bar.

Darcy listened for a few moments, obviously enraptured. "She's good."

"She is," Clay confirmed.

"Hey, Clay, is a Long Island Iced Tea the sweetened or unsweetened kind? And where do we keep it?" Nick, the new bartender, cupped his hands around his mouth so Clay could hear his shouted question.

Hiding a groan, Clay held up a finger to indicate he'd be with Nick momentarily.

Darcy leaned over the bar and asked, "Did your bartender really just ask that?"

"He's new. A friend from high school."

"You want me to help him out?"

He wanted Darcy to take it easy and get well. "I'll handle it. You enjoy the music."

"Not a problem," Darcy said, her eyes on Jenna. "I'm going to find a table nearer the stage."

She left before Clay could say anything more. He frowned, realizing he hadn't thought past getting Jenna to Memphis. He didn't plan to keep her connection to Darcy a secret, but neither had he considered how to break the news.

"I got a customer waiting." Nick sidled over to him, panic in his wide, unknowing eyes. The seats at the bar had started to fill up, something Clay had failed to notice.

"A Long Island Iced Tea is a mixed drink, Nick. Equal parts vodka, rum, gin, tequila and lemon, with a splash of Coke for color. It's listed in that bartender's guide to mixed drinks I gave you."

Nick's brow furrowed. "Vodka, gin, whiskey and what else?"

"Not whiskey. Rum and tequila. But never mind. I'll make it. You help some other customers."

The next half hour passed in a blur even though the bar wasn't near capacity, mostly because of Nick's inexperience.

"I asked for a Vodka Collins and got a Vodka Martini," a customer groused to Clay. "Took a long time to get it, too. If not for the music, I'd be out of here."

"We've got a new bartender," Clay said. "Tell you what. The martini's on the house, and I'll personally make your next drink. How's that sound?"

"It sounds like I'm staying through the next set. Where's the duo from anyway? They're terrific, especially the singer."

"Little Rock. First time performing in Memphis. Tell your friends," he said into the silence that signaled the band was taking a break. Music from the jukebox kicked in.

He glanced at the wall clock, noted the time at nearly eleven and looked up to check on Darcy only to find the table where she'd been sitting empty. Unease pricked the back of his neck as he scanned the bar. Surely she'd have told him if she planned to leave.

Vicky approached, curly red hair streaming behind her, barking out a drink order to Nick as she came. "Three Bud drafts and a glass of white wine."

Clay made sure Nick pulled out the right glasses, then met Vicky at the bar. "Hey, Vick. Do you know where Darcy is?"

Vicky nodded toward the exit. "She followed that singer outside a couple minutes ago. Said she wanted to tell her how much she likes her singing."

CHAPTER THREE

AFTER SPENDING THE PAST few hours inside Clay Dillon's bar, Jenna expected the fresh air to invigorate her but humidity still hung heavily over the night.

"You were good in there," a man old enough to have listened to his share of the blues told her. "Kind of reminded me of Etta James."

"Thank you." She couldn't hide her delight at being compared to a blues great. Getting out into the humid air had reinvigorated her after all.

Peyton's Place was situated at a portion of the street that had a much quieter feel than the busiest part of Beale.

Not many people milled about except for herself and a quartet of young men, drinks in hand, clustered around a young blonde who'd exited Peyton's Place. Sensing trouble when the tallest and broadest of the four released a piercing wolf whistle, Jenna started toward them.

"Wanna party with us?" the big guy asked the blonde.

"Sorry, boys. I don't drink," the blonde said firmly but sweetly.

"Who said anything 'bout drinking?" The shortest of the four slurred his words and took what Jenna perceived as a threatening step toward the young woman.

"Mind your manners," the blonde scolded, still in the same sweet tone. "What would your mama say if she heard you?"

The other three erupted into good-natured laughter, ribbing their drunk friend until he was laughing, too.

"Give Peyton's Place a try tonight," she told them. "My brother owns the bar and he brought in a fabulous rhythm-and-blues duo."

The sweet little blonde who'd deftly handled the four raucous young men was Clay Dillon's sister? Able to drum up business for her brother's bar with the brilliance of her smile?

"We'll do that," the man who'd whistled at her said.

"You won't be sorry." She walked away from the men, straight toward Jenna, not stopping until she reached her. "I just had to come out here and tell you how much I love your singing."

"Thank you," Jenna said. "I'm a fan of yours,

too. I saw the way you handled those guys just now."

"Oh, that was nothing." She waved a hand in the general direction of where the men had been. "They were harmless. Just had a little much to drink, is all."

A slight southern accent softened her syllables, adding appeal to her voice. No more than five feet four with delicate features and golden-blond hair, she looked fabulous although dressed casually in jeans and a blue V-necked tee. Jenna couldn't determine the color of her eyes, but she was betting on blue.

"I heard you say Clay's your brother." Jenna didn't mention that she'd never guess they were related if she hadn't.

She brightened. "My big brother. Couldn't ask for a better one. A smarter one, either. He hired you, didn't he?"

Jenna laughed. "We'll see how that works out for him. Corrine and I aren't exactly an established act."

"But you're so good," she enthused, then made a face. "I'm gushing, aren't I? My excuse is that I was bowled over by your singing. Are you saying you're just starting out?"

"Starting over is more like it. Corrine's the professional musician. I'm an amateur who hasn't sung in ages."

"Why not?" No sooner had she asked the question than the young woman put a hand to her lips. "Listen to me, prying into your private life when I haven't even introduced myself. I'm Darcy."

"Darcy Dillon, that's cute. I'm Jenna."

"The name's actually Darcy Wright. Clay and I have different fathers."

All sound—tires swooshing over pavement on a cross street, guitar music from a street-corner musician, the voices of the other people nearby—seemed to cease.

Darcy Wright.

Although she hadn't heard the name spoken in years, Jenna recognized it immediately. It had been branded into her brain on that day her grandmother called to report her father's new wife Margo had given birth to a baby girl.

A baby girl named Darcy who had grown into a pretty blonde who looked uncannily like Jenna's memory of Darcy's mother. Jenna had only seen Margo Wright once, with Jenna's father in front of a restaurant when Jenna's parents were still married, but she'd never forgotten.

"Jenna. Are you alright?" Darcy cocked her head, her bow-shaped mouth pursed in concern.

Jenna hadn't used her surname in the introduction, and her first name obviously hadn't resonated with Darcy. The limited contact Jenna and her brother had with their father had dwindled in the years after their parents divorced until his visits had stopped. Eventually, so had his phone calls and birthday cards. Jenna didn't imagine her father had often spoken of her to his second family, if at all.

"I'm fine." Jenna gestured to the bar. "It's just that I've got to get back inside."

"Oh, yes. Clay will be wondering where you've gone, especially when his customers start clamoring for you to start singing again."

The shock of finding herself face-to-face with Margo's daughter wearing off, Jenna belatedly processed the information and realized exactly who Clay Dillon was. Margo's son. The eight-year-old who'd moved into her father's grand old house after Jenna, Jeff and their wounded mother had been shunted aside.

The knowledge that Jeff had been right about Clay Dillon shocked her to her core.

Clay and his offer really had been too good to be true.

CLAY SWEPT PAST THE FOUR young guys who came into the bar carrying plastic cups of beer, not bothering to direct them to a table or tell them it was against bar policy to bring in outside alcohol.

He burst through the exit into the humid night, his frantic gaze searching the immediate vicinity. The streetlight caught the sheen of Darcy's blond hair, but he was too late.

His sister stood facing Jenna Wright, who held herself more stiffly than the giant replica of the Statue of Liberty that one of the downtown Memphis churches had erected a few years back.

He half walked, half jogged toward the two women, intent on damage control.

"Clay, there you are." Darcy greeted him with her customary smile. "If you're here for Jenna, I'm through flattering her. So you two can go on back inside."

Darcy hadn't guessed who Jenna was, he thought, his mind turning over ways to tell her. His gaze moved to Jenna, whose glare could have frosted the Memphis air.

Jenna had figured it out.

A car horn sounded from the cross street. He looked up and saw his mother's Jag idling at the curb.

"I called Mom to pick me up so I've got to run. Jenna, nice meeting you. Maybe next time I'll be able to keep my eyes open longer so I can hear more of you." Darcy stood on tiptoes, kissing Clay on the cheek. "Bye, Clay."

She headed toward the Jaguar, her steps not as

quick as they could have been. Was she leaving because she didn't feel well? Or had her stamina simply given out? Her next dialysis treatment, Clay knew, was ten the next morning.

"That's her in the car, isn't it?" Jenna's voice couldn't have been colder. "That's Margo."

The way she said his mother's name spoke of unresolved anger, another variable Clay hadn't anticipated. He thought any residual anger on her part should be directed at her late father.

Jenna didn't wait for his reply. "This isn't a co-incidence, is it? You knew who I was all along."

"I can explain," Clay said.

"I doubt that." Her eyes flashed with the inner fire she'd displayed in a much more positive light on stage. Her hair seemed fiery, too, the street-lamp highlighting the auburn hue. "There's no possible way you can justify not telling me who you were the minute you introduced yourself."

"I did tell you. Clay Dillon, owner of Peyton's Place."

"Don't play games. You knew I didn't recognize your name." Her voice trembled with anger. "You knew, and you didn't tell me."

"Like I said, I can explain."

"Go ahead," she challenged, taking a step closer and glaring up at him. "Explain."

Clay hesitated. If he told Jenna about Darcy's

need for a donor kidney now, before she had time to process what a truly amazing person Darcy was, she'd walk away and never come back.

"I'm waiting," she snapped.

He rubbed the back of his neck, unsure of what he could say that wouldn't make the situation worse. "You're right. It wasn't a coincidence. I found out you were singing at the Blue Mockingbird and went to Little Rock to persuade you to get to know Darcy."

"Why?"

Although he couldn't reveal the whole truth yet, he could tell her part of it. "It seemed wrong that you two had never met. She's as much your half sister as she is mine."

"I don't think of her that way. How could I after your mother broke up my parents' marriage?"

Clay bristled. He suspected his mother had been involved with Donald Wright before Donald was divorced, but he loved her all the same. "My mother wasn't the one who left your family. She didn't make any vows to anybody."

"You're twisting things around." With a slash of her hand, Jenna completely dismissed his argument. "Nothing you say can justify you tricking me into coming to Memphis, anyway. What kind of a man does something like that?"

A man desperate for his sister to live a long, healthy life, he thought.

"I didn't plan it. I was blown away by your voice. Even if you weren't Donald's daughter, I'd have tried to hire you."

Skepticism descended over her face. "That doesn't explain why you didn't tell me you were Margo's son."

"Would you have agreed to sing at my bar if I had?"

"Definitely not."

"You've proved my point."

She aimed a finger at him. "Your point seems to be that you feel justified in manipulating me. And manipulating your sister, too. She obviously doesn't know who I am."

Clay didn't like the way her accusation made him sound but could hardly argue. "I meant to tell Darcy, the same way I meant to tell you, but I haven't managed to find the right time."

"Don't tell her," she retorted. "She seems like a nice girl, but she's not someone I want in my life."

"That's crazy. She stops by the bar pretty regularly." He threw up his hands. "How can you expect to keep something like that from her?"

"Easy. I'm not going to keep singing at your bar."

His breath caught at the implication of what that would mean to Darcy. "But Corrine signed a contract."

"And you'd hold us to it? After the secret you kept from me?" She annunciated every word, her expression incredulous.

He'd do almost anything to help his sister, but forcing Jenna to sing at Peyton's Place wouldn't accomplish that goal. Helping her reach the decision not to abandon the gig was a different matter.

"Maybe not," he said. "I know you're not looking to make singing your career, but Corrine's eager for a chance to prove herself."

He started to ask if Jenna could take that chance away from Corrine but swallowed the question when he realized how manipulative it would sound. He wasn't so blinded by Darcy's condition that he couldn't understand Jenna's anger.

She glared at him, her dislike as visible as the neon signs that dotted the Beale Street establishments. He didn't like himself very much at the moment, either.

"Jenna, where the hell have you been?" Corrine, her face appearing pale beneath her fall of black hair and matching dark clothes, rushed toward them on stacked heels. "We were supposed to go on ten minutes ago."

The guitarist tapped the toe of her right shoe, communicating her impatience.

Clay couldn't have orchestrated a scenario that would demonstrate more clearly how Corrine felt about performing at Peyton's Place. He glanced at Jenna, but she wouldn't look at him.

"It's my fault, Corrine." Clay returned his attention to the guitarist. "So it's okay with me that you're running behind schedule."

"I'd hate for the customers to get restless and head off to find live music somewhere else." Corrine talked fast, as though every moment spent away from the stage pained her. "Are you coming, Jenna?"

Clay felt his gut tighten as he waited for Jenna's answer. Corrine started to walk toward the bar, but Jenna didn't move, didn't speak. Time seemed to lengthen, although no more than a few seconds elapsed.

Obviously realizing Jenna wasn't following her, Corrine stopped and turned. "Jenna. Come on."

Jenna cast a final fierce glance at Clay before replying, "I'm coming."

Clay tried to relax as he watched Jenna trail her smaller friend into the bar, but relief wouldn't come. Jenna would perform as scheduled tonight, but there was no guarantee she'd take the stage tomorrow.

CORRINE WAITED UNTIL JENNA left the hotel room in search of coffee and a danish on Saturday morning before she auto dialed her home phone number. She listened to the phone ring at the house in Little Rock, her hands sweating so badly she could hardly grip the phone.

One ring.

Her husband Maurice loved to indulge himself on Saturday mornings by sleeping late, claiming he didn't have the chance any other day of the week.

Two rings.

Although Maurice had been known to sleep as late as ten, he usually rolled out of bed at around nine-thirty.

Three rings.

Corrine couldn't remember the last time he'd awakened before eight-thirty.

Four rings.

The time on the hotel's bedside alarm clock read seven fifty-nine.

"Yo. Talk to me, man."

Corrine's relief at hearing Maurice's trademark greeting was so great she almost dropped the phone. "Maurice, I—"

"If you're someone me or Corrine wants to talk back to, one of us will give you a call."

A beep sounded, confirming that the answering machine, and not Maurice, had picked up her call. He must have forgotten to tell her he'd changed the recorded greeting.

She disconnected the call without leaving a message, then cradled her head in her hands. He should have answered. They kept a phone beside the bed, because Maurice couldn't stand the thought of not being reachable if one of his aging parents should need him.

A full five minutes must have passed before she told herself not to jump to premature conclusions and lifted her head. Maurice always kept his cell on when he wasn't home. She speed dialed his number, the way she had last night when she couldn't reach him at home. He picked up on the third ring.

"Yo."

"Maurice, it's Corrine."

"Hey, babe," he mumbled, as though he'd been awakened from a sound sleep. "Didn't we just talk a couple hours ago?"

He'd claimed to be at his friend Eddie's house at a poker game that was just breaking up. He'd said he was heading home.

She swallowed and supplied the excuse she'd invented to justify her early morning call. "I was afraid the dehumidifier would flood the basement. I think I left it running."

"I'll check," he said.

She listened carefully, she wasn't sure for what, but couldn't hear any noises in the background.

"I called home before I tried your cell." Her heart beat so fast she thought she might pass out. "Why didn't you pick up?"

"I must have been outside getting the newspaper. I thought I heard the phone."

She didn't ask why he hadn't checked the answering machine for a missed call when he got back inside the house. He'd have an explanation. Maurice always had an explanation.

"You're up early today," she remarked.

"Couldn't sleep. Didn't have you next to me." He pitched his voice low and sexy, reminiscent of the way he sounded when they made love.

Despite her suspicions, she melted. A favorite memory of him getting down on one knee flashed through her mind. She could hear him proposing, saying he wanted to spend the rest of his life with the woman he loved.

She was probably letting her imagination get the best of her. Yes, he'd smelled of what she thought was perfume after poker night last week, but he'd had a ready excuse. It wasn't perfume at all, but the air freshener his friend's girlfriend used to mask the scent of smoke in the house.

The hotel room door swung open. Jenna

entered, holding two stacked coffee cups in one hand and anchoring them with her chin. She held the key card in the other.

"I should go," Corrine told Maurice. "Jenna just got back with caffeine."

"Tell Jenna I appreciate her being good to my girl. Love you, babe." He hung up, leaving Corrine listening to nothing.

"You, too," she whispered, then flipped her cell phone closed.

"The restaurant was crowded so I skipped the danish and got coffee to go. I thought you might like one, too." Jenna handed Corrine the extra cup. "Double cream, double sugar, right?"

"Right. Thanks."

Jenna sat down at the plush chair beside the mahogany desk and removed the plastic lid from her cup. "Were you talking to the charming Maurice?"

"You think Maurice is charming?"

Jenna's eyebrows shot up. "Don't tell me you haven't noticed your husband has a way with words?"

And with women.

"It's hard to miss." Corrine deliberately changed the subject. "It's just that you ignore Clay's charms so well, I was starting to think you were immune."

Jenna brought her coffee cup to her lips and drank before asking, "Why would you say that?"

"I saw the two of you talking last night. He's obviously into you."

"Not for the reason you think."

"What's that mean?"

Jenna cradled her coffee cup in both hands, staring down at the brown liquid before looking up at Corrine. "Nothing. He likes the way I sing, is all."

"I'd be surprised if that's all he's interested in."

"That's all it is," Jenna reiterated firmly. "What are you going to do today?"

"Catch the duck parade, then I was thinking about heading to Graceland." The idea of visiting Elvis Presley's former home had just occurred to her, but it seemed like a good one. Elvis could help take her mind off Maurice. "Want to come?"

"No, thanks. I brought some work with me, and this afternoon would be the perfect time to do it."

"No way," Corrine exclaimed in dismay. "The weekends are supposed to be about the music."

"I'll be singing the blues Monday morning if I don't get this stuff done, but we could go to the exercise room together. The caffeine's starting to kick in, so I have enough energy for a workout."

Corrine noticed for the first time that Jenna was dressed in yoga pants and a dri-fit top. "Are you kidding me? I burn plenty of calories playing my guitar, thank you very much."

After Jenna's laughter faded and Corrine was once again alone in the hotel room, her gaze fell on the cell phone she'd left on the bedside table.

If she called home now and Maurice answered, she'd know he was telling the truth about getting the newspaper when she phoned the first time. If not…

She heard the seconds tick by on the bedside clock radio until one minute had passed, then two. Before the minute display could click over a third time, she anchored her hands on the bed and rose.

As she rummaged through her suitcase for the clothes she'd change into after her shower, she pointedly ignored the phone still lying where she'd left it.

JENNA STEPPED INSIDE Peyton's Place and removed the sunglasses that had shielded her eyes from the brightness of the Saturday afternoon sun.

The bar looked different than it had the night before, the green of the tile and the booths more vivid, the wooden surface of the bar more glossy, the crowd even thinner.

But she could still feel the energizing thrill that

infused her when she sang to the crowd—and the anger that had engulfed her when she learned the reason she'd gotten the opportunity.

Determination had replaced the sharp edge of the anger, fueling her steps as she marched up to the bar. She'd finished her accounting work hours ago, but now needed to take care of the real reason she'd skipped the trip to Graceland.

"Is Clay Dillon around?" she asked a tall, shaggy-haired bartender of about twenty-five who hadn't been on duty the night before.

"He's in the kitchen. Should be right out. Can I get you a drink while you're waiting?" He had an engaging manner which made Jenna like him instantly.

"I'd love a double shot of whiskey," she said, thinking it would help her get through the confrontation to come, "but I don't drink in the afternoon."

His grin transformed his long, narrow, freckled face into something special. "How about a cola then?"

"No, thanks," she said. "All I need is for you to let Clay know I'm waiting."

"Sure thing."

She chose a booth farthest from the bar and a good distance from the other customers. Then she drummed her fingers on the table, fighting fatigue from her poor night of sleep. She wasn't sure whether her tossing and turning had kept Corrine awake or vice versa.

It hurt that Corrine hadn't confided what was bothering her, but then Jenna hadn't shared her problems, either. From past conversations, Jenna was well aware that Corrine believed she should become acquainted with Margo's daughter.

Corrine didn't understand how Jenna felt. She couldn't. Corrine hadn't been the one who'd watched her mother struggle to rebuild her life. Or who'd grown up in a house with a gaping hole where a father should have been.

A warm, male laugh drew Jenna's attention. Clay, his dark eyes crinkled at the corners, his lips split into a grin as he traversed the passageway leading from the kitchen. The grin disappeared as the bartender gestured to her table, but Clay didn't waste time in approaching her.

He moved with the grace of an athlete and the confidence of a man comfortable in his own skin. The soft blue shirt he wore with faded jeans of almost the same shade softened his appearance, but Jenna wouldn't make the mistake of underestimating what he'd do to get his way.

"Jenna. I didn't expect to see you." If he were anxious about encountering her at Peyton's Place in the middle of the afternoon, he didn't let on.

"You didn't expect to see me right now or you didn't expect to see me at all?" she challenged.

He slid into the booth across from her, his expression guarded. "I'm an optimist. I was betting on you showing up tonight."

"I'll be here tonight. And I'll keep coming until the terms of the contract are up."

He nodded, neither gloating nor showing surprise, as though he'd expected her to say what she'd said. It ticked her off all over again, because he didn't know anything about her.

"We moved to Little Rock after the divorce, because my mother couldn't stand the thought of running into your mother," Jenna said. "She got child support but no alimony, so she worked menial jobs during the day and went to school at night. I was seven. My brother Jeff was twelve. He watched me night after night, because my mother didn't have the money for a babysitter."

Clay said nothing, his eyes steady on her as she talked.

"We moved into a tiny house that was too cold in the winter and too hot in the summer. We were all homesick for Memphis. Those first few years, my mother cried all the time. We rarely saw my father. But eventually things got easier and we got through it."

"Why are you telling me this?" Clay asked when she paused to gather her thoughts.

"Because my mother used to say the three of us were all the family we needed." She sucked in some oxygen, finding the tale hard to tell. "That's the way it was. That's the way it still is. So I want to make it clear I won't have a relationship with your sister."

He crossed his arms over his chest. "How about me? Will you have a relationship with me?"

She fidgeted, annoyed at herself for reading nuances into the question that weren't there. He was talking about a business relationship, not a personal one.

"I realize it would be impossible not to because you own the bar. But we don't have to be…" She groped for a word. "…friendly."

He uncrossed his arms, leaned his strong forearms on the table and looked at her from under long, male eyelashes. "So sitting here like this, talking together, that's out?"

She had to clear her throat before she could manage a reply. "Unless it's about business, yes."

"Will you be unfriendly to Darcy, too?"

"Not if you don't try to push us together. That's why I came here today. To get assurances from you that you'll respect my desire not to get to know her."

He expelled an audible breath through his nose. "I can hardly tell my sister she's not welcome to drop by my bar."

"That shouldn't be a problem. If she shows up, I'll keep my distance."

His shoulders rose and fell in a sigh. "Okay, you've talked. Now it's my turn."

Her jaw clenched. "Whatever you have to say, I don't want to hear it."

"You mean you're too stubborn to listen to reason?"

"Reason?" Her voice spiked, and some of the customers at the bar slanted them curious looks. She made a concentrated effort to speak more softly. "Look who's talking about being reasonable. The man who manipulated me into coming to Memphis."

"I already told you why I did that. I thought it was time you and Darcy met."

Hadn't anything she'd said sunk in? She felt the blood rushing through her veins and pounding in her ears and couldn't remember the last time she'd been so angry. "I'm not about to let you or anyone else jerk me around. I make my own decisions."

"There's trouble." He uttered the remark under his breath but Jenna heard him.

"If you respect my wishes, there won't be any trouble," she retorted hotly.

"I wasn't talking about you." Clay nodded toward the entrance. A red-faced man wearing a backward baseball cap canvassed the interior of the bar, his fists clenched at his sides. The man wasn't overly tall, but his sleeveless shirt showed off arms rippling with muscle. "I was talking about him."

"Who is that?"

"Vicky's boyfriend Seth."

Jenna recognized the name of the petite waitress who'd worked last night. The redhead was nowhere to be seen, but Seth didn't seem to be looking for her. When Clay half stood, the enraged man charged like a bull drawn by the red of a matador's cape. He spewed cuss words as he came.

"You better run while you still can, Dillon, because I'm gonna beat your ass senseless," he cried.

Clay drew to his full height, not even flinching in the face of the other man's ambush. "I'd sure like to know why we're fighting first."

"'Cause you're screwin' Vicky, that's why," the man bellowed. He stood near enough to the booth that Jenna heard his harsh breathing and smelled the faint scent of sweat.

"Did Vicky tell you that?" Clay asked.

"I'm not an idiot," he roared. "Why else would she dump me?"

Jenna could think of a half-dozen reasons, and she hadn't officially met the man.

"I'm not sleeping with Vicky," Clay said.

A vein throbbed in the man's thick neck. "I don't believe you."

Jenna didn't doubt that under normal circumstances Clay could take care of himself, but Seth looked like one of those guys who spent his free time lifting weights and chugging protein shakes.

"It's the truth," Jenna heard herself say.

Seth spun to face her, his face even more flushed than it had been when he entered the bar. "How the hell would you know?"

"Because Clay and I are together." Jenna refused to flinch as she met his furious gaze. "You better believe I'd know if Clay were sleeping with someone besides me."

She avoided looking at Clay, focusing instead on Vicky's ex. Something shifted in the muscled man's expression. He scratched his head, then some of the fight leached out of him.

"Well, shit." He took off the baseball hat and rapped it against his thigh. "Then who is she sleeping with?"

"Maybe nobody," Jenna ventured.

"Like hell. Why else would she have broken up with me?"

Jenna could have told him jealousy wasn't an

attractive trait but couldn't risk making the situation worse.

"You need to leave the bar and not come back, Seth," Clay said firmly. "I can't have you coming in here making scenes."

Seth's massive chest expanded and for a moment it looked like he might still take a swing at Clay, but then his whole body seemed to deflate.

"I'm gonna find out who it is she's cheating with," he muttered before turning on his heel and stalking out of the bar.

Jenna's racing heart had slowed with Seth's retreat but picked back up when she became aware of Clay's penetrating gaze.

"Why'd you stick up for me?" he asked.

She fidgeted, not sure she could explain to him what she didn't understand herself. "Why does it matter? It worked, didn't it? He left."

"Yeah, he did. But I'd still like to know why you were chewing me out one minute and defending me the next."

"Maybe I didn't want to see you get punched in the face."

"I appreciate that, but I can take care of myself. I wouldn't be so sure he'd have gotten the better of me."

She took in his broad shoulders, lean musculature and the strength that emanated from him and knew he had a point. "It just seemed silly to watch him light into you because of a misunderstanding."

"That's another thing I don't understand." He anchored both hands on the lip of the table and leaned over it so far that Jenna pressed her back against the booth. "How can you be sure it was a misunderstanding? How do you know I'm not sleeping with Vicky?"

Her eyes flicked to his. "You're not, are you?"

"I did tell her she should think again about marrying Seth. But, no, I'm not sleeping with her. But why were *you* so sure of that?"

She searched her mind for a reason and couldn't dredge up one that made sense.

"Could it be because deep down you don't think I'm such a bad guy, after all?" he asked softly.

Because she was unwilling to acknowledge that his observation held the truth, she slipped out of the booth and stood up. "If I thought you were such a great guy, I wouldn't have asked you to stay away from me, now would I?"

She followed the same path Vicky's angry ex had taken, past the mostly empty tables and out into the sunlight. As an exit, it wasn't bad.

The damnable part was that in a few hours

she'd be back at Peyton's Place—and she probably still wouldn't know why she'd been positive Clay hadn't been having an affair with his waitress.

CHAPTER FOUR

CLAY NEEDED TO TELL DARCY about Jenna.

He'd reached that ironic conclusion less than an hour ago even as Jenna had tried to get him to say he wouldn't reveal the connection.

He carefully hadn't made any promises, unwilling to add lying to the wrong he'd already done by keeping the secret. Jenna's defense of him, in a strange way, had served to strengthen his resolve to come clean.

He wanted to be the sort of upstanding man she'd told Seth he was.

He pulled his Hyundai into the driveway of the house on Riverside Drive, spotting his mother poised to get into her late husband's Jag. She looked cool and sophisticated in a white cotton skirt and a pale pink cardigan set, her blond hair pulled back in an elaborate braid.

He briefly considered asking her to postpone leaving so he could include her in his confession, then rejected the thought. It would be best to sort things out with Darcy first.

He shut off the engine and got out of his car. "Hey, Mom."

No reply. He took stock of her wooden posture and the stark unhappiness on her face. Noticing unshed tears glimmering in her blue eyes, he quickly closed the distance between them. "What's wrong?"

She carefully wiped the moisture from beneath her eyes with the pad of a finger. "Nothing, really. I'm being a baby. It's just that Darcy had dialysis this morning and, well, you know how hard it is for her."

He was also well aware how difficult it was for his mother to watch her daughter suffer. He laid a hand on her shoulder, which felt knotted with tension.

"Dialysis is doing the work Darcy's kidney can't," Clay said.

"I know." Her pink-tinted lips trembled. "But at what cost? The treatments exhaust her. She came home and went straight to bed."

"Is she still sleeping?"

His mother sniffed. "She's awake now, but she seems so tired. I hate to leave her, even for a few hours, but she shooed me out of the house, insisting she'd be okay."

"I'm sure she'll be fine." He gently squeezed his mother's shoulder. "But I'll check to make sure."

"She was on the second floor terrace when I left the house." His mother laid a hand on his cheek. "You're such a good brother, Clay. Darcy's lucky to have you. We both are."

He thought about his mother's claim while climbing the interior stairs to the second floor of the house. A good brother? Would Darcy agree with that after he told her about Jenna?

The stairs led to a landing of white marble, beyond which were French doors opening onto a skinny terrace that ran the length of the back of the house. Clay immediately spotted Darcy, her forearms resting on the white railing as she gazed at a view he knew well. The house sat on a high bluff on the east bank of the Mississippi River, providing a view of Riverside Drive, a wide strip of greenery known as Tom Lee Park and the scenic river.

Darcy turned at the sound of the French doors opening, that familiar sweet smile of welcome curving her lips. "Hey, Clay. I'm surprised to see you. I thought you'd be at the bar by now."

Peyton's Place was busiest on Saturday nights so he usually arrived early to get ready and stayed until closing. Jenna's unexpected visit had changed his plans.

"I'll be at the bar all night." He joined her at the railing, feeling the sun beat down on them. "What are you doing out here, Darce? It must be ninety degrees."

"I can take the heat for a little while for a view like this."

Below them, the Riverbluff Walkway was empty save for a cop who patrolled the area on bicycle. The blue sky was cloudless, the sun that shined down on the river in the distance causing it to shimmer as a lone riverboat chugged by. Birds sang the day's praises while a soft breeze rustled the leaves of the trees.

Yet Clay could only focus on the lines of fatigue on Darcy's face and the Band-Aid on her arm at the needle site. Before undergoing dialysis at age sixteen, she'd had a procedure to fuse a major artery to a vein, creating an access site for blood to be removed and returned to her body.

After she'd gotten well, she used to joke about the cheap thrill she could get by touching the fused artery and vein. Instead of a drug rush, she said, she got a blood rush.

"Dialysis go okay today?" he asked.

"It went fine."

"I wasn't sure whether you'd still be napping."

"I set my alarm so I wouldn't sleep the day away." Her voice hitched. "I needed to return a phone call from the director of the day care where I thought I'd be working this summer."

Darcy had recently finished her junior year at the University of Tennessee, which they couldn't have afforded if Darcy hadn't taken out a student loan and received a few minor scholarships. A college counselor at UT had helped her secure a summer job at a Memphis day care.

"Thought you'd be working? What happened?"

A muscle in Darcy's jaw flexed before she answered. "The center needs someone full-time. The director said she was sorry, but they can't work around my dialysis schedule. So she gave my position to someone else."

The urge to criticize the director for her inflexibility clashed with Clay's concern that the job would have been too taxing for Darcy. His concern won.

"If it's any consolation, a day care center isn't the best place for you to work right now," he said. "Kids tend to get sick and pass around their germs."

"Mom told me the same thing, but I really wanted to work there. Seemed like it would have been the perfect summer job."

"I'm sorry, Darce." He laid a hand on her arm, which felt cool to the touch despite the heat.

"I know you are, but I'll be okay. I've already got some other ideas about how to earn money this summer."

Plenty of dialysis patients held down jobs and led productive lives, but the treatments didn't affect all of them as severely as they did Darcy. Clay didn't see how she'd be able to work on the days she received dialysis.

"You don't need to get a job if you don't want," Clay said. "There's enough money."

"I'm not naive, Clay. I know you're paying some of Mom's bills and that this house is about the only asset she has. I can't let you support me, too."

"You're my sister. My money's your money."

"I'm twenty-two years old. If I hadn't skipped that year in high school, I'd be graduated from college. I can get a job."

"Doing what?"

"Remember when I freelanced for that Web design firm last summer?" she asked. "I have a call in to see if they'll shoot some work my way."

"That's great," he said, although he also recalled that she'd changed her mind about majoring in computer science because of how impersonal it seemed.

"So you can stop worrying about me, because I'll be fine," she said in what had become a familiar refrain. "I even have a big night planned."

"With Kenny?"

Her smile dimmed. "Kenny still has that cold. Me and Mom are having a girls' night. She's picking up some chick flicks. And microwave popcorn without butter."

"Mom was only going to the video store?" Clay thought back to her pretty summer outfit. "I'd have guessed she was meeting somebody."

"I heard her on the phone arranging for an early dinner. I think she changed her plans so she could spend the rest of the night with me."

"An early dinner with who?"

"The guy she's dating, Simon something or other. She's been talking about him a lot lately. But enough about me and Mom. Tell me how things are going at the bar. Did the crowd get bigger after I left last night?"

"Marginally," Clay said.

"I bet business picks up tonight. Word's bound to get around about how good Jenna and Corrine are. I loved listening to them. Especially Jenna. Where'd you find her, anyway?"

The light wind blowing off the river made the temperature tolerable, but a thin trickle of perspiration dripped slowly down the side of Clay's face. He couldn't be sure whether to attribute the sweat to the heat—or anxiety over what he needed to disclose. "A bar in Little Rock."

She scrunched up her nose. "I didn't know you'd been to Little Rock. What were you doing there?"

A perfect opportunity to tell her Jenna was her half sister. "I, um, heard about her and knew that's where she'd be singing."

"Lucky you did," she exclaimed. "So now, how about telling me what you're really doing here?"

She blinked up at him, the dark circles under her eyes underscoring her vulnerability.

Could he really add to her burden by disclosing that the singer she admired was the half sister who wanted nothing to do with her?

It suddenly seemed wrong to add emotional distress to the physical problems Darcy was already experiencing. Besides, a lot could change in the remaining weeks that Jenna and Corrine were under contract to Peyton's Place.

Making his decision, he chucked her lightly under the cheek. "Since when do I need a reason to visit my little sister?"

VICKY RUSHED UP TO JENNA when she arrived at Peyton's Place that Saturday night, stood on tiptoes and hugged her, the contact as brief as it was puzzling.

"Thank you. Thank you." The pretty redheaded waitress gazed up at her as though she'd saved the world from a nuclear attack, her face glowing and her smile wide.

"For what?" Jenna asked.

"For making sure Seth didn't do something we'd all regret. Clay told me all about it."

Jenna squirmed under the praise, uncomfortably aware she didn't deserve it. She'd lied to Vicky's ex-boyfriend not for Vicky's sake, but for Clay's. Admitting as much to Vicky was out of the question, especially because Jenna still wasn't sure why she'd done it.

At the thought of Clay, she sensed him watching her. She located him behind the bar, his tall form angled in their direction. She quickly averted her gaze but not before it touched on his. Ignoring the uncomfortable shivery sensation that danced down her arms, she focused her entire attention on Vicky. "Think nothing of it."

"Oh, but I do. I appreciate it so much." Vicky grimaced. "That's why it's hard for me to ask for another favor."

"Another favor?" Jenna repeated, her mind still on Clay.

They stood not far from the bar's entrance, in the path of a half-dozen customers making a noisy entrance. Vicky grabbed Jenna's hand and tugged, pulling her over to a relatively quiet corner of the bar.

"I have a feeling Seth's going to show up here tonight to check out your story," Vicky said. "He'll want to see for himself I don't have anything going on with Clay."

"What does that have to do with me?" Jenna feared she already knew the answer.

"Seth'll get suspicious if he thinks you weren't telling the truth about being involved with Clay. So if Seth does show up, just for tonight, could you pay extra attention to Clay?"

Jenna stared mutely at the waitress, who couldn't possibly realize the magnitude of the favor she asked. The hell of it was Jenna couldn't tell her, not without getting into the whole, embarrassing story.

"I'm not asking you to make out with Clay in public," Vicky quickly added, causing Jenna to automatically envision what it would be like to kiss him. She imagined pleasure. Her face heated. "Just talk to him during your breaks. Maybe look over at him and smile while you're singing. Stuff like that."

Exactly the kind of "stuff" Jenna had planned to avoid.

She started to tell Vicky she couldn't help, but something in the other woman's expression prevented her from refusing. Hope, mixed with a trace of desperation.

"You and Seth aren't back together, are you?" Jenna asked.

"Hell, no," Vicky immediately refuted. "Once Seth cools down, he'll realize we aren't right for each other, the same as I did. Seth isn't a bad guy, but his pride's wounded. I'd hate for him to do something he regrets."

"Clay won't stand for that," Jenna predicted. "He made it clear this afternoon that Seth wasn't welcome in the bar."

"Peyton's Place doesn't have a bouncer, Jenna. The only way to get Seth to leave would be calling the cops."

"Then Clay will call the cops."

"Not if I ask him not to. I dated Seth for almost a year. I don't want to get him in trouble, especially because I'm leaving Memphis." She lowered her voice even though nobody was near enough to hear. "My sister invited me to live with her in California."

"You're letting Seth run you out of Memphis?"

"Of course not, but the move will be good for both of us. He'll have to let me go, and I'll be able to go back to school. My sister said she'd pay for night classes if I babysit her kids during the day. It's the perfect situation."

The situation seemed significantly less than perfect later that evening when Seth waltzed into the bar, his shoulders thrown back and head high.

Jenna, on stage belting out a rowdy Ma Rainey blues tune, watched Vicky intercept Clay before he could approach Seth. The waitress spoke with her hands, obviously pleading her case.

Arms crossed over his chest, Clay's displeasure couldn't have been more clear had he shouted it. He nodded a few times, then left Vicky to speak to Seth, his features stern. The upshot was that Seth never left the stool.

Jenna sang on, finding nothing in the muscular man's manner or appearance that seemed threatening. She noticed that Clay observed Seth, too— when his dark gaze wasn't focused on her. The set, inevitably, came to an end.

Corrine set down her guitar. "You want to head outside for some air?"

Jenna pursed her lips, the decision upon her whether she'd do as Vicky asked. "I can't. I have to talk to Clay."

"And here you say there's nothing between the two of you." Corrine winked at her before leaving the stage.

Just what she needed, Jenna thought. Her best friend joining the movement to push Jenna toward a man who hadn't been honest with her about who he was.

Locating Clay as he returned to the bar from the direction of the kitchen, Jenna intercepted him, not missing the narrowing of his eyes. Or the mussed look to his hair, as though he'd repeatedly run his fingers through it.

He wouldn't be as attractive with shorter hair, she thought with a jolt. A strange observation from a woman who'd never dated a man with hair that ended anywhere near his collar.

Clay bent down so that his mouth was in line with her ear even though the music from the jukebox wasn't overly loud. "I thought we were staying clear of each other."

His warm breath sent a shiver cascading over her skin, but she didn't back away in case Seth was watching. "Vicky asked me to keep up the pretense that we're involved."

"Because of Seth?" Clay smiled at her. "I appreciate that, but I really can take care of myself."

"I'm not doing this for you," Jenna said, not quite sure she believed her own words. "Vicky practically begged me to help her protect Seth from himself."

He expelled a shot of air. "Vicky's too soft-hearted. But she's right about Seth. Once he understands that she wasn't cheating, he'll accept the breakup. He has to, with her moving to California."

"You know about that?"

"Sure do. I've been telling her for months to take her sister up on her offer."

"But she's your best waitress."

"Vicky's my friend, too. She's not happy waiting tables. I'm glad she'll be able to do something else with her life." Determination etched his strong features, as though he meant to help Vicky accomplish her goals through sheer force of will.

"You really care what happens to Vicky," Jenna observed.

"Yeah, I do." He scowled, his voice heavy with irritation. "What kind of a guy do you think I am?"

Jenna hadn't made up her mind. She should hate him for the sneaky way he'd gotten her to Memphis, but then he'd do or say something that made hating him impossible.

"Don't answer that. I don't want to hear what you think of me." His distress at what she might say seemed so genuine that she touched the front of his chest.

"What if I'm revising my opinion?" Her hand where she touched him suddenly felt hot. She removed it, already regretting the softly spoken words. "But even if I am, I'm not saying I forgive you."

His smile crinkled the skin at the corners of his eyes. "You're saying you don't think I'm all that bad."

"*All that* being the operative two words in that sentence."

He threw back his head and laughed, a deep, pleasant sound that resonated inside her. The warmth that spread through her inspired something else: Panic.

"That doesn't mean I've changed my mind about getting involved with you." She cringed at her clumsy wording and rushed to explain. "I didn't mean that the way it sounded, like I think you're attracted to me. Because I don't think that."

"Then you haven't been paying attention," he said softly.

Had she heard him correctly? "Excuse me?"

"When I came to that bar in Little Rock, I didn't only like what I heard." He touched her lightly on the cheek. "I liked what I saw, too."

The heat in his eyes cemented the meaning behind his words, and the air between them crackled with awareness. Jenna knew she should bat his hand away, but couldn't make her own hand move. Saying nothing, she stepped slowly backward until he no longer touched her.

"I've got to get something to drink," she

blurted, more off balance than she'd been in years. Maybe even since she'd developed a crush on a middle-school student teacher, who was as off-limits to an adolescent girl as Clay Dillon was to Jenna.

She walked blindly to the bar, telling herself attraction didn't have to be reciprocal. As an adult woman, she could handle the interest of a man who didn't interest her.

Vicky, carrying a tray of drinks, waylaid her before she reached her destination. "Thanks," the waitress mouthed. "That was perfect."

Jenna caught sight of Seth sitting at one of the bar stools. His body was angled in her direction, his eyes on her. Raising his beer mug, he gave her a smile of pure satisfaction.

Jenna might have congratulated herself on her acting abilities had circumstances been different. But the truth was she'd completely forgotten Seth at about the time Clay touched her cheek.

CHAPTER FIVE

NOTHING ABOUT DOING the laundry appealed to Corrine. She detested sorting clothes, pretreating stains and figuring out which washing machine settings to use.

She disliked most of all returning from a weekend on the road and discovering Maurice had let the dirty clothes pile up, leaving the chore to her on Sunday evening.

She paused in separating the whites from the darks and stuck her head out of the small laundry room that was adjacent to the kitchen. Maurice was at the refrigerator, taking out a bottle of water.

"You know, it wouldn't kill you to do a load yourself," she told him.

"You're right." He screwed the top off the water bottle and took a swig, his strong throat muscles working as he swallowed. "Sorry about that, babe."

He kissed her neck on his way past the laundry

room to the den, where she could hear the audio of the televised baseball game he was watching.

She thought about following him and pointing out that he hadn't done a lick of laundry in the two years they'd been married, but instead stroked the place where his warm mouth had touched her skin.

She didn't want to start an argument. Not tonight, when Maurice finally had an evening off.

She'd caused enough friction lately by complaining he was never home at night. His usual response was to accuse her of not being supportive, pointing out many of his clients could only meet in the evening hours because they held down jobs.

Maurice was wrong. She was proud of him for building up his business. She just missed him. As soon as she got this latest load of laundry going, she'd snuggle up to him and show him how much.

She stifled the urge to throw all the darks into the cold water slowly filling the machine. A forgotten tissue had been inside one of the pants pockets the last time she'd done that. When she'd removed the clothes from the machine after the spin cycle, little bits of the tissue had clung to the wet clothes like dandruff.

She dropped items of clothing into the machine one by one, checking the pockets of the pants by rote. Every last pocket was empty until she got to her favorite pair of Maurice's jeans, the ones that hugged his butt and thighs and made him look oh so fine.

She pulled a folded piece of hot pink paper from the back pocket of the jeans. Her heart went so still that she might have been declared dead if she'd been on an operating table.

Trash it, a voice inside her head yelled.

Her hand made a motion toward the waste can in the corner of the room, but her fingers gripped the paper so tightly it crinkled. Pulling her hand back toward her body, she slowly unfolded the note.

The name *Imelda,* elegantly scrawled in black ink, stood out against the pink background. Following the name was a telephone number. A divorced woman named Imelda, who dressed in tank tops and short skirts, had recently moved into the house two doors down from theirs.

I'm stuck in a cliché, Corrine thought mere seconds before her brain rebelled. *No, no. There's probably a logical explanation.*

She marched into the den, pink paper in hand, and held it out to Maurice. He waited until the baseball player at the plate grounded out before looking up at her.

"Want to explain what this is?" Her voice

shook, but she wasn't sure whether with rage or fear.

His expression hooded, he reached for the paper, examined it and took his time in answering. "It's Imelda Santos's phone number."

"I guessed that. But what's it doing in the pocket of your jeans?"

This time there was no hesitation. "Imelda's thinking about hiring me as her personal trainer. She gave me her number so I could provide her with more information."

Questions sprang to Corrine's mind. Why hadn't he given Imelda the information when he was talking to her? Why hadn't he handed her a business card and told her to contact him? Corrine didn't ask either of them because they sounded like the questions a wife would ask of a husband she didn't trust.

Maurice's eyebrows rose. "Why did you think I had her phone number?"

Because Imelda Santos was beautiful. Because Maurice hadn't answered the phone Saturday morning when Corrine called. Because she was a jealous idiot.

"I'm sorry," she said. "I don't know what I was thinking."

"If you want me to accept your apology," he said in a smooth, playful voice, "you'll have to do a lot better than that."

"But the laundry—" she began.

"Can wait," he interrupted. "Your husband can't."

He reached for her hand and tugged, pulling her on top of him and wrapping his arms around her. She was still giggling when his mouth captured hers, blotting out all thought of Imelda Santos.

BREATHING IN THE SCENT of freshly mowed grass, Jenna walked under the low-hanging branches of a mimosa tree and past a couple of lovingly tended gardenia bushes around the periphery of her mother's house that Wednesday.

Clusters of red and pink dragonwing begonias grew alongside an open-view wooden fence stained a dark cedar. Jenna spotted her mother in the backyard, kneeling in front of a bed of purple and white flowers. Her back was to Jenna.

Jenna unlatched the wooden gate and swung it open, calling to her mother as she did so, "I was on my way home from work and stopped by to say hey."

No response. Her mother didn't so much as pause in whatever task engaged her, which upon closer inspection was pulling weeds. She wore gardening gloves to go along with what Jenna recognized as her yard clothes, a faded T-shirt and grass-stained shorts. She'd pulled back her brown hair, which Jenna suspected she was dying to keep the gray out.

Jenna ventured closer, her high heels sinking slightly in the soil beneath the lush green lawn. "Hey, Mom," she called.

Still no response.

Her mother repositioned herself to tackle more weeds, then must have caught movement in her peripheral vision because she whipped her head around.

Her mother stood up, brushing the dirt from her knees but missing the smudge on her face. She exuded health, from her trim figure to the touch of color on her face. Before her mother smiled a greeting, Jenna thought she detected a grimace.

"Why didn't you answer—?"

Her mother held up a finger, then removed her earplugs. Only then did Jenna notice the portable MP3 player clipped to the waistband of her shorts.

"Since when do you have one of those?" Jenna asked.

"Since your brother showed me how his worked and I found out they could play books on tape. It's a godsend when you're in a book club," her mother said. "What brings you my way on a Wednesday?"

That was her mother. Direct and to the point. Jenna couldn't bring herself to be quite so blunt, especially because she'd come to tell her mother she'd met Clay—and Darcy.

Not an easy decision, especially considering Jenna had yet to tell her mother she was singing again. The two things—her singing and her association with Margo Wright's children—went hand in hand.

Since she'd returned from Memphis on Sunday, a part of Jenna longed to believe the old saying about ignorance being bliss. But as Monday stretched into Tuesday and then Wednesday, she'd second-guessed the wisdom of keeping such a daunting secret from her mother. Jenna certainly hadn't taken it well when Clay Dillon withheld information from her, but then she hadn't appreciated him speaking his mind, either.

I didn't only like what I heard. I liked what I saw, too.

At the memory of his comment, an annoying sliver of unease pulsed through her. She'd tell Clay Dillon this coming weekend that anything more than a working relationship was out of the question. For now, she needed to focus on the present.

"You don't seem happy to see me," Jenna said.

"I'm always happy to see you, Jenna. It's just that I didn't realize how late it was getting."

Jenna checked her watch. "It's only a few minutes past six. That's not late."

"Not for you. You usually don't leave work until around seven, right?"

"Right," Jenna said. "But I remembered you're off Wednesday nights and thought you and I might spend some time together."

Her mother worked almost as much as Jenna. A massage therapist employed by a health club in suburban Little Rock, she tailored her schedule to fit the needs of her clients yet still managed to cram a dozen other things into her schedule. Book clubs, volunteer work, fund-raisers. You name it, she'd probably been involved at some point or other.

"Oh, honey. I wish you'd called first."

"I did." Jenna hadn't reached the final decision to visit until about an hour ago, at which time she picked up the phone. "But nobody answered. So I took a chance and dropped by."

"I must have been working in the yard. Or I could have told you I'm going out to dinner with the girls."

The "girls" consisted of a group of neighborhood women in their forties and fifties who occasionally got together to compare notes on their lives.

"Oh," Jenna said, thrown off balance. Now that she'd decided to come clean, she didn't want to postpone her confession until another day. "How long do you think dinner will take?"

"Not too long, I hope. I'm supposed to meet Ned Voight for a drink at ten."

"Mr. Voight? Tammy's dad?"

"That's right. You remember his wife died a few years ago, don't you? Terrible tragedy, the cancer that took her. The whole thing was really hard on Ned. He's just starting to reconnect with old friends."

"At ten o'clock at night?"

Her mother laughed. "Ned manages an office supply store that doesn't close until nine-thirty."

"I didn't realize you were seeing anybody, is all."

Her mother scrunched up her face. "I'm not *dating* him. I'm meeting him for a drink."

A drink she seemed to very much look forward to. Jenna didn't state her observation but figured it was about time her mother let a man into her life.

"I'll get right to the point of why I came over then." Jenna drew in a deep breath, then decided to ease gently into the subject. "You know Corrine's a guitarist, right?"

Her mother snapped her fingers. "That reminds

me of something I meant to tell you. I saw Corrine's husband with a woman a couple weeks ago at Corky's Barbecue."

Jenna switched mental gears and readily came up with an explanation. "Maurice is a personal trainer, Mom. Corrine says he's always having lunch with potential clients. If they don't hit it off, he advises them to hire someone else."

"It wasn't lunch, it was dinner. And he was holding this woman's hand."

"It could have been innocent," Jenna muttered even while she thought back to how subdued Corrine had acted over the weekend. Did she suspect Maurice of cheating on her?

Her mother raised her eyebrows but didn't offer a further opinion. "So what is it you wanted to tell me? I gather it has something to do with Corrine?"

"Yes, it does." She relegated Maurice to the back of her mind, hoping there was an innocent reason for what her mother had seen. "The band Corrine was managing fell apart when she had a gig outstanding. She asked if I'd perform with her so she didn't have to cancel."

Her mother's shoulders tensed. "So you're singing again?"

"Temporarily. And just as a favor to Corrine."

Her mother's shoulders relaxed. "Good. I'd

hate to see you jeopardize your future at Morgan and Roe."

"That won't happen. I'm singing only on weekends and only until the beginning of July. That's only six weekends total."

"Tell me where and when, and I'll try to catch a performance."

"The gig's in Memphis," Jenna said.

"Memphis," her mother repeated the name of the city as though it were a dirty word. "I can count on one hand the times I've been back there since…"

She didn't finish her sentence, but then she didn't have to. "If you're singing in Memphis, I won't be coming to hear you. It may be irrational, but I won't take the risk that I'll run into *her*."

Not so unreasonable, Jenna thought. Clay's mother might very well show up at Clay's bar.

"Sorry," her mother said before Jenna could reply. "I still can't think of that woman without resenting what she did to our lives."

"It's been a long time," Jenna ventured.

"Twenty-three years, two months since the divorce was final. Nearly twenty-four since she called to tell me she was having an affair with my husband."

Jenna felt her mouth gape open. "Why didn't I know that?"

"I never told you. But since it's come up,

maybe it will explain why I've always hated her so much." Her expression hardened. "I can still remember what she said even after all this time. *He never loved you like he loves me.* Can you imagine telling a man's wife that?"

"No." The response was the only one Jenna seemed able to give.

"I'm sorry, Jenna. I shouldn't be talking about this to you. But that woman stole your father from us."

Her mother had never kept her views about Margo Wright to herself. Even though Jenna's father had been granted liberal visitation rights by the family court, he hadn't arranged for his children to visit him in Memphis, a failing Jenna's mother blamed on "that woman."

"Listen to me. Getting so worked up for nothing," her mother said. "Your father's dead, God rest his soul. There's no reason we ever need to have anything to do with that woman."

The outburst answered one question for Jenna. Time hadn't dimmed her mother's hatred of Margo Wright.

"Are you okay, honey?" her mother asked.

Jenna smiled. "Sure. Why wouldn't I be?"

"It's not like you to drop by unannounced like this. Why don't you come out to dinner with me and the girls? They'd love to have you."

"Thanks," Jenna said, "but I have some work I need to finish up tonight."

"Then I've got to run. I haven't showered yet, and Peggy's picking me up at seven. If you call tomorrow, maybe we can set something up for later in the week."

"I'm swamped this week, Mom."

"Well, then next week or the week after. We can get the whole family together. I don't see my grandsons as often as I'd like, and it's been too long since we were all together."

"We can try," Jenna said, knowing how difficult it was to mesh their busy schedules.

Her mother fixed her gaze on her. "Are you sure there isn't anything else you want to talk to me about?"

"I'm sure," she said.

The saying about blissful ignorance came back to Jenna, but this time it made more sense. Because there was absolutely no reason her mother needed to find out who owned Peyton's Place.

DARCY GLANCED AT HER watch that Wednesday night to discover that only one minute had passed since she'd last checked the time, which meant Kenny was now fourteen minutes late.

She picked up her cell phone, which continued

to show no missed calls, and verified she still had full reception. Did Kenny?

She'd tried calling him twice since arriving at the Italian restaurant, and both times had been bumped to voice mail. Was his phone turned off or didn't he have reception where he was? And why hadn't he called to let her know he'd be late?

He'd chosen the restaurant and the time, claiming it would be easier to meet her because he was coming straight from a basketball game he was refereeing.

Could he have gotten into a car accident? He drove too fast, even though she was always telling him to slow down. She mentally reviewed the route between the restaurant and the gym. All city roads. He didn't even need to hop on a highway.

"Darcy? Hey, how's it going?"

A tall, young man with floppy brown hair, freckles and a wide, friendly smile stopped at her table. Thin arms hung out from his navy-blue, short-sleeved shirt and his khaki pants seemed too baggy for his narrow hips.

"Hey." She tried to remember where she knew him from and failed so posed an open-ended question. "What are you doing here?"

"Ordering some takeout before I head home. I just got off work so I'm looking forward to putting my feet up, maybe watching a movie."

She searched for a clue in what he'd said but her mind came up blank.

"You don't know who I am, do you?" He still wore the smile, but it no longer lit his eyes.

She grimaced. "Sorry. I know you. I just can't place you."

"We met last week. My name's Mike." He must have realized she still couldn't figure out who he was, because he added, "but I was probably introduced to you as Puff."

Puff. Now *that* jogged her memory. She vaguely recalled Clay introducing him in passing on a day her mind had been preoccupied. Whether her worry had been her failing kidney or Kenny, she couldn't say. "You bartend at my brother's place."

"I do," he said.

"Isn't it early for you to be done for the night?"

"If I was coming from the bar, it would. I work weekdays making deliveries for a florist. Wednesday's my new night off from bartending. Clay switched my schedule around after that bartender he just hired quit."

"Nick quit already? What happened?"

"He got a job that paid more, I think as a bouncer. Didn't even give notice, which is why I'm working six nights a week. Clay's understaffed, considering Vicky left, too."

Darcy imagined the resistance she'd get from Clay if she offered to help out, even though she'd worked at the bar last summer.

"You sound busy," she told Puff, wishing the same for herself. "Is that why people call you Puff? Because your schedule's so exhausting, it has you huffing and puffing?"

He laughed. "That's a new one. And, believe me, I thought I'd heard them all. My last name's Puffenbarger so the nickname—" he made a face "—is inevitable."

"What if I call you Mike?"

He smiled, using his eyes again. "I'd like that very much. Speaking of names, were you named after the character in Pride and Prejudice?"

"I'm impressed you know there's a character named Darcy in that book."

He looked sheepish. "Only because I saw the Bridget Jones movies. Somebody explained the name of the Colin Firth character is an inside joke."

"Can you keep a secret?" Darcy asked, eliciting a nod from Mike. "Sometimes I tell people Mr. Darcy was the inspiration, but my mom heard my name while she was watching the Miss America pageant. Darcy the contestant didn't even win."

"If you entered, you would."

She laughed at his extravagant compliment. "Why, thank you for saying that. But I'd have invited you to sit with me while you wait for your take-out order anyway."

"You wouldn't mind?"

"Not at all. I'm meeting my boyfriend, but he's late. I feel sort of conspicuous sitting here all by myself. So come back and keep me company after you place your order."

While Mike ordered his food at the take-out counter, Darcy tried Kenny's cell phone one more time. He picked up on the second ring.

"I'm on my way," he said before she could identify herself. "I stopped home to shower and ran into some traffic. See you in a few."

Relief that Kenny hadn't been in an accident washed over her. It didn't occur to her to ask why he hadn't called to warn her he'd be late until he hung up.

"Something wrong?" Mike Puffenbarger slid into the seat beside her, his eyes soft and concerned. They were an indeterminate color, somewhere between green and brown.

"It's just my boyfriend. He's been acting funny lately." She nearly clamped her hand over her mouth. Now why had she told Mike Puffenbarger something so personal?

"Funny, how?"

Now that she'd started confiding in him, she surrendered to an urge to finish. "He's not as attentive as he used to be. Not as thoughtful."

"You mean, like, suggesting you have dinner at an Italian restaurant?"

That was exactly what she meant. Italian sauces tended to be high in sodium, phosphorus and potassium, all substances she needed to avoid. "Now how did you know that?"

"The menu doesn't have good choices for someone going through dialysis."

She stiffened. There was absolutely no way he could have known that. Unless… "Did Clay tell you I needed another kidney transplant?"

"No." He shook his head, his expression suddenly serious. "I saw you go into the transplant center when I was delivering flowers to the hospital across the street."

And now she'd not only confirmed she was a dialysis patient, but that she needed a transplant. Another one, yet. But something else didn't make sense. "How did you know about the dietary restrictions?"

A sheepish look crossed his face. "After I saw you, I researched dialysis on the Internet."

She expended so much effort pretending she wasn't sick that she should have been annoyed but wasn't. Mike Puffenbarger, she decided, was adorable. "I'd appreciate it if you didn't mention my kidney problems to anyone at the bar."

"Consider it done," he said, "but there's no shame in having kidney failure."

"I know that. But people look at me differently when they find out I need a transplant, as though I'm less than whole."

"That would be hard to take."

"Even though dialysis really wipes me out, I'm not an invalid. Kidney disease might slow me down every now and then but I like to think there's nothing I can't do. Like helping Clay out at the bar."

"He is shorthanded."

"Tell me about it. I've been thinking about trying to switch my dialysis schedule from Tuesday, Thursday, Saturday to Tuesday, Thursday, Sunday so I could help Clay out on weekends. But he probably wouldn't hear of it."

She bit her lip, surprised at herself. She hadn't spoken that frankly since discovering she needed the second transplant. Not to her mother. Not to Clay. And certainly not to Kenny. Yet she'd blurted out her thoughts to a man she'd have passed on the street without recognizing.

"If you want me to talk to Clay for you, let me know," he said. "And if there's ever anything you want to talk about, I'll listen."

"Thanks, Mike." She fought back tears, not sure why they tapped at the backs of her eyes. His hand rested inches from hers and she had a powerful desire to grasp it.

The restaurant door banged open, letting in a blast of hot air and Kenny. He walked purposely to their table, his golden-brown hair darkened from the shower. He wore a simple white shirt open at the neck and black jeans, clothes that would have looked unremarkable on most men. With his muscular, athletic body, Kenny looked like a dream.

"Hey, Darce. Sorry to keep you waiting." He kissed her full on the mouth before sticking out a hand to Mike. "Kenny Coleman."

"Mike Puffenbarger." Mike rose to shake Kenny's hand, and Darcy was surprised to discover Mike topped Kenny by a few inches. The more self-assured Kenny seemed taller.

"Good to meet you, Puff." Kenny pulled out a chair, the legs scraping on the hardwood floor. "It's okay if I call you Puff, right?"

Mike reclaimed his seat, slanting a pained look at Darcy before answering, "Everybody else does."

"Are you here for dinner?" Kenny asked.

As if on cue, the woman at the take-out counter signaled to Mike that his food was ready. "I was just leaving," he said.

"Don't go on my account," Kenny said.

Darcy looked sharply at him. The extroverted Kenny enjoyed being around others but inviting another man to dine with them was out of character. When they'd first started dating, he insisted on having her to himself.

"Thanks, but I've got to run." Mike's gaze touched on Darcy. "You know where to find me if you ever feel like talking."

She smiled her gratitude.

"He bartends for Clay," Darcy explained after Mike was out of sight.

"Oh." Kenny picked up a menu and examined it.

She frowned. "Why'd you ask him to have dinner with us?"

"He seemed like a nice guy," he said absently, still perusing the menu.

"How did you know he wasn't hitting on me?"

Kenny looked up, his expression mild. "Was he?"

She thought about his remark about the Miss America pageant, but immediately dismissed it as one of those things people say when they're trying to be nice. "No."

"There you go." He went back to considering the menu. "I'm having the bow tie pasta with Italian sausage. How about you?"

She'd had plenty of time to look over the menu while waiting for Kenny to arrive. "I'm going to ask if they'll bring me plain pasta with garlic and butter."

"That doesn't sound very appetizing."

"There's not a lot on this menu I can eat."

He closed the menu and placed it on the table. "Speaking of diets, did I ever tell you about the ref who scarfed down chocolate bars at halftime for energy? He lost fifty pounds since I last saw him."

"I'm supposed to stay away from candy." Darcy brought the conversation back to her restricted diet, although she hardly understood why. She didn't usually complain about her condition and limitations.

"Scooter's not eating chocolate anymore, either."

Darcy pursed her lips, thrown that Kenny hadn't picked up on her desire to talk about her condition. She squashed the ridiculous disappointment that rose up in her, reminding herself she'd finally gotten her wish. One of the most important people in her life wasn't hovering over her.

Yet the relative stranger who'd kept her company had a better feel for her needs than the man who'd occupied a part of her heart for half of the past year.

CHAPTER SIX

FRIDAY NIGHT, AND ALL was not well.

Clay intended to have a strategy by Jenna's second weekend in Memphis. A strategy that would persuade her to reconsider her staunch refusal to get to know Darcy, but he'd barely had time to think.

First Vicky quit, then Nick, leaving Clay in the unenviable position of locating quality help on short notice. Vicky would have stayed until he found a replacement waitress, but he couldn't justify delaying the start of her new life. Nick, on the other hand, had refused to give him a week's notice.

"C'mon, man. I've got to look out for my wife and baby," Nick said. "We both know I'm a lousy bartender, anyway."

True enough, but Clay could have stationed Nick beside the door to collect the cover he'd decided to charge tonight. That extra revenue could go a long way toward making the bar more profitable, a necessity if he was to continue helping his mother out financially. He kneaded his forehead, trying to figure out how to spring another employee to collect the cover.

Impossible.

He needed Puff behind the bar, and the reclusive Manny wouldn't emerge from the kitchen even if he wasn't responsible for cooking up their limited selection of bar food.

Clay would be lucky if Trudy, the waitress who usually worked side by side with Vicky, didn't rebel at the extra workload. He planned to help out wherever and whenever he could but in truth could use more than two helping hands.

After mopping up a spill in the kitchen, he slipped behind the L-shaped bar and asked the nearest customer what he'd like to drink. Taking a clean mug from a shelf beneath the bar, he placed it under the tap dispensing lite beer and pulled up the handle.

"A Vodka Collins and a couple of drafts," a familiar voice ordered.

His head jerked up and he saw Darcy's reflection in the mirror. His sister stood at the bar, her long blond hair tied back in a ponytail, an expectant expression on her pretty face.

Beer flowed over his fingers, clueing him to shut off the tap. Holding the mug in one hand, he grabbed a towel and wiped the beer from his other. Then he turned to confront the young woman who'd cast the mirror image. "What are you doing here, Darcy?"

"Helping," she answered, as though he hadn't been sitting next to her when the doctor broke the news about her failing kidney. "I know you're understaffed, so don't you try to tell me differently."

He held up a finger, set the beer in front of the customer who'd ordered it and came around the bar to where Darcy waited. He gently cupped her elbow and ushered her a few steps from the bar, aware they still didn't have privacy. Then he noticed she was wearing the kelly green apron he issued to waitresses.

"Where'd you get that apron?" he asked.

"Does it matter?"

"What matters is I'm not so desperate for help that I'll let you wait tables," he said in a low voice.

At the stricken look that appeared on her face, he said, "Sorry. That came out wrong. I meant to say you have a serious health problem. Waiting tables can't be good for you."

"I didn't have dialysis today, so I feel fine." She spoke in a whisper he had to strain to hear. "The center is experimenting with Sunday hours so I changed my schedule so I could have Fridays and Saturdays free."

The stubborn tilt to her lips reminded him of the expression he sometimes saw when he gazed into the mirror.

He gentled his voice. "I appreciate what you're trying to do, but I've got it covered. When it gets really busy later tonight I'll help Trudy out. Hopefully by tomorrow night I'll have hired another waitress."

"You'll still be understaffed."

"Not so understaffed I need you to wait tables."

"There must be some way I could help out." She blinked up at him. "How about if I sit at the door and collect the cover charge?"

He narrowed his eyes. "How'd you know I planned to collect a cover tonight?"

"You didn't tell me that?"

"No, I didn't."

She shrugged. "Corrine and Jenna are so good I figured a cover was a given. You are planning to charge one, aren't you?"

It was the smartest way to bring in more money. "Yeah, I was."

"Then what are you waiting for? Set me up at the door." She untied the string that held the apron around her waist, folded the material neatly into a square and handed it to Puff on her way past the bar. She winked at the bartender, giving Clay a pretty good idea of how she'd gotten the apron and discovered he planned to charge a cover.

It dawned on him that he'd been conned. If Darcy had offered straight away to collect the cover, he'd have refused, afraid the job would be too taxing. But of course collecting money wasn't anywhere near as strenuous as waitressing.

He stopped at the cash register and put together a wad of bills from which his sister could make change. Then he dragged a tall stool over to the door, where Darcy waited.

"You planned to collect the cover all along, didn't you?" he asked.

"Oh, yeah." She beamed at him, brightening the atmosphere inside the bar so he felt like the sun was shining upon them.

Despite his misgivings, he couldn't help but smile back.

"WHAT ARE YOU SMILING about?"

Jenna dropped a few coins in a guitar case belonging to a street corner musician singing a Beatles song before answering Corrine's question. "Nothing in particular."

Corrine laughed. "I didn't mean you should stop smiling. I meant you seem to be looking forward to tonight."

Jenna couldn't fault Corrine's powers of observation. The closer she and Corrine got to Peyton's Place and the start of their Friday-night performance, the more excited Jenna became.

"I am." She couldn't pinpoint when she'd had a reversal of opinion about performing in Memphis, but figured it must have begun last weekend when she'd sung before the appreciative audiences. "During the week I kept thinking about how much fun it was to be on stage."

"You say that like fun's a bad thing. You really need to lighten up, Jenna."

Jenna was trying. She no longer entertained thoughts of skipping out on the contract, but not entirely because abandoning the gig would devastate Corrine. Singing in Memphis was exactly what she wanted to be doing.

As for Clay Dillon, she'd started to forgive him. She realized she'd jumped to his defense last weekend because something inside her recognized him as a decent man.

Not telling her he was Darcy's half brother had been a lapse of judgment, but she liked other things about him. His willingness to help a friend who needed a job and his understanding about an employee who needed a change, to name a few.

"Do you see that?" Corrine asked when they reached Peyton's Place, pointing to a small sign in the corner of one of the bay windows. "Clay's charging a cover tonight."

Corrine clapped her hands, more in keeping with the way she usually acted than the long silences that had marked her behavior last weekend. She still seemed preoccupied, but whatever had been on her mind no longer seemed so worrisome. Maybe it had nothing to do with Maurice, after all. Or maybe Jenna wanted to believe that because she hadn't told Corrine about what her mother had seen.

"I take it you think a cover's a good idea," Jenna remarked.

"A great idea. It means people are coming for the act and not just the beer. We're on our way up in the world." Corrine squeezed her arm. "Doesn't it make you feel special?"

Jenna laughed and linked her arm with Corrine's. They entered the front door side by side, but Jenna's enjoyment of the moment crashed and burned when she saw who manned the entrance.

"Hey, Jenna." Darcy smiled at her. The medium golden-blond shade of the hair she'd tied back from her face and the graceful line of Darcy's neck made Jenna think of that long-ago look she'd gotten of Margo Wright. "It's good to see you again."

Jenna's throat thickened, preventing her from replying, let alone uttering the lie that she was pleased to see Darcy, too.

Corrine unlinked her elbow from Jenna's and stuck out a hand. "I don't think we've met. Corrine Sweetland."

"I heard you last weekend, so I know who you are," Darcy said. "I was blown away by that guitar solo you did on 'Texas Flood'. It took some serious guts to imitate Stevie Ray Vaughan but somehow you pulled it off."

Jenna searched for something to dislike about Darcy, but the younger woman didn't give off the air of self-importance common to many beautiful woman. Her friendliness seemed genuine, her praise sincere.

"I'm impressed you knew enough to be impressed," Corrine said. "Do you play?"

"A little, but I'm not very good. That's probably why I can appreciate a talented guitarist, which you very definitely are. I'm Darcy, by the way. Clay's sister."

Corrine tilted her head and regarded Darcy quizzically. "You're his sister? I'm not seeing a family resemblance."

"We get that a lot. But our mother says our ears are the same shape. Clay's are just bigger and a lot higher off the ground." She tugged on one of her lobes, making Corrine laugh, but Jenna couldn't even form a smile.

She was too busy thinking about Darcy's mother. Margo Wright. The woman who'd broken up Jenna's family, moved into the big Victorian house where they'd all been so happy and supplanted Jenna and Jeff in her father's heart with Darcy and Clay.

"I'm looking forward to hearing you two play tonight." Darcy indicated her stool with the sweep of a hand. "A good thing about being stuck here at the door is I'm guaranteed a seat. We're filling up fast."

A trio of men entered the bar, talking noisily as they produced bills to pay the cover. Corrine and Jenna moved out of the way, and Darcy gave them a little wave, then greeted the men with her appealing smile.

The bar was significantly more crowded than it had been the weekend before, with nearly every table, booth and bar stool already occupied. The smell of smoke, beer and greasy hamburgers permeated the air, the prevailing scents in bars everywhere. Clay's back was to them as he filled beer mugs at the tap, but the floppy-haired bartender waved.

"I like Darcy," Corrine remarked after they'd climbed onto the stage and she went about the business of removing her guitar from its case. "She's good-looking and friendly. Exactly the kind of face you should put on a bar. Clay made a smart move putting her at the door."

Jenna squashed her inclination to rush across the bar and demand Clay explain why Darcy was working for him. She'd heard talk of the bar being understaffed, and Darcy was his sister. It made perfect sense for her to help him out. Why make a big deal when there was absolutely no reason Jenna had to talk to either Darcy or Clay for the rest of the night?

Jenna amended the playlist, pouring her frustration over the situation into songs by artists like Jerry Lee Lewis and Jimi Hendrix that were high energy instead of mellow. She felt almost calm by the end of the set. Until she looked down to see Darcy at the foot of the stage.

"I didn't want you to spend your break waiting at the bar like I did," Darcy said, holding out two tall glasses of ice water.

Corrine reached for one of the glasses and guzzled down some water. "I think I love you."

Darcy beamed at her. "Not half as much as I love your music."

Jenna took her glass more reluctantly. "Thank you."

"Anytime," Darcy said. "I've got to get back to

cover-charge duty, but I was wondering if the two of you will be in town tomorrow morning."

"Sure," Corrine said. "Why?"

"I'd love to take you on the Sun Studio tour." Darcy winced, looking charmingly unsure of herself. "That is, if you want to go."

"Do I want to go see the studio where Elvis, Muddy Waters and Roy Orbison recorded?" Corrine said. "Do you even have to ask?"

"Cool." Darcy gave Corrine a relieved smile, then turned to Jenna. "What about you, Jenna?"

Jenna looked away from the hope on Darcy's face, her gaze landing on one of the bright orange flyers somebody had posted all over the bar advertising a 10K race/walk. "Sorry. But I'm doing the charity run tomorrow."

"Since when?" Corrine asked. "This is the first I've heard of it."

"I just decided tonight. You know I run for exercise, Corrine, and the hotel's treadmill gets old real fast."

"Do you want us to wait to take the tour until you're through?" Darcy asked.

"Oh, no," Jenna said quickly. "You two go ahead. The run's early in the morning. I imagine I'll need some downtime when it's over."

After Darcy had returned to her station at the door, Corrine sidled closer to Jenna. "Downtime?

What happened to running to get more energy? Why don't you want to take the tour?"

Now was not the time to explain. "No reason," Jenna said vaguely.

Corrine might have pressed her for more of an explanation if a fan hadn't approached asking about her method of playing guitar. While Corrine explained her technique, Jenna talked to a few fans, then retreated against a far wall that featured a poster of B. B. King.

She scanned the bar, not exactly sure what she was looking for until her eyes fell on Clay. He was near the entrance, his dark head bent toward Darcy's blond one. Even from half a bar away, Jenna spotted the way his features softened when he talked to his sister. Darcy pointed to one of the orange flyers, and he straightened.

His head turned slowly, his gaze fixating on her. She felt her muscles bunch as he walked straight toward her, a fight-or-flight instinct. By the time her mind chose flight, he was close enough for her to see the faint shadow of a beard on his face. Her back literally against a wall, there was no room to flee.

"Before you say anything, I didn't ask Darcy to collect the cover," he said by way of an opening. "She heard I was shorthanded and just showed up. She didn't give me much choice."

Jenna wished he'd kept that information to himself. It reinforced her impression of Darcy as kind and thoughtful. It would have been so much easier to avoid her if she wasn't.

"But that's not why I came over here. At the risk of sounding too friendly," his brows rose slightly, "I just found out from Darcy you turned down the Sun Studio tour because you're doing the 10K."

She tried to hear the censure in his voice but found none. "That's right."

"I'll be there, too. I run it every year. It's at a park on the outskirts of Memphis called Deer Lake. You do realize it's a trail run, right?"

She hadn't read the flyer closely enough to figure out what kind of run it was. "I ran cross-country in high school, so it shouldn't be a problem."

He seemed about to say something else, then merely nodded. "Then I'll see you there."

His gaze swept over her before he headed back to the bar. She ignored the shivery sensation that danced over her skin and lamented her bad luck at successfully dodging Darcy's invitation only to commit herself to an event where Clay would be present.

But surely hundreds of runners and walkers would turn out for the 10K. It wasn't as though she'd be forced to hang out with Clay Dillon.

Unless, of course, she wanted to.

A FEW HUNDRED RUNNERS milled about the grassy area beside the starting line when Clay arrived at Deer Lake Park the next morning, some going through stretching exercises, others doing slow, warm-up jogs.

Clay couldn't spot Jenna Wright among them.

He shouldn't be surprised. He was fairly sure she'd used the run as an excuse to get out of hanging with Darcy, but he'd expected her to at least show. Then again, he knew very little about her. Maybe she'd even lied about the high-school cross-country team.

Not sure why the thought depressed him, he asked the nearest participant—a guy wearing a shocking pink headband around his shaved head—if he knew the location of late registration.

"Over by those trees." The man indicated a spot not far from the loop trail that followed the shoreline around the lake. With the extra area it was a distance close enough to six point two miles that organizers had been able to advertise the race as a 10K. "But you have a race T-shirt. Aren't you already preregistered?"

"Just want to say hello to the director," Clay replied, trying to keep from staring at the pink headband but obviously not managing it.

The man made a face. "I lost a bet."

"I hear you," Clay said sympathetically. "I'm probably about to lose one myself."

He walked through the slightly dewy grass in the direction the poor guy had pointed, still searching for Jenna, still not finding her. Until he looked in the last place he'd expect her to be.

"Jenna. What are you doing at the registration table?"

"Helping." She took a personal check from a short woman in cut-off jeans shorts, handed her a number and thanked her before explaining. "I was registering when the director got called away on an emergency. So I volunteered."

"Why?"

"Because nobody else was around. And because it's for a good cause." She tapped the stack of pamphlets on the table top that told about For the Children, the nonprofit charity the event benefited. "The profits go to help abandoned and neglected children."

He'd underestimated her, he realized. Not only had she shown up at the race, she'd wholeheartedly gotten into the spirit of the event.

"I'm sorry." Rachel Goldstein, the director of For the Children, rushed up to the table. Some of her dark hair had escaped from her ponytail and her official yellow T-shirt had come untucked from her shorts. Energy vibrated off her, the way it always did. "I didn't think I'd be gone for more than a couple minutes. Would you believe somebody sprained an ankle before the race even started? And our trainer wasn't here yet?"

"No problem," Jenna said, getting up from her chair behind the desk.

She looked great in a white dri-fit sleeveless tee with navy running shorts, every bit as alive as she looked on stage.

"I'm sure you handled it fine, Rachel," Clay said. "Things are going great. Look at this turn-out."

"Partly thanks to you." Rachel flung her arms around his neck, stood on tiptoe and kissed him on the cheek. When she let him go, she told Jenna, "I don't know how I let this one get away. He handed out my flyers to all the businesses on Beale, then double-checked to make sure they were up."

"Glad to do it," Clay said while Rachel took her position behind the registration table. "I assume you've already met Jenna," Clay pointed out.

"You two know each other?" Rachel looked back and forth from Clay to Jenna, her dark eyes growing large. "Oh, damn. You're dating, aren't you? Jenna, I don't want you to get the wrong impression. I'm happily married."

Clay laughed. "Jenna and I aren't dating, Rachel."

"Then is Jenna one of your exes like me?" Rachel asked. Before Clay could answer, Rachel told Jenna, "Because Clay stays friends with his exes. But I thought I knew them all."

"Actually, Clay and I just met," Jenna said, amusement in her voice at Rachel's effervescence. Rachel had that effect on a lot of people. "I'm singing in his bar."

"Jenna saw one of your race flyers hanging up at Peyton's Place," Clay said. "She used to run cross-country."

"Oh, a ringer," Rachel said.

"Hardly," Jenna jumped in to clarify. "I'm great at keeping a steady pace, but I can only run seven-minute miles."

"I get it now," Rachel concluded. "You're here to help Clay win his bet with Mark."

"Mark?"

"My husband," Rachel supplied. "Don't tell me you don't know about the bet? The one who finishes last pays up. Clay usually leads most of the race, then loses steam in the end."

"I've won once or twice," Clay said.

"Once, five years ago. Mark mentioned it this morning on the way over." Rachel took cash from a runner who jogged up to the table and instructed him to write down some particulars on a form. "Thanks for helping, Jenna. If Clay has a prayer of winning the bet, you better get him over to the starting area. The race is about to begin."

"So will you do it?" Clay asked when they approached the start of the race at a slow jog, Jenna's shorter strides somehow a match for his longer ones. Her low socks left most of her slender legs bare, and her ponytail swung as she ran.

"Do what?"

"Pace me." They reached the cluster of runners waiting for the starter's command. Since the path was only wide enough to accommodate three or four runners at a time, they were already back in the pack.

"Hey, Dillon. You ready to lose?" Mark Goldstein called to Clay from his spot a few dozen runners in front of them. A big man who spent a lot of time in the weight room, Mark stood head and shoulders above the crowd.

"I'm thinking I might pull it off this year," Clay yelled back.

Mark guffawed. "Dream on, man. Dream on."

"I take it that's Rachel's husband?" Jenna asked. "Is he always such a braggart?"

"Always."

"Then, yes. I'll pace you."

JENNA BREATHED IN THE smell of evergreen and listened to the crunch of running shoes on packed gravel as she ran alongside Clay, the only other sounds the occasional song of a bird and the even cadence of their breathing.

She'd run with a lot of different partners over the years, but seldom had she found someone whose style meshed so comfortably with hers. Or one who looked so good running. The short-sleeved shirt showed off the definition in his arms, the shorts his muscular, hair-sprinkled legs.

Unlike some others she'd trained with, Clay didn't feel the need to keep up a constant stream of conversation. The occasional comment, she could handle. As long as he didn't mention Darcy.

The sun peeked through the trees and shone on the surface of the glimmering lake. The terrain was mostly flat, with occasional bays jutting out from the main body of water and sending the trail in unexpected directions. They caught occasional glimpses of Mark, who was about a hundred feet in front of them.

"You really do run a steady pace," Clay said when they'd finished mile one.

"Slow and steady wins the race," she said, and he laughed.

At a little past the mile two marker, they caught up to Mark. At mile three, they passed him.

"You'll come back to me," Mark yelled as they went by, his breathing sounding slightly labored. "You might as well get out your wallet, Dillon."

"How much is this bet for, anyway?" Jenna asked.

"A hundred bucks."

Clay had risked a hundred dollars on whether he could beat some loudmouth in a race? Jenna could understand how the other man could have goaded him into it, but it seemed a case of too much testosterone. The two men seemed more like adversaries than friends. Did Clay's past relationship with Mark's wife have anything to do with that?

Telling herself the answer was none of her business, she kept her pace steady. She glanced over her shoulder at the four-mile mark, but Mark was no longer in her sight line. They reached a stretch of trail open to the sky. The sun beat down, the heat of the day seeming to rise from the ground so Jenna felt like she was getting toasted from both ends.

"Why hold the race in June?" she asked Clay.

"July and August are too hot," he answered, as though he wasn't affected by the rising temperature.

It became harder and harder for Jenna to draw a deep breath, harkening back to days she thought were over. She kept putting one foot in front of the other, but it felt as though somebody was sitting on her chest. She could hear her breaths become ragged.

"Jenna, are you all right?"

"I'm fine," she said, willing it to be the truth. She struggled for another hundred yards before her tightening lungs forced her to slow to a walk.

"You go ahead," she told Clay, practically gasping the words.

He ignored her, walking along beside her as runners passed them on the left. "What's wrong?"

"Asthma," she said between wheezes.

"Where's your inhaler?"

"Thought I'd..." She stopped and drew in another ragged breath until she was able to finish the thought. "Outgrown... it."

"Put your hands over your head. Then breathe in through your nose, out through your mouth," he ordered, repeating a tactic to deal with asthma that she should have remembered.

She did as he instructed, the pressure on her lungs gradually easing. More and more runners passed. She motioned for Clay to go on ahead, but he ignored her. Concentrating hard on her breathing, she was finally able to lower her arms.

A few moments later, Mark passed them. He waved, a grin splitting his face.

"You're gonna lose again, sucker," he called to Clay, apparently oblivious to Jenna's breathing difficulties.

"Go after him," Jenna said, relieved she could again speak without panting. "There's only a mile to go. You can take him."

"Maybe," Clay said, "but I'd rather stay with you."

"I'll be okay. I just need to walk the rest of the way."

"Then I'll walk with you."

"But the bet—"

"Isn't as important as making sure you're okay."

"I am okay. Really. It's just the heat." She stopped talking, loath to admit she couldn't handle her problem herself but finding it harder to talk than she'd thought.

They walked on, with Clay sending frequent glances her way. The pale yellow T-shirt he wore with For the Children printed across the front looked good with his dark hair. Despite having run nearly five miles, he wasn't breathing hard. The definition in his chest and arms told Jenna he did more for exercise than run.

"Your breathing sounds a lot better now," he said after a few minutes.

"It is," she agreed. "The humidity must have triggered it, the same as it did when I was a kid."

"You ran cross-country despite having asthma?"

"It was no big deal." She shrugged off her condition, the feeling of not wanting to be fussed over coming back to her. "I carried an albuterol inhaler, which usually took care of it. I didn't think I still needed it."

"Did the asthma give you problems when you sang?"

"Never. It was exercise induced. I didn't even know I had asthma until I joined the cross-country team. And I only did that because the choir director said running would increase my lung capacity." She made a face. "That kind of back-fired."

"Sounds like you were hooked on the singing."

She nodded slightly, unwilling to reveal how deep her love of singing had run.

"Corrine said you hadn't sung in public since college. So why'd you give it up?"

"Because reality intruded and I had to get on with my real life." She sensed he was about to probe deeper into her reasons for abandoning her passion, reasons she didn't even like to examine herself. She changed the subject. "So how about you? How'd you get into the bar business?"

"On a lark," he answered. "I saw the 'for sale' sign and something clicked. I majored in business administration at Austin Peay and worked at three or four places before realizing I hated being accountable to a boss. Buying the bar was a gamble, but I thought, why not go for it?"

How different they were, Jenna thought. No matter how much she loved singing, she hadn't been willing to risk her future.

"How's that working out for you?"

"Not bad. We're having growing pains, but the bar's finally turning a profit. You and Corrine will help. I should have brought in live music sooner."

They rounded a bend, and she was surprised to see the finish line. Time had passed swiftly as they walked the final mile, even more speedily than if they'd been running.

"Thanks for staying with me," she told him. "I'm sorry it meant losing your bet."

He smiled at her, the lines at the corners of his eyes crinkling. "It's no big deal. Mark won't let me hear the end of it. But if it wasn't about the race, he'd find something else to rag me about."

Mark lived up to his reputation, approaching Clay less than a minute later, holding a bottle of blue Gatorade and wearing a satisfied grin. "The best man wins again."

"You got me." Clay took Mark's outstretched hand. The men shook, then half embraced, slapping each other on the back and grinning. So much for Jenna's theory about them being adversaries.

"I thought you went out too fast, but I wouldn't have figured you for a walker," Mark said.

"It was—" Jenna began.

"Too hot for me today," Clay finished before Jenna could take the blame. Had he sensed how much it bothered her for anyone to know about her weakness? He introduced Jenna to Mark.

"You'll have to come over to our house sometime with Clay," he told Jenna, repeating his wife's mistake of thinking they were a couple. "Rachel's a great cook. Isn't she, buddy?"

"The best."

"She's waiting over at the registration desk to take your check," Mark said.

"You're letting your wife have the hundred dollars?" Jenna asked in surprise. Mark didn't seem the type to authorize anyone to collect on his bets except Mark.

"Sure am." Mark seemed confused by her question. "She is the director."

Everything finally clicked into place. "The money's going to For the Children," she said, almost to herself.

"Does every year," Mark said. "You didn't think Clay was going to hand over the money to me, did you?"

The truth was she'd hardly thought the situation through at all. But now that Mark had cleared the cloud that had been in front of Jenna's eyes, she could see Clay more clearly.

She had to admit she liked what she saw.

CHAPTER SEVEN

"IF YOU TELL ME what's eating you, I'll listen."
Corrine stood at the closet in their hotel room,
holding a hanger containing the flowing black top
she evidently planned to wear to dinner and then
to the bar. "I've known you long enough to tell
when something's wrong."

From where she stood at the mirror applying
makeup, Jenna cut her eyes at her friend. The
irony was that Jenna could have expressed the
same sentiment.

"Nothing's wrong," Jenna said.

Corrine swept by her, the material of the shirt
on the hanger brushing Jenna's arm as she passed.
"If you want to pretend it's nothing, fine, just
don't expect me to believe it."

Jenna put down her tube of brown mascara,
the urge to confide in Corrine as strong as the scent
of the coffee her friend had just brought up from
the lobby. She stepped around the corner so she
could face Corrine and braced her back against a

half wall. "If I tell you, do you promise not to judge me?"

Corrine dropped the garment on one of the beds, which were covered with golden spreads that should have lent the room a soothing feel. She perched her hands on her hips, the open draperies behind her revealing that day would soon turn to night. "When have I ever judged you?"

"When I told you about my father's daughter with his second wife," Jenna answered. "You said it was a shame I hadn't made an effort to get to know her."

"Oh, that." Corrine sat down on one of the cushy mattresses with a soft plop. "It is a shame, but what does your dad's daughter have to do with anything?"

Jenna sucked in a breath, bolstering her courage. "Darcy's his daughter, Corrine."

Corrine's eyes turned to saucers. "Clay's your *brother?* Now that's awkward."

"No, of course he's not my brother," Jenna refuted. "Clay was eight years old when his mother married my father. He and Darcy share a mother. Darcy and I have the same father."

Corrine wiped a hand across her brow. "Whew. Thank God he's not related, considering what's going on between the two of you."

"There's nothing—" Jenna began.

Corrine didn't let her finish her denial. "So Darcy is your *sister?*"

"My half sister," Jenna corrected.

Corrine brought both hands to her face, placing them on either side of her cheeks. "That's why you didn't take the Sun Studio tour with us. Because you don't want to be around her."

Her observation sounded like an accusation. "Don't make me the bad guy here, Corrine. That title should go to Clay."

"Because he brought you to Memphis?" She dropped her hands, her eyes narrowing with understanding. "Or because he's the son of the woman your father left your mother for?"

"He didn't tell me about Darcy before he hired us, Corrine. He didn't give me a choice in whether to meet her."

The tips of Corrine's top teeth became visible as she bit her bottom lip, her expression thoughtful. "You've got a choice now. You can choose to get to know your half sister."

Jenna released a frustrated breath and straightened from the wall. "See. This is why I didn't tell you. I knew you wouldn't understand."

"So explain it to me."

"If I get involved with Darcy, it would only hurt my mother. I couldn't even tell her I was singing in Clay's bar. When I brought up Memphis, she talked about how upset she still was. And about how much she still hates Margo."

"Her issues, not yours."

"I can't just ignore how she feels. She was everything to me and Jeff growing up. You don't think I have a right to decide not to get involved with Darcy for my mother's sake?"

"You had that right, but the playing field's changed," Corrine said. "Clay took that out of your hands."

"Exactly," Jenna said. "I just wish I could be angrier with him for it."

"You like him, don't you?"

"Too much," Jenna said, giving her a brief rundown of what had happened during the 10K. "If he'd asked me out today, I think I would have said yes."

"What's so bad about that?"

She rolled her eyes. "I can't get involved with him for the same reasons I can't get involved with Darcy."

"Because of your mother?"

"Right."

"Then keep it light. We're not in Memphis for long. Why not have fun while we're here?"

"You make it sound so easy."

Corrine rose from the bed, crossed the plush carpet to where Jenna stood and patted her arm.

"I don't mean to. I know this is hard for you. But you'll work it out. And whatever you decide, I'm in your corner."

Corrine walked back to the bed, took off her casual white cotton top and replaced it with the flowing black number. She'd already changed into skinny black pants and high-heeled half boots and looked like a woman who hadn't a care in the world. Jenna knew better.

"I'm in your corner, too," Jenna said, then plunged ahead. "So you can tell me anything. Even about the trouble you're having with Maurice."

Jenna watched Corrine closely for a reaction, hoping her comment was off the mark. Her friend grew still, her neck and shoulder muscles tensing.

"What makes you think Maurice and I are having trouble?" Corrine asked casually. Too casually.

Jenna pursed her lips, not sure how to tactfully proceed with the subject now that she'd brought it up. "You've been preoccupied the past couple of weeks, not quite yourself. I just wondered if things between you and Maurice were okay."

"It's more than that." Corrine's attempt at casualness was gone, replaced by steel-jawed determination. "I know you, Jenna. You wouldn't have brought up my marriage unless you knew something about it. What is it?"

"Nothing important," Jenna murmured, then cringed inwardly at her evasive response. How had it come to this? How had a woman who valued honesty, and who'd practiced it for the first thirty years of her life, become such a liar?

She'd already kept the identity of Peyton's Place's owner from her mother. Could she really compound her sins by withholding information from Corrine?

Here goes, Jenna thought.

"My mother saw Maurice with a woman at Corky's Barbecue last Saturday," Jenna said in a rush.

The only part of Corrine that moved was her lips. "So what? Maurice has meals with women all the time. She was probably thinking about hiring him as her trainer."

"That's what I said." *Tell her the rest,* Jenna's internal voice screamed. "But my mother said he was holding her hand."

Corrine's head shook with the rhythm of a metronome. "Your mother must have confused Maurice with someone else."

Jenna's mother had been a guest at Corrine and Maurice's wedding only two years before. "She insists it was Maurice."

"Then she got it wrong. You know Maurice. He's a toucher. Always has been. If he was touching this woman's hand, that's just Maurice. That's normal. It didn't mean a thing."

"Maybe not," Jenna said, but without much conviction.

"You think he's cheating on me, don't you?" Corrine's voice rose, and her eyes flashed. "That's why you brought this up."

Jenna sighed inwardly. "I don't know if Maurice is cheating, but it felt wrong not to tell you what my mother saw."

"So much for your faith in my marriage." Corrine picked up her small black purse and headed for the hotel room door, her steps clipped and her lips flatlined.

"Corrine, I—"

"I'll see you at the bar." Corrine opened the door, then let it close behind her with a soft thwack.

Jenna stared helplessly after her, resigned to eating dinner alone. So much for honesty, she thought.

IF ROMANCE COULD ACTUALLY be in the air, Darcy suspected the oxygen at Handy Park would be rich with it.

Saturday night seemed to have transformed the city park into a lovers' paradise as people gathered to listen to a free rock concert at the end of Beale Street.

An elderly couple wore T-shirts, complete with arrows, that proclaimed "I'm with him" and "I'm with her." A younger pair had wrapped their arms so securely around each other's waists they resembled Siamese twins. A couple of teens shared a very hot, very public kiss in front of the statue of W. C. Handy, the man widely known as the father of the blues.

Everybody seemed to be holding hands, including the two men at the edge of the grassy area in front of the stage. Everybody, that was, except Darcy and Kenny. They stood under the trees near the back of the park, a hand's width between them.

Darcy's fingers clenched as she remembered how Kenny would grab for her hand when they first started dating, as though he couldn't bear not to touch her. What was stopping her from reaching for his?

She closed the fingers of her right hand around his left. Did Kenny's fingers remain rigid for a few seconds before they curved around hers? Or had she imagined it?

"I'm glad you're coming to the bar tonight," Darcy said when the rock band took a break. "You can pull up a chair and sit next to me while I collect the cover. You'll absolutely love Jenna."

"So you've said," Kenny remarked, his gaze

straying from her to take in the typical weekend night commotion. A group of guys winding through the crowd with beers in hand, a buxom woman in an ultra-short skirt, a street corner saxophonist filling in the gap before the rock group started again.

"I asked Jenna to take the Sun Studio tour this morning but she did a 10K instead," Darcy continued.

"You already told me that."

Darcy supposed she had covered that subject, but silence reigned between them unless she kept the conversation going.

She'd inquired after Kenny's summer job waiting tables at a popular chain restaurant. He preferred refereeing basketball games.

She'd questioned him about whether he'd declare business as his major when he returned to the University of Tennessee for his junior year. He would.

And she'd asked if anything was wrong.

"What could be wrong?" he'd responded.

What indeed? They were young, they were together and they were listening to music. Even more vital, Darcy felt fine. She'd napped after the studio tour, but only as a precaution. On nondialysis days, she could pretend she was just like any other girl.

A woman passed a few feet from them, the burnished color of her hair drawing Darcy's attention.

"Jenna," she cried in delight.

Jenna started, obviously surprised to hear someone call her name. She turned, her lips stretched into a partial smile. "Hello, Darcy."

"We were just talking about you," Darcy said. "How was the run this morning?"

"Fine." Jenna shifted her weight from one foot to the other, giving Darcy the impression that she was uneasy about something.

"Corrine and I had a blast on the tour," Darcy said. "She kept saying you would love it. I don't mind going again. So let me know when you're up for it."

Jenna's eyes shifted. She didn't reply for a moment, then said, "I'm not much for tours."

Jenna didn't want to hang out with her. The realization hit Darcy like a slap in the face. Could Darcy be more dense? Jenna had already passed on the tour once. Darcy should have picked up before now on the strange vibe Jenna had been giving off.

"We're heading to Peyton's Place to hear you sing," Kenny said smoothly, oblivious to Darcy's distress. "Darcy's been telling me how good you are."

Darcy's mind churned with reasons Jenna might have for avoiding her, but Kenny's comment reminded her she hadn't introduced them. "I'm sorry. Jenna, this is Kenny Coleman. Kenny, this is Jenna…"

She paused, realizing Jenna had failed to furnish her full name when Darcy had initially introduced herself. "I'm sorry, Jenna, but I don't know your last name."

Jenna said nothing for long moments, the sax in the background filling in the silence, before finally admitting the truth. "My full name is Jenna Wright."

Shock traveled through Darcy, like a jolt of electricity delivered by lightning. Jenna Wright was the name of her late father's daughter, of her own half sister.

A gale storm of emotions swirled inside her, the most paramount of which was wonder. This talented, accomplished woman with whom she'd felt an immediate connection was her sister. Her sister!

Now that she knew the connection, Darcy could see that Jenna was tall like their father with hair a similar shade of auburn and eyes the same golden-brown. Even her oval face and wide mouth reminded Darcy of him.

If she'd been looking for the similarities, Darcy would have seen them immediately. But why should she? According to her mother, Jenna and her brother Jeff had made it clear they wanted nothing to do with Margo. Or with Darcy.

"Nice to meet you, Jenna." Kenny seemed blind to the undercurrents, failing even to comment on their shared surname.

Jenna's eyes fastened on Darcy. They didn't look like the eyes of a woman glad to make the acquaintance of her sister. Jenna's dodge of Darcy's invitation suddenly made sense, but nothing else did.

"How?" She uttered only the single syllable.

"Clay didn't tell me who he was when he hired us," Jenna said woodenly. "I didn't figure it out until I was already in Memphis."

Kenny gazed from one woman to the other, obviously at a loss, but Darcy was no longer in the dark. The pieces clicked together until the picture came sharply into focus.

"I've got to go." Jenna left without another word, walking quickly away, leaving Darcy staring speechlessly after her. Jenna wasn't due to perform for another hour and a half.

Kenny frowned. "What was she talking about?"

"You know my father was married before he met my mother, right?" Darcy didn't wait for his answer, her gaze on Jenna's rapidly retreating form. "Jenna's his daughter from his first marriage."

"Imagine that," he remarked, but didn't say more, as though Clay's reasons for hiring Darcy's half sister weren't worth exploring.

Questions ran through Darcy's head, crowding it so she could barely think. Did Jenna know Darcy needed a kidney transplant? Had Clay brought Jenna to Memphis in the hopes that she would become a donor? Was that the reason Jenna was avoiding her?

Darcy's heart clutched, the pain almost physical. But she couldn't be sure of anything until she got some answers, and the only one who could provide them was Clay.

THE FEDEX FORUM IN THE heart of the Beale Street Entertainment District buzzed with activity during the pro basketball season, but sat silent save for the occasional concert, circus or wrestling meet during the summer months.

Clay immediately noted that the forum wasn't hosting an event tonight. The vast paved area in front of the large, sprawling building was nearly deserted.

A skinny, pig-tailed girl of about ten years old chased a miniature version of herself in a game of tag, obviously not trying too hard to win. A man, woman and a third girl, all working on ice cream cones, watched them play.

"Run faster, Mandy," the man called. "Don't let your sister catch you."

Mandy let out a stream of high-pitched giggles as she zigzagged to get away from her slow-moving sister.

Beyond where the two girls played, Darcy sat on one of the short stack of steps leading to the building. From a distance, she looked small, vulnerable and utterly alone.

Clay quickly closed the distance, curious to find out why she'd called him on her cell and asked him to meet her here during his busiest night of the week.

"Hey, Darcy," he called when he was near enough for her to hear.

She inclined her head but said nothing. He couldn't spot even the ghost of a smile on her lips.

He hadn't spent twenty-two years around Darcy without learning something about her. His sister radiated happiness even on her darkest days when she dug deep to put a positive spin on the most negative of situations.

His first thought was of Kenny. Hadn't she planned to be with her boyfriend tonight?

"Why are you by yourself?" he asked.

She took her time answering. "We ran into

some of Kenny's friends on the way over here. They asked him to hang out with them."

"And he left you?"

"I told him to," she said, which Clay thought was no excuse. Although it was barely past eight, he didn't like the thought of his sister walking the downtown area by herself. "I wanted to talk to you alone."

He sat down beside her on the steps, getting a bad feeling. Darcy usually kept her problems to herself, or at least tried to, but something weighed heavily on her mind. She said nothing for long moments, watching the young girls play tag.

The older girl finally caught the younger, wrapping her arms around her in a bear hug. The little girl's giggles grew louder.

"I want to play, too," the third girl shouted. Now finished with her ice cream cone, she ran to join the other two.

"Kenny and I ran into Jenna at Handy Park," Darcy finally said, her voice a monotone. "I realized I didn't know her last name when I went to introduce them. It's Wright." She cut her eyes at him. "But you already know that."

Clay often thought Darcy's voice sounded honey coated, so sweetly did she deliver her words and phrase her sentences. Now she just sounded disheartened. His heart clutched.

"How could you have hired Jenna without telling her who you were?" she asked.

He scratched his head, wondering how he could explain. "I wasn't sure she'd come to Memphis if she knew."

"Knew what? That you were my brother? Or that I need a kidney transplant?"

"Both," he admitted.

"What did you say when you had her under contract? Oh, by the way, can my sister have your kidney?" Her voice cracked at the end of the question. "No wonder Jenna didn't want me to know who she was."

"That's not the reason," Clay refuted.

Darcy dashed a tear from her cheek, as though angry she'd let it fall. "How can you possibly know that?"

"Because Jenna doesn't know you're sick. She reacted so strongly to finding out you were her half sister that I didn't tell her."

"Strongly? That's a strange word for it." She wrapped her arms around her midsection. "She hates me."

"Jenna doesn't hate you, Darcy." He resisted the urge to put his arms around her, sensing she wouldn't welcome his comfort. "She feels a strong sense of loyalty to her mother, who still has a lot of resentment toward our mother."

"Even now that Daddy is gone?"

"Even now."

"So Jenna doesn't know my kidney is failing?"

"She doesn't even know about your first transplant."

She uncrossed her arms and sat up straighter. "Then you can't tell her," she declared.

Every protective instinct he owned rebelled. "I have to tell her."

"This isn't your call, Clay." She looked fierce, like a lioness protecting her cub, except in this case she was safeguarding the secret of her damaged kidney. Or maybe her injured pride. "This affects me. Not you."

"Everything that happens to you affects me."

"I appreciate that you feel that way, but I'm the one who needs a kidney transplant. And I couldn't bear for Jenna to feel pressured to give up her kidney to a stranger."

"You're not a stranger," he argued. "You're her sister."

"I'm her half sister, one she apparently wants nothing to do with." A few tears slid unheeded down her face.

He wiped the moisture from her damp cheeks with the pads of his fingers, feeling like he wanted to cry himself at the sight of her distress. "I've gotten to know Jenna a little since she started singing at the bar. She's a good person, Darcy. If we told her you need a transplant, her feelings toward you might change."

"I don't want her to give me a kidney out of pity. Or guilt; that would be even worse. Dialysis is hard on me, yes. But not so hard I can't manage until a cadaver kidney becomes available."

Clay didn't point out it could be a very long time until she moved up high enough on the transplant list to receive an organ. Darcy already knew that. "You'd manage better with a kidney donated by a relative."

"Maybe so, but most donors don't surrender a kidney to a relative they were tricked into meeting," she said hotly. "Besides, we don't even know if Jenna's kidneys are a match."

"We don't know they're not," he said.

The fight and the anger seemed to seep out of her as quickly as it had appeared. "It just occurred to me to look at this from your view point," she said softly. "You'd do anything for me, wouldn't you?"

"You know I would."

"Then listen very carefully." She grasped both of his hands in both of hers. "I want you to promise not to tell Jenna my kidney is failing. You can't tell Mom about Jenna, either. I couldn't take it if Mom started pressuring me to ask Jenna to get tested."

He'd never seen his sister so serious, not even that night six years ago when he'd driven her to the hospital for her kidney transplant.

"Promise, Clay," she urged.

She was right, he acknowledged. He couldn't deny her anything, especially when she looked at him that way. He inhaled slowly, knowing there was only one answer he could give. "I promise."

"Thank you." Darcy leaned closer to him and kissed him softly on the cheek before letting go of his hands.

The night seemed quieter than it had before, the noise from the crowded part of Beale Street barely audible even though only a few low buildings separated them from the commotion. The three girls and the couple had gone, their laughter no longer carrying on the gentle breeze.

"I'm not coming into the bar tonight," Darcy said into the silence. "I'm sure you understand."

The sadness in her voice tugged at him, but he nodded. Short of breaking his promise to Darcy, there was absolutely nothing he could think to do to make things better.

JENNA KNOCKED ON THE DOOR to Clay's office, where Puff had directed her once the first set was over. No answer. She rapped her knuckles again, more sharply this time. Still no answer.

She tried the knob, found it unlocked and let herself into a room so tiny it barely contained enough space for a desk, chair and filing cabinets.

Clay sat at the desk, his elbows on the smooth dark surface, his head in his hands. He looked up, his expression lacking the warmth that had been present earlier that day at Deer Lake Park.

"I'm sorry," she said. "I knocked, but you didn't answer."

He said nothing. She closed the door, muting the buzz of conversation and jukebox music. He straightened in his chair, sliding his elbows from the desk.

"Can I help you?" he asked.

She shifted her weight from one foot to the other, wondering, as he obviously did, what she wanted from him. Posters of Elvis and Jerry Lee Lewis hung from the walls, but a framed photograph on his desk of Clay flanked by two beautiful blondes drew her attention. Jenna's memory had served her right. Darcy looked just like her mother.

"I noticed Darcy wasn't collecting the cover tonight and wondered why," she ventured. Mark Goldstein was stationed at the door instead, chatting up everyone who came through it, bragging about how he'd beaten Clay in the 10K earlier that day.

Clay released a shot of air through his nose. "You know why. She found out her sister doesn't want to get to know her."

Jenna's stomach pitched and rolled, even though Clay was correct in assuming she'd already guessed the reason. Having it verified made her feel even worse.

"She can't possibly think of me as a sister," she said. "We didn't have any contact at all growing up."

"That wasn't Darcy's decision."

It hadn't been Jenna's, either.

"I have a right not to be friends with her." Jenna heard the defensiveness in her voice.

"The way I see it, you have no right to punish an innocent young woman."

"That's not what I'm doing!"

He rose, coming around the desk and closing the distance between them until he was close enough for her to see his glittering dark eyes.

"Oh, no? Then why are you here in my office? If you didn't feel how hurt Darcy was, you wouldn't be asking about her."

"I'm not trying to hurt her."

"Then get to know her. Let her get to know you. Darcy has a big heart. Give her half a chance, and she'll let you into it."

If there had been enough space in the tiny

room, Jenna would have paced to get away from what he'd said. She fought back with the only argument she had. "That's because *her* mother wasn't the wronged party."

"I've told you this before, but it bears repeating," he said softly. "Darcy wasn't the one who wronged anybody."

Jenna lapsed into silence, averse to acknowledging the truth in what he said. She had an urge to say she'd changed her mind about Darcy. But, of course, she couldn't. She wouldn't.

"I don't appreciate you turning the tables and making this my fault," she said. "None of this would have happened if you hadn't tricked me into coming to Memphis. If anybody should feel guilty, it's you."

"Oh, believe me. I feel plenty guilty." He rubbed the back of his neck. "But it's not because I tried to get you and Darcy together."

She said nothing, feeling the room grow warmer and awareness spark the air as he continued to stare at her. He raised a hand. It hovered inches from her cheek before he dropped it to his side.

"I read you wrong, Jenna," he said. "You're not the kind of woman I feel good about letting myself be attracted to."

CHAPTER EIGHT

JENNA LEFT MEMPHIS NOT long after the sun came
up Sunday morning but couldn't escape Clay's
reproach. His words kept coming back to her
during the week, whether she was shopping for
groceries or advising corporate clients of short-
and long-term strategies to manage cash flow.

A man had never before admitted he was attracted to her in one breath, then condemned
himself for it in the next.

The echoes of his disapproval were loudest at
night, his voice sounding over and over in her
mind, keeping her awake even as her body craved
sleep.

The week dragged by until Friday arrived and
Jenna was back in Memphis, waiting to do what
she should have a week ago.

She checked her reflection in her compact,
verifying that she really did look as tired as she
felt. Her eyes appeared sunken and her skin
pallid, courtesy of her restless nights.

She snapped her compact shut and dropped it back into her purse. Then she tried to get comfortable in the Queen Anne chair tucked into a lonely corner of the Peabody Hotel lobby while she watched and waited.

Darcy Wright finally entered her field of vision, looking effortlessly lovely in a cotton print dress.

Bracing herself, Jenna half rose, lifting a hand to draw the young woman's attention. She approached Jenna not with the exuberance that seemed so much a part of her but with slow, measured steps. Her smile, however, was still bright.

"I'm so glad you called and asked me to meet you," Darcy said.

"I'm glad you agreed." Jenna gestured to the bar situated in the middle of the lobby, where men and women dressed in work clothes were starting their weekend early. "Want to get a drink?"

"Not really." Darcy sat down on a love seat at an angle from Jenna. Jenna wasn't in the mood for a drink, either, but suddenly wished she had something to keep her hands occupied. She folded them in her lap.

"Where's Corrine?" Darcy asked.

"She stopped to visit her cousin on the way to

Memphis so we didn't drive together." Jenna suspected the real reason was Corrine hadn't forgiven Jenna for suggesting Maurice had been unfaithful. Why else would Corrine have booked a separate room?

"I left work early," Jenna announced, although she didn't know why. Darcy couldn't possibly understand how big of a deal that was.

"Where do you work?" Darcy asked politely.

"An accounting firm in Little Rock called Morgan and Roe."

"You're an accountant? I wouldn't have guessed that."

"How about you?" Jenna asked. "What do you do?"

"I'm majoring in elementary education at the University of Tennessee. I'll be a senior in the fall."

They fell silent, and it occurred to Jenna they'd conversed like complete strangers. She knew Darcy was twenty-two, but beyond that the young woman was an enigma. Jenna's mother certainly never discussed her. Looking back on that long-ago weekend when she'd met her father for a drink, Jenna couldn't remember him revealing details of Darcy's life, either. He hadn't even mentioned her.

"This is awkward." Jenna stated the obvious

"I should get to the point. I didn't ask you to meet to make small talk. It was so we could come to an understanding."

Darcy's brow crinkled, the same way Clay's did when he was puzzled. "An understanding?"

"I felt bad last Saturday when you weren't collecting the cover charge. I don't want you to feel so awkward around me you stay away from the bar when I'm singing."

Darcy scooted forward in her seat, all manner of stiff formality gone. Her eyes flashed blue fire. "I'm so mad at that brother of mine, I could just spit. He had no right to put you in this position."

Jenna's mouth dropped open. Hadn't she expressed that same sentiment to Clay?

"If you were interested in meeting me, you'd have arranged it a long time ago. I accepted that." Darcy stated her position in a matter-of-fact, non-judgmental tone, but Jenna's conscience panged.

"I was a child when you were born," Jenna said.

A child whose mother cried over her busted marriage when she thought nobody could hear.

"You haven't been a child in a long time. I'm not naive, Jenna. I know you and Jeff don't think of me as part of your family."

She was right, they didn't. But stated that way, it sounded…harsh.

"But Clay, he doesn't see things like I do. He identifies what he thinks is a problem and will move heaven and earth to solve it." Her chest rose up and down in a heavy sigh. "I won't lie and pretend I don't wish things were different between us. I'd love to get to know you. But I don't have a problem with the way you feel about me. I even understand it."

Jenna felt Darcy's pain as though it were her own. "It's not you I have a problem with, Darcy. None of this has anything to do with you. It's just…complicated."

"Because of how your mother feels about mine?"

"I haven't even told her I'm singing at Clay's bar. It would reopen too many wounds."

Darcy looked more bewildered than enlightened. And why shouldn't she be confused? It was possible, even feasible, that Darcy was unaware of the premarital affair Margo had carried on with their father.

"While I'm singing at your brother's bar, I hope we can be, well, not friends exactly. But two women who aren't uncomfortable around each other," Jenna said.

"You mean, like, acquaintances?" Darcy asked.

"Exactly like acquaintances."

They smiled at each other, not full-fledged smiles, but not adversarial ones, either.

"Am I glad that's over," Jenna confessed. "I get this little tic below my eye when I'm nervous. Drives me crazy."

"I noticed."

Jenna clamped a hand over the offending eye. "Why didn't you say something?"

"I didn't want to embarrass you."

"I think I'm mortified."

"Don't be. I sometimes have the same problem. When I first went out with Kenny—that's my boyfriend—my eye twitched so much he asked why I kept winking at him."

Jenna laughed. "You're joking."

"I wish. Talk about embarrassing."

"I can top that. I once double-dated with a friend and thought her date had a tic. I found out he was winking at me when he got me alone and tried to kiss me."

"I bet you let him have it," Darcy said.

"I sure did. With the cola in my glass."

Darcy giggled. The conversation flowed so swiftly that Jenna didn't realize how much time had gone by until her stomach grumbled. She checked her watch, confirming it was nearly when she usually ate dinner.

"Would you like to grab a bite to eat?" she asked Darcy.

"I'd love to," Darcy replied instantly. "There's a new place around the corner where Corrine and I ate lunch last week that has the best salads."

"Salads are good," Jenna said.

Jenna stood up, then walked side by side with Darcy out the door and down the street to the restaurant. As they walked and talked, Jenna waited to regret the impulsiveness that had led to the invitation.

But, somehow, the regrets never came.

SOMETIMES A MAN COULD trust his gut when it came to a woman, Clay thought as Jenna sang the last note of the evening.

What was left of the Friday night crowd, which was pretty much all of it, applauded loud and long. Jenna, her face lit with pleasure, executed a theatrical bow while Corrine played a showy guitar riff.

"Y'all come back Saturday night, y'hear," Jenna said, slipping into a deep southern twang. The crowd even applauded that, obviously believing Jenna could do no wrong tonight.

Clay agreed.

Darcy had shared the details of her meeting with Jenna, restoring Clay's initial impression of

Jenna as a woman worth knowing. He didn't fully understand Jenna's resentment toward his mother, but she'd proved she had a good heart by realizing she was being unfair to Darcy.

The night owls headed for the door, probably to frequent the Beale Street bars that stayed open until 5:00 a.m. He said all the right things to his customers, but kept his eyes on Jenna. She'd collapsed in a back chair, looking tired but happy.

He approached her after the last straggler left. The hair around her face was slightly damp and the lipstick she applied between sets long gone, but she didn't need any enhancement.

"Where's Corrine?" he asked.

"The restroom," she answered, then squinted at him. "What are you smiling at?"

"The most talented singer in Memphis. The most beautiful, too."

"Beautiful?" She cocked an eyebrow. "I look like a lot of things at the end of a night, but beautiful isn't one of them."

"You're wrong there. But I'm not only talking about the way you look on the outside."

Wariness settled over her, so visible it was as if a cloud hovered above her head. "What's going on, Clay? You told me last weekend you were ashamed at being attracted to me. When I arrived tonight, you avoided me."

He sat down in a chair beside her. "That was because I wasn't looking beneath the surface to the person you really are."

"Darcy told you I asked her to meet me, didn't she?"

He nodded.

"You were right about me being unfair." The forced casualness of her shrug told him the realization had been a difficult, painful one. "I needed her to know I don't hold anything against her personally even though I can't be her friend."

"But she said you had dinner together."

"Yeah, we did." She turned her head so that one of the stage lights brought her face into soft focus, illuminating the warm tones of her skin and hair. "That part about not being her friend isn't working out too well. I like her, Clay."

A sort of peace settled over him, spurred by the knowledge that he hadn't been so wrong to lure Jenna to Memphis. At the very least, the half sisters would get to know each other. "I knew you'd like Darcy if you gave her half a chance."

"Liking her complicates things."

"What's complicated about two people who like each other spending time together?" He smoothed a vaguely damp strand of hair back from her face, taking as an encouraging sign that she didn't slap at his hand. "I happen to know

Darcy's busy tomorrow so why not spend time with me?"

"I don't think—"

"That's good," he interrupted. "Because if you do think, you'll talk yourself out of it. But we had fun during the 10K, didn't we? What's the harm in getting together again?"

"I swear, Darcy's not the only one who's hard to resist. What exactly are you proposing?"

"Meet me in the lobby of the Peabody at ten tomorrow morning and find out."

"Ten? It's already after two."

"Then you won't have long to wait, will you?"

"You won't even give me a hint?"

"Wear your walking shoes," he said with a wink. "And bring an open mind."

He almost added she should bring an open heart, too. But that might have been going too far and he didn't want to risk ruining what had been a superb evening.

THE BASKETBALL TOURNAMENT was in full swing when Darcy took a seat in the bleachers Saturday morning. Ten boys barely into their teens, half of them dressed in maroon and the other half in white, sprinted down the court, passing the ball in whiplike fashion. Almost to a player, they were impressive athletic specimens: tall, fleet and muscular.

Darcy barely glanced at them, her focus on the tan young man in the black-and-white striped shirt, a whistle dangling from a lanyard around his neck.

Two of the players jumped for a rebound and collided in midair. One hit the court as though he'd been shot while the other came away with the basketball and prepared to dribble upcourt.

Kenny put the whistle to his mouth and blew, pointing to the player with the ball and motioning that he'd fouled the other player while pulling down the rebound.

"C'mon now, ref," the player protested loudly.

Kenny didn't respond verbally but leveled him with a don't-mess-with-me stare. The player raised both hands in the universal gesture of apology, then backed off.

The game clock across the gym showed two minutes remaining. From the relatively low score, Darcy figured halftime was approaching. The fans in the stands groaned and applauded on every possession, one man with a foghorn voice screaming "money ball" whenever his team made a shot. Darcy sat silently, watching Kenny instead of the game.

The buzzer sounded, signaling the first half had reached an end. She started to rise to draw Kenny's attention, but he walked straight toward her. Funny. Because he hadn't spared her a glance since she'd entered the gym, she'd been under the impression he hadn't seen her.

"Hey, Kenny." She sent him a smile he didn't return.

He took the bleacher steps two at a time, then plopped down next to her, his chest filling out the referee shirt, a length of long tanned legs visible below the hem of his shorts. He even looked hot in a referee uniform, she thought.

"What are you doing here, Darcy?" he asked.

"I was in the area so stopped by to see if you wanted to take in a movie or go out to dinner later." She might have been stretching the truth with her claim of being "in the area," but her house was only three miles away.

"And you thought tracking me down at the gym to ask was a good idea?"

While she tried to read between the lines of what he'd said, her gaze landed on the clock, which showed four minutes remained in the halftime.

"I left messages on your cell but you didn't call back, so I thought it might be on the blink." She read the truth in the guilty look that descended over his face. "There's nothing wrong with your phone, is there?"

"No," he said flatly without looking at her.

"Then what's going on, Kenny? Why are you avoiding my calls?" There, she'd asked the question she must have subconsciously wanted to ask all along. Otherwise, she wouldn't be here in this stuffy gym before noon on a Saturday.

He glanced over at the clock, which was at three minutes and counting. "This isn't the time to get into it, Jenna."

"I don't agree. I want to know what's going on."

He rubbed his beautifully shaped nose. The dark blue eyes that used to gaze upon her with adoration looked pained.

"I never meant to talk to you about this in a gym. But I think we should stop seeing each other."

On some level Darcy had known what was coming, but pain still lanced through her. She and Kenny were perfect for each other. All their friends said so. "Are you seeing someone else?"

"Nothing like that," he said.

"Then why?" She could hardly form the question.

"It's going to sound like a line, but this is the truth. It's not you, it's me."

"What does that mean?"

He rubbed the back of his neck. "Call me shallow, but I can't deal with this kidney stuff you're going through, okay? I like to go clubbing and stay out late and drink too much, then turn around the next morning and swim or raft or ride my bike. I need a girlfriend who can do those things with me."

"Once I have the transplant," Darcy heard herself saying, "I'll be able to do lots more than I can now."

"Yeah, but you don't know when that'll be. It took a while for this to sink in, but I'm not cut out to be around somebody who's sick. I thought I could handle it. But I can't."

That was why he'd dumped her at the curb when she'd gone in for her initial dialysis treatment, she realized. That was why he never asked how she was feeling or whether it scared the crap out of her that her kidney was failing.

"This isn't being fair to you. You need somebody who can give you a lot more support than I can," Kenny said. "I can't even keep straight which days you're doing that dialyson."

"Dialysis," she corrected.

"Yeah, that."

A buzzer sounded, the alert that one minute remained in the halftime.

"I've got to go, Darcy." He stood up, descended one step, then looked back at her with that handsome face she once thought she'd never tire of looking at. "I'm sorry. I feel like a jerk for telling you something like this at halftime of a basketball game."

She nodded, surprised her eyes were still dry. With her body retaining excess water because of her kidney disease, she should be sprouting tears.

Kenny ran lightly down the bleacher steps and over to the scorer's table, not affording her another glance. As though the sick girl who needed a kidney transplant was already part of his past.

Because she'd pressed the issue, she couldn't blame him for breaking up with her at halftime of a basketball game. But she could blame him for lying.

It wasn't him, as he'd claimed. It was her.

CLAY WATCHED JENNA AS the black Doberman rushed toward her, the muscles of its powerful chest bunching with every stride, its impressive set of teeth bared.

She didn't so much as flinch. Instead her face split into a grin, she bent down, took the Frisbee from the dog's mouth and hugged his thick neck.

"You're a good boy." She laughingly leaned back when the dog tried to lick her cheek. "Yes, you are. A great, big, slobbering good boy."

She stood up, bent her arm at the elbow and flung the disk with surprising authority over the grassy field.

"I can't believe I'm jealous of a dog," Clay said. "I should tell him to keep his paws to himself."

Clay half expected Jenna to list the reasons she couldn't get involved with him, but she laughed.

"No need. It looks like your rival is leaving the park." She gestured to the teenage boy fastening a leash onto the dog's collar. The dog pulled against the restraint, dark eyes shining with love for Jenna, but the boy held fast. The boy waved, calling, "See you around. Thanks for playing with Bubba."

"If I had a dog, I wouldn't give him a boring name like Bubba," Jenna remarked. "I'd call him something cool like Jerry Lee or Stevie Ray or maybe even the Big Bopper."

Clay grinned, wondering if she'd sing to her musically named pup. "Why don't you own a dog?"

She'd wasted no time in making her acquaintance with Bubba. After Clay picked her up at the Peabody Saturday morning and drove her to the park, she quickly noticed the teenager listlessly throwing the Frisbee to his dog and offered to take over.

"I work so much it wouldn't be fair to the dog," she said. "But if I lived in Memphis, I might be tempted to get a dog just for a reason to come to the park."

Jenna swept her hand to indicate the open green space hugging the banks of the Mississippi that was known as Tom Lee Park. Children flew kites, joggers and walkers shared the sidewalk and young families sat on blankets, watching the boats pass by.

"Isn't enjoying the view reason enough?" He looked at her instead of the river. "Although I've been here plenty of times and I can't remember the view ever being this beautiful before."

She crinkled her nose. "Does that kind of flattery usually work on women?"

"No, but there's always a first time."

She threw back her head and laughed, a throaty sound that reminded him of her singing. Clay spread out the blanket he'd gotten from the trunk of his Hyundai and motioned for Jenna to sit down. They sat in comfortable silence, gazing out at the blue of the Mississippi.

The sun lit up her face and the breeze played with the ends of her hair, making her look a little wild, the way she did on stage when she belted out a tune. "I can't envision you as an accountant."

"My coworkers would have a hard time picturing me as a singer."

"Not after they heard you," he said. "Have you ever considered singing full-time?"

She hugged her knees and looked at the river instead of him. The temperature would rise as the day wore on, but for now the breeze kept it cool enough to be comfortable.

"I suppose I might have dreamed about it before I started college, but I'm far too practical for that. I learned from what happened to my mother how important it was to get an education and have a stable career."

"What does your mother do?"

"She's a massage therapist. But she didn't get her license until after she and my father divorced."

Realizing their conversation treaded on controversial ground, Clay returned the subject to Jenna. "Singing could be your career."

Her head shook before he finished his sentence. "Singing jobs don't come with health benefits and a 401K plan."

"If the singer's talented, she can make enough money and those things won't matter."

"Corrine's a very talented guitarist, and for years I've watched her struggle. Things are easier now that she's married, but there were a few times when she could barely pay rent."

He breathed in the smell of the river and freshly cut grass. "Do you think Corrine regrets doing what she loves?"

A frown touched Jenna's lips. "I'm sure she'd like to be more successful."

"Sometimes it's more important to be happy. I called Vicky in California and she's decided to go into social work. She doubts she'll make a lot of money but it's what she wants to do."

"Then I'm happy for her," Jenna said.

"If singing makes you happy, you could make a success of it," he repeated.

"Thank you very much for the vote of confidence, but I'm not a gambler. The gig at your bar is as far as it goes for me." She turned to face him fully. "Let me ask you something I've been wondering about. Why name your bar Peyton's Place? You couldn't have been a fan of that old soap opera."

He plucked a blade of grass, debating whether to let her get away with changing the subject, deciding she'd said all she would about her singing.

"I didn't name the bar after the soap." He needed to be careful how much he told her. "I named it after a person."

She seemed to digest that before asking, "Female or male?"

His answer was bound to give her the wrong impression, but there was no getting around it. "Female."

When he failed to elaborate, she nodded, as though she understood when she couldn't possibly. "I'll say one thing for the name. It's catchy. Once you hear it, you remember it."

"I hope so," Clay said. "But business has never been as good as these past few weeks. I didn't get into the music scene before hiring you and Corrine because I thought I couldn't afford it yet. I see now that was a mistake. You've got to spend money to make money. Which brings us full circle back to you."

She regarded him quizzically. "How so?"

"Sometimes you've got to bite the bullet and take a chance."

"I wouldn't be here with you if I wasn't taking a chance," she said. Before he could accuse her of deliberately misunderstanding him, she pointed to a row of expensive houses atop a bank on the other side of the street. "Is there a sidewalk on top of that hill?"

He let her get away with changing the subject from her singing. Again. "Around these parts, we call that hill a bluff. The neighborhood's known as the South Bluffs and the sidewalk's called the Riverbluff Walkway. See those steps carved into the bluff? That's where they lead."

"Can we go for a walk up there?"

"You should know something first," he said

slowly, reluctant to say anything that might ruin the lighthearted mood but knowing he must. "My mother owns one of those houses."

She visibly started. "I thought she lived in the house on Locust Lane."

That five-bedroom Victorian had been the house in which Jenna had lived during the first eight years of her life, the house where Clay and Darcy had later spent a good chunk of their childhood.

"They sold that house after the city put in the walkway and people started renovating the houses on the bluff," he said. "My mother fell in love with the view of the Mississippi."

Jenna nodded but said nothing.

"We probably won't run into her, but I'd understand if you want to pass on that walk."

"No," Jenna said a little too brightly. "Let's go."

THE MISSISSIPPI APPEARED even mightier from the vantage point of the Riverbluff Walkway than it had from the park. Jenna had a better appreciation of the scope of the great river and the dramatic view to the Arkansas flood plain.

The gorgeous riverside houses that backed up to the walkway were nearly as impressive as the scenery, with huge picture windows, modern designs and stunning landscaping that spoke of exclusivity.

She asked the question pounding at her brain. "Which house is your mother's?"

"It's on the next block," he said. "Two stories with a gray stucco exterior and a second-floor terrace."

Margo's house blended so nicely with the others that Jenna might not have awarded it a second look. Now that she knew who lived there, she couldn't smother her curiosity.

"Is that a bedroom that leads onto the terrace?" she asked.

"Two of the bedrooms open onto the terrace. The master suite on the left and Darcy's bedroom on the right."

Jenna focused on the flowering plants lining the terrace outside Darcy's bedroom, easily imagining the luxury within: Plush carpeting, fancy furniture, expensive bedding. Darcy and her mother would want for nothing.

After Jenna's mother had moved her and Jeff from the house on Locust Lane, Jenna's bedroom had been a tiny four-wall box.

"Let's go back." Jenna didn't wait for Clay to agree, pivoting sharply and retracing their path, walking a good foot ahead of him.

He caught up to her when they reached the

steps leading back to the park, stopping her retreat with a hand on her shoulder. "Care to tell me why we're running?"

"This was a mistake," she muttered.

His dark brows furrowed. "Going for a walk?"

"Going anywhere with you. Having dinner with Darcy. Singing in your bar. All of it."

"Because my mother lives in a nice house?"

"It sounds petty put that way, but, yes. Before today, I'd have sworn my mother was the reason I was reluctant to get involved with you and Darcy. Looking at that house, I realize that's not entirely true."

"I don't understand."

She kneaded her brow, feeling a headache coming on. The sun had risen higher in the sky since they'd gone for their walk, significantly raising the temperature. "You probably already know Jeff and I hardly had any contact with our father growing up. He paid child support, but that was it."

"Is that why you didn't come to his memorial service?"

"What?" The wind seemed to leave her lungs, reminding her of the time she'd tripped while racing her brother and fallen on her stomach. "No. Of course not. Your mother didn't tell us he was dead until after he was buried."

"She wouldn't do that," he refuted.

"Why not? She kept Jeff and me away from our dad by never inviting us to Memphis. If our dad didn't come to Little Rock, we didn't see him."

"What makes you think my mother decided when and where your father exercised his visitation rights?"

"Are you saying she didn't influence him?"

"I'm saying your father wasn't what I'd call a family man. Hell, neither is mine. My mother never even married him. He moved to Hawaii to work in a hotel years ago, and I'm lucky if I see him once every five years."

"Darcy saw my father every day."

"Not true. Like I said, he wasn't much of a family man."

His argument carried the ring of truth, but Jenna felt compelled to offer a counterpoint. "At least he cared enough about Darcy to be there for her some of the time."

"I don't like to speak ill of the dead, but if he'd really cared, he'd have left Darcy and my mom in better financial shape. He had so much credit card debt that the house is my mother's only real asset."

"Then she should get a job, like my mother did."

"I've told her that again and again. It's only

lately that it's finally started to sink in. But she doesn't have the same level of education as your mother. Any job she gets wouldn't pay much."

"I can't say I feel sorry for her, considering it was her fault I missed my own father's funeral."

She heard him breathe out through his nose. "She really didn't notify you in time?"

"She really didn't," Jenna said, then felt she needed to qualify her answer. "We heard she thought Dad's former law partner had called us."

"That's no excuse," he said. "No matter what the circumstances, she should have made sure you and your family knew in time to go to the funeral. I'm sorry."

"Thank you," Jenna said with as much dignity as she could muster. "And I'm sorry for going off like that. I know none of this is your fault."

"Or Darcy's fault, either," he added.

She smiled at him sadly. "Here's the thing. I'm not sure I'm a big enough person to continue to have a relationship with the children of the woman who was at fault. At least partly."

On the street below them a car horn sounded. In the park a dog barked. A warm breeze whooshed through the leaves of the nearby trees. Clay said nothing, merely holding his hand out to her.

She took it, and he kept her hand securely in

his grip for the silent trip down the steep steps. At the bottom of the bluff, they waited for the traffic to pass so they could cross the street to the parking lot. He squeezed her hand.

"By the way," he said in a soft tone that alerted her to the importance of whatever he was about to say, "you're a bigger person than you think you are."

She didn't reply, not at all certain he was right.

CHAPTER NINE

JENNA ENDED THE FIRST SET Saturday night with a Joan Baez song about a simple twist of fate, then exaggeratedly wiped a hand over her brow as the bar crowd applauded.

"Am I glad you liked that one or Corrine would never let me hear the end of it." Jenna gestured to her partner. "I had to talk her into including it."

Corrine leaned slightly forward to speak into her microphone. "We cut a deal to do Stairway to Heaven after the break because of the cool guitar riffs, so it'd help if you could applaud that one, too."

Jenna laughed, announced they were taking a short break and waited while Corrine stowed her guitar. Her friend started to leave the stage, barely glancing at Jenna.

"Corrine, wait." Jenna was heartened when her friend stopped instead of sweeping by, uncomfortably aware that their on-stage banter had been an act on Corrine's part. "I hate that this distance between us is getting bigger."

Corrine said nothing, the same reaction she'd had the other times Jenna had tried to apologize for suggesting Maurice could be having an affair. A heavy weight settled over Jenna's heart. "Just tell me if you're okay."

"I'll tell you what I am," Corrine said. "I'm still married."

Corrine left the stage without a backward glance, fighting her way through the crowd and the tables to the front door. Jenna repressed an urge to chase after her, knowing it wouldn't do any good. Spending her break with Clay wasn't an option, either, since he and Puff looked busy behind the bar.

"You probably get tired of hearing this, but you are one awesome singer," a girl who couldn't have been much past drinking age told her when she stepped off stage.

Jenna usually enjoyed chatting about music to the bar patrons, but discovered a palpable need to be alone to sort out her thoughts. Not only about Corrine, but about Clay and Darcy.

"Thanks for letting me know you think so," she told the girl with a smile. She excused herself, heading toward the back of the bar where there must be a rear exit.

Yes, there it was, along with a small sign alerting customers to use the front exit. Ignoring the instructions, she pushed through the door, craving the fresh air.

The door led to an alley that Jenna thought was deserted until she heard a soft snuffling. She cast a panoramic glance around the area, taking in the narrow paved road, the shadows, the dumpsters—and a blonde with her back pressed against a building who looked exactly like...

"Darcy," Jenna cried, rushing over to her. The young woman's head lifted, obviously surprised to see somebody else in the alley. "Honey, are you okay?"

Darcy immediately brushed tears from her cheeks, but they still leaked from her eyes. "I'm fine."

"You don't seem fine." Jenna smoothed the hair back from Darcy's damp cheeks. "What's wrong?"

The younger woman gave up on trying to smile, her lower lip trembling. "I'm being a baby. I asked Amanda—that's Clay's new waitress—to cover for me at the door because I felt the tears coming. But I never cry. Especially not in front of people."

"Just tell me what's bothering you."

Darcy took a shuddering breath. "Kenny broke up with me this morning."

"This morning?"

"During halftime of a basketball game he was reffing." She sniffed, blinked a few times and must have read the indignation on Jenna's face. "I know it sounds bad, but it was my fault, really. I knew things weren't right and I made him tell me why."

It pained Jenna that Darcy was making excuses for the young man who'd hurt her. "Oh, Darcy, I'm sorry."

Darcy's throat constricted as she swallowed. She wiped a tear from under her eye. "I thought he loved me, Jenna. Boy, was I wrong."

"Then he's not the right man for you."

"That doesn't make me feel any better. Kenny's not even dating anyone else. He just doesn't want to be with me."

"Then Kenny's a loser," Jenna declared.

Darcy's face crinkled. "Do you mean that?"

"Of course I do. You're a sweet, wonderful young woman with a heart even more beautiful than you are. If Kenny can't see that, he's blind."

The words hung between them, pregnant with meaning. Jenna looked at Darcy and felt as though she saw her clearly for the first time. Clay was right. She did have room in her heart for her half sister.

"You really believe those things about me?" Astonishment infused Darcy's voice.

Jenna nodded. "I really believe it. And I'll tell you something else. The next man who dares hurt my sister will have to answer to me."

This time the tears that ran in rivulets down Darcy's face had a different source: Joy.

Jenna could identify the source because, as she hugged Darcy close, it was the same emotion fueling her own tears and coursing through her heart.

MIKE PUFFENBARGER HAD never deluded himself into believing he had the kind of face that turned a woman's head.

His eyes were too close together, his nose a tad long, his lips a bit thin. He wasn't unattractive as much as he was nondescript. That wasn't conjecture; that was a fact of life.

He'd once delivered roses to his favorite high-school teacher. He'd sat front row center in her class for two school years, through both algebra and geometry. She sent him away with a tip and a "thank you, young man."

Females with whom he'd attended high school came into Peyton's Place and showed no indication they'd ever seen him before. The prettier the young woman, the less likely she was to remember him. Or to notice him, if the woman was someone he hadn't yet met.

Darcy Wright was an exceedingly pretty young woman, the kind who dated great-looking guys like Kenny Coleman. Except a self-centered guy like Kenny Coleman couldn't make Darcy happy.

He'd wager anything that Kenny was behind Darcy's subdued behavior. The sweet smile with which she greeted customers wasn't as sweet, her gestures not as expansive, her manner not as friendly.

She'd even asked Amanda to cover for her at the door. He was about to go hunt for her, the customers be damned, when he spotted her walking past the bar.

He ignored a customer vying for his attention and nearly plowed over Clay in his zeal to reach Darcy, immediately noticing the slight swelling around her eyes. Nobody would blame her for crying over the scary health problems that would devastate other women her age, but that jerk Kenny was probably the cause.

"Hey." He wouldn't ask how she was doing, a question she had to be sick of hearing. "I noticed you left your post."

"Kenny broke up with me," she blurted.

Darcy wouldn't be so upset over a simple breakup, Mike thought. That idiot had said or done something to make Darcy doubt herself. If

Mike was patient, one day Darcy might trust him enough to tell him what it was.

"If you want me to beat him up, I'll try," Mike said. "I can't promise I'll succeed, but I will try."

She smiled, the response he'd been angling for even though he was far enough gone over Darcy that he would gladly take a swing at Kenny.

"Just knowing you'd be willing to is enough," she said.

"I'm sorry, Darcy." He *was* sorry, not that Kenny was out of Darcy's life but that she'd ever let him close enough in the first place. "He's the loser, Darcy, not you."

"Jenna said the same thing."

She smiled at him, and he felt like the warmth of the sun's rays had just hit him.

"Can you keep a secret?" she asked.

He could do anything she asked. "Sure."

"Jenna's my half sister. But the knowledge is kind of new so I don't want to tell just anybody."

"That's great." He referred both to her news and the fact that he'd transcended the level of "just anybody."

"Between the nice things you and Jenna tell me, I'm going to get a huge ego," Darcy said.

"You? Never." Mike shook his head. "But now we have a consensus. Kenny doesn't deserve you."

"Thank you." She kissed him on the cheek. "It's weird. I hardly know you, but I already consider you a good buddy."

His heart clutched. She thought of him as a *buddy?* Even though he'd suspected as much, the disappointment was palpable.

Tell her you'd like to be more than a buddy. The timing wasn't ideal, but he might not get a better chance. Somebody as great as Darcy would have a new boyfriend in no time.

A boyfriend who wasn't the instantly forgettable type.

"Hey, barkeep, can I get a beer over here?" a man yelled.

"You better go," Darcy told him. "I'll catch you later, okay?"

She walked away, taking his chance to confess his feelings with her. For how could a guy like him ever get the courage to tell a woman like Darcy he was nuts about her?

JENNA THOUGHT NOTHING WAS quite so sexy as having a desirable man's eyes following your every move. The eyes tracking her were so dark they were almost black, somehow making his stare seem more intense.

Those ebony eyes had watched her sing to the crowd, deflect the attention of more than one overexuberant male fan and wrap Darcy in a heartfelt hug before the young woman left for the night.

And they'd watched her watch him.

That the eyes belonged to Clay might have been the sexiest thing of all. Nobody else in the bar—nobody else in her *life*—had ever made her feel as if he was caressing her with a mere look.

While she fended off yet another admirer, this one a young man at least ten years her junior, she furtively watched Clay pick up empty and half-empty glasses from the nearby tables.

"Thanks very much for inviting me to party the night away," she told the young man, "but I'm seeing somebody."

"That's the story of my life," the young man said, taking her rejection in stride before trudging out of the bar.

Clay abandoned his task as soon as the man was gone. He approached her, the heat still in his eyes. It gave Jenna hope she'd told her youthful admirer the truth about a special man in her life.

"Where's Corrine?" he asked.

"Gone." Jenna didn't offer an explanation for why Corrine had called a taxi rather than waiting to walk back to the hotel with her. "I'm on my way out, too."

"I can't let you leave by yourself. I've seen

how men react to you while you're singing. You can't be too careful."

Jenna peered at him from under her lashes. "Does that mean I should be careful of you?"

He grinned. "Hell, yeah, but I'm hoping you don't let that stop you from accepting a ride back to the hotel from me."

She couldn't help but smile back.

After Clay asked Puff to close the bar, he drove her to the Peabody, parked and walked her to the elevator. They talked of inconsequential things. Her song selection. His new employees. The police presence in the Memphis downtown.

The back and forth felt so right Jenna nearly asked when things had changed so drastically between them that the mere touch of his hand on her elbow electrified her skin.

"I'll walk you to your room," he offered when a tone sounded the arrival of the elevator car.

Their conversation dried up when the elevator doors slid shut, enclosing them in the close confines of the car. Jenna wondered if the emotions rendering her speechless had also taken hold of Clay's tongue. Even though they didn't touch, she could feel the heat of his body, hear the cadence of his breathing, smell the scent of his skin.

He waited for her to exit the elevator, then accompanied her down the hall, showing no indication he heard the rapid thumping of her heart. Would he think she was too forward if she invited him in? Was it too soon?

"If you weren't sharing with Corrine," he remarked, "I'd be angling for an invitation."

Of course. He'd set up the hotel arrangements so he naturally believed Corrine was behind the door, which meant he had no expectation of sharing her bed when suggesting he walk her to her room. That endeared him to her even more.

"Corrine and I aren't rooming together this weekend." She heard her voice crack but couldn't help it. She valued her friendship with Corrine too much to trivialize, even with a gorgeous man outside her hotel room door. "We didn't drive to Memphis together, either."

The heat that had been in his eyes fled, replaced by concern. "Want to tell me what's going on with you two?"

She didn't need to think about her answer. "Yeah, I do."

"I promise not to get the wrong idea if you invite me in. I'll even keep six feet between us at all times so you're not tempted to jump me."

She rolled her eyes even while secretly thankful he'd lightened the mood. "I can control myself, thank you very much."

"Does that mean you might *want* to jump me?"

She laughed, unlocked the door with her key card and stepped back so he could enter. The filmy nightgown she'd worn to sleep the night before lay strewn across one of the beds, a discarded bra beside it, making being with him inside her room seem intimate. She gathered up the items and threw them in a drawer.

Her throat suddenly parched, she crossed the room to the minibar and crouched down in front of it. "I don't usually use these things because everything's so overpriced, but I'm dying for a bottle of water. You want anything?"

"Water's good."

He sat down in the swivel chair beside the desk while she removed the water from the minibar. She handed him a bottle, watching the strong lines of his throat as he swallowed. She drank, too, then put her bottle down on the desk and sat on the edge of the bed so she faced him. She appreciated that he said nothing, instead letting her take her time.

"I told Corrine my mother saw her husband with another woman, and she didn't take it well. I've apologized more than once but she's still angry."

Clay visibly winced.

"You think I should have kept quiet, don't you?" Jenna voiced her own concern.

He didn't answer for long moments, the whir of the room's air conditioner sounding strangely loud. "I get that you were trying to be a loyal friend, but you don't know her husband's having an affair."

"I realize that."

"You do?" He sounded unconvinced.

"Sure I do. Why wouldn't I?" Even though he remained silent, she guessed at the reason for his skepticism. "You think I'm predisposed to believe men cheat because my father cheated with your mother."

He stroked his chin, which had developed a five o'clock shadow hours ago. "I wondered about that. I even wondered if that's the reason you aren't married."

She straightened her spine. "I'm not married because I haven't found the right man."

He leaned forward in the chair, balancing his elbows on his thighs, his hands dangling between his spread legs. "You mean a man who loves you so much he'd never consider being with another woman?"

She'd never consciously assigned that criteria but recognized the truth in his question. Maybe that was one of the reasons her past relationships tended to last about as long as it took milk to sour. "Is that so corny?"

"Not to me. I'm waiting for a woman who makes me forget about every other."

It occurred to Jenna to ask him about Peyton, the woman after whom he'd named his bar. Jenna had gotten the strong impression this Peyton held a special place in Clay's heart, but Clay couldn't be thinking of Peyton now. Not when he looked at Jenna so intently, as though she was the woman who could make him develop tunnel vision.

"I saw you hug Darcy when she left the bar tonight," he said into the silence. "Why'd you do that?"

She heard what he didn't ask: Had she changed her mind about continuing a relationship with Darcy?

"You know about her breakup with Kenny, right?" she asked, and he nodded. "She was pretty torn up about it, especially because I gather he was pretty callous about the whole thing. I know relationships sometimes just don't work out, but seeing Darcy hurting like that made me want to hunt down Kenny and make him pay."

He rolled the chair closer to the bed over the thick carpeting and captured her hand, reigniting the sexual tension that had simmered between them in the hallway. "I told you."

She pretended not to understand. "I don't

remember you mentioning anything about me having vigilante tendencies."

He didn't let her trivialize the moment. "I meant I was right. You are a better person than you think you are."

"Because I can't resist Darcy?"

"Yeah." He turned her palm over and lazily drew a circle on it with his forefinger, sending her pulse skittering. "And now I'm praying Darcy isn't the only one you can't resist."

"Weren't you supposed to keep six feet away?" she asked in a hushed voice.

"If you ask me to, I'll move."

Silence fell between them, so absolute she could hear their breathing above the still-humming air conditioner and the sound of a door closing in the hall. The quiet stretched for one beat, two, three.

"You haven't told me to back away," he said softly.

The resolve to fight what she felt for him dissolved, like droplets of water in the sun. The battle, she acknowledged, had been lost long before this moment. Maybe even as far back as the 10K when he stuck stubbornly beside her even though it meant losing his bet. "That's because I want you to come closer."

A smile of pure male satisfaction curved his lips and reflected in his eyes. Without letting go of her hand, he rose from the chair and sat down next to her on the bed, gathering her close to his heart.

"Ah, Jenna. I can already tell you I won't be able to get close enough." He nuzzled her cheek, the feel of his lower face slightly scratchy against her skin. She turned and their breath mingled before her mouth met his in a soft, gentle kiss that still managed to sear her insides.

His lips leisurely explored her own while the hand that wasn't holding hers glided up and over the bare skin of her arm, stopping to play with the soft hair at her nape.

She gasped and he deepened the kiss, his tongue sliding silkily over hers, his fingers tangling her hair and cradling the back of her head. Sensations danced inside her, causing her body to come jarringly alive despite the early morning hour.

Heat built up deep inside her, demanding release. Only Clay could affect her this way with a kiss, she thought dizzily. Certainly no other man ever had. As the kiss went on and on and on, it became more difficult to think. She certainly couldn't puzzle out the reason he was stopping.

"Open your eyes, Jenna," he commanded.

Her eyes blinked open, her senses so dazed he appeared in soft focus.

"Look at me, Jenna. I want you to see who

you're kissing. I don't want you to regret inviting me into your hotel room."

She touched his face, stroking the arch of his cheekbone, discovering the small bump on his nose, tracing her fingers over his wonderfully masculine mouth. Then she found her voice.

"I'll tell you a secret." She spoke in a breathy whisper, the only sound she seemed capable of making. "I think I must have known this would happen when I invited you in."

The corners of his mouth lifted. "Oh, really?"

"I only have so much willpower." She unbuttoned the top button of his shirt and slowly worked her way down, baring to her gaze a muscular chest sprinkled with just the right amount of dark hair. She reached the button to his jeans before she spoke again. "And that willpower? I'm pretty sure it's all gone."

"It couldn't have left at a better time." He wrapped her more securely in his arms. Their mouths fused, their hands eagerly trying to rid each other of clothes, the hours ahead filled with the promise of pleasure.

Throughout every one of them, Jenna kept her eyes wide open.

CLAY AWAKENED TO THE sound of chirping and a naked woman nestled against him. His fuzzy brain couldn't identify the noise until Jenna turned over and switched off the alarm clock, taking her warmth with her. His arm snaked around her waist, pulling her back into the crook of his arm.

"Hey, where do you think you're going?" His mouth found hers for a thorough kiss, his body responding the same way as it had last night. He smiled into her eyes. "Good morning, gorgeous."

She smiled back, softly running her fingers through his hair. "You're even charming first thing in the morning."

"I'm trying to convince you to stay in bed. What time is it anyway?"

"Nine o'clock."

He made a face. "Who gets up that early on a Sunday morning?"

"I set the alarm before I left for the bar last night. Checkout's at eleven. Even if it wasn't, I've got to get back to Little Rock."

"I have an idea about that." He smoothed his hand down the side of her body, pausing to explore the satiny curve of her hip. "Why don't you spend the day with me?"

"If you're suggesting we spend the day in bed, you make an offer that's hard to refuse."

He chuckled, a warmth he recognized as happiness radiating through him. "The offer's for a morning in bed and an afternoon on the water. A friend lets me borrow his motorboat. I'm free until six. If you leave for Little Rock then, you'll get back in plenty of time to get ready for work tomorrow."

"But not in time for my brother's cookout." She sounded regretful, which didn't stop disappointment from gripping him. "That's why I set the alarm. My whole family's going to be there."

Clay stopped running his hand over her sleek skin and sat up in bed, the sheets falling to his waist. In a perfect world, Jenna would invite him to accompany her and he'd accept without reservation. But neither of those things would happen.

"Who's coming besides your brother and mother?" he asked.

She anchored one elbow on the bed and supported her head with a hand. "Jeff's married to a fantastic woman named Nancy, and they have three sons. Chad's eleven, Ben's nine and Kevin's seven. It's ironic we're having a cookout today considering that Jeff will do most of the work."

"Ironic how?"

"Today's Father's Day. Don't tell me you forgot to send your dad a card."

"I mailed him a gift certificate last week," he said. "Like I told you before, he's in Hawaii. We're not close."

"My family is close," she said.

"Did you tell them you've been spending time with Darcy and me?" he asked, fairly certain of the reply.

"I thought I'd tell them today."

"Tell them what exactly?" He watched the fall of her chest as she breathed in and out, but stopped himself from reaching for her.

"That I'm singing in your bar. That I met Darcy. That I like her."

He noticed she said nothing about informing her family about her very personal involvement with him. "How do you think they'll take it?"

"Not well. But I can always hope." She sat up beside him, baring her beautiful breasts to his gaze. "I should get going."

"What time does the cookout start?" he asked.

"Noon."

When she made no move to leave the bed, he pulled her snugly against him, finding it impossible to let her go. "I'm thinking hard about persuading you to be late to that cookout."

"I wish you would," she said, lips smiling, eyes shining.

Even as he kissed her, he acknowledged that the secret he still kept represented an even bigger risk to their relationship than her family.

Jenna had forgiven him for tricking her into

getting to know Darcy, but she might get angry all over again when she learned Darcy needed a kidney donor. She could even conclude he'd used sex to soften Jenna up so she'd get tested.

Jenna kissed him back, and his mind vehemently rejected that last thought as having no merit. Clay's only reason for making love to Jenna, he realized, was because he was falling in love with her.

CHAPTER TEN

THE CUTE LITTLE split-level home Corrine shared with Maurice was quiet when Corrine stepped across the threshold on Sunday morning. Too quiet.

She hadn't been able to sleep in her lonely hotel room and had gotten an early start back from Memphis, but not so early that Maurice shouldn't be up and around.

Her husband wasn't a churchgoer so Corrine couldn't think of a plausible reason for him not to be home—unless he'd stayed out all night.

The large open family room with the cathedral ceiling that had sold her on the house showed no signs of life but he could be elsewhere in the house.

She shut her eyes tight. Oh, please, let him be home. Silence greeted her prayer, followed by the soft fall of footsteps. She almost gasped in relief.

"Hey, babe. I didn't expect you back so early." Maurice appeared from the direction of the kitchen, where he'd probably been drinking decaffeinated coffee while reading the Sunday newspaper. His snug-fitting gray T-shirt accentuated the sleek muscles in his arms and chest, and his lightweight sweatpants hung low on his waist. Even first thing in the morning, he was a fine specimen of a man, the perfect advertisement for the type of work he did. "I missed you."

He gathered her into his arms, and her whole body went pliant. Whether it was from relief of the effect of being close to him, she didn't know. He kissed her with practiced ease, tasting of cocoa beans and smelling like soap and shampoo, as though he'd showered recently.

Maurice usually took a shower at night.

He lifted his head, a satisfied smile creasing his handsome face as he stepped away from her. Was the smile because she was home or because he believed his ardent kiss could curb her suspicions? She nearly cried out in dismay as she silently acknowledged the doubt that had never truly left her. Instead, it had lurked in the back of her mind, waiting to resurface.

She made her voice casual. "How long have you been awake?"

"A few hours. I got up and went for a run."

Of course. How could she forget her husband was a health and fitness nut? The very way he was dressed, in that T-shirt and those low-slung sweatpants, should have tipped her off.

"How was Memphis?" he asked.

"The gig's going great." She didn't tell him about the rift that had developed between herself and Jenna, growing so wide she'd barely spoken to her friend all weekend. "How'd you keep yourself busy while I'm gone?"

"The usual. You know how packed my weekends are with clients." He took her by the hand before she could phrase more specific questions. "Come with me. I've got a surprise for you."

She let him lead her into their eat-in kitchen. On the table sat the newspaper and a small box wrapped in shiny red paper and topped with a bow.

"Sit down and open it." He pulled out the nearest kitchen chair so she could take a seat.

She untied the bow and unwrapped the package, revealing a square, black box imprinted with the name of a prestigious jeweler. She snapped open the box, where a bracelet consisting of a string of tiny white pearls was nestled against black velvet.

"Do you like it?" Maurice prompted.

"It's beautiful." Beautiful and completely impractical. Corrine preferred oversized costume jewelry that drew the eye while she was performing. The delicate pearl bracelet might snap if she brushed against something.

"I thought of you when I saw it," Maurice said.

She'd never worn pearls or expressed a desire to own them. "Really? Why?"

"Because they're lovely." He leaned down and kissed her on the mouth. "Just like you."

Maurice had always been masterful at delivering compliments. He sustained eye contact and spoke in a tone quieter than his normal speaking voice, creating the impression that whatever he was saying was extremely important.

He used the same tactic on everyone, whether the recipient of the compliment was Corrine, a potential client or the clerk at the grocery store.

She weakened, the same as she always did, but this time an internal voice screamed a question. A question she needed to ask. "What's the occasion, Maurice? It's not my birthday and our anniversary is months away."

It was, in fact, Father's Day. Since Maurice claimed he wasn't a shopper, she'd bought the cards and presents for both of their dads.

He didn't answer immediately and that voice in Corrine's head provided a number of solid reasons Maurice had overcome his aversion to shopping.

Because Corrine had found a woman's phone

number in his jeans. Because guilt drove a man to compensate for the wrong he'd done. Because he didn't want her to suspect him of adultery.

He tipped up her chin so that she had to look into his soft, brown eyes. "I didn't realize I needed an excuse to buy the woman I love a present."

If she'd been an ice cube, she would have melted into a puddle. Maurice loved her. No, he hadn't been as attentive lately as she would have liked but they were no longer newlyweds.

Corrine needed to readjust her expectations. She had a hardworking husband who invested time and energy into building up his client list and growing his business. Some of those clients, understandably, were female. The sooner she tamped down the jealousy, the stronger their marriage would become.

"Love you, too," she said.

Something that looked like triumph flashed in his eyes at the same moment she spotted a faint mark on his neck that hadn't been there when she'd left for Memphis.

Just like that, she had another question: Had a woman put it there?

JEFF WRIGHT LIVED IN an upscale Little Rock neighborhood where home owners took pride in their properties. His two-story contemporary home boasted modern styling, high ceilings and bay windows. But in Jenna's estimation the best part of the house was the backyard deck that overlooked an in-ground swimming pool.

She'd visited her brother's house dozens of times, usually ringing the doorbell to gain admittance. On Sunday afternoon she took a chance that Jeff had unlocked the gate of the privacy fence that enclosed the backyard.

She stood with her hand poised on the latch, listening to water splashing as her three nephews whooped it up in the pool and smelling the inviting aroma of burgers cooking on the grill.

The small group of people she'd always thought of as her family was beyond the fence, literally and figuratively closed to the possibility of adding anyone else into the mix. Until she'd met Darcy, Jenna had also viewed their family as a self-contained unit.

She didn't want to think about where Clay fit into the equation, although she couldn't get him out of her mind. She still felt the imprint of his body on hers as vividly as she felt the afternoon sun.

Squaring her shoulders, she unlatched the gate and walked into a cookout already in full swing. Ben and Kevin, the youngest two boys, whipped a ball back and forth from one side of the pool to the other. Chad stood on the diving board. He spotted Jenna first.

"Hey, Aunt Jenna. Watch this." Chad sprang into the air, wrapping his arms around his knees and hitting the water with such a resounding smack that a wave of water sloshed out of the pool.

"Stop it with the cannonballs, Chad. I don't want to have to add water to the pool." Jeff called from behind the grill. The sun caught the auburn highlights in his hair, the giveaway that he was Jenna's brother. Of medium height and weight, he kept himself in shape by running every morning and trying to keep up with his three sons. To Jenna, he said, "Hey, Sis. It's about time you got here. We were starting to wonder if you were going to make it."

"I stopped home to change into shorts after driving back from Memphis." Jenna left out the part about loitering in bed with Clay for the better part of the morning.

"I heard you were singing again." Jeff's wife Nancy crossed the deck to envelop her in a warm hug. Nancy wore her dark hair in a pixie cut that should have looked incongruous with her tall, thin body but didn't. "You look incredible. Performing obviously agrees with you."

Making love to Clay agreed with her, Jenna thought. "I've got to admit I enjoy being back on stage."

Her mother emerged from the house carrying condiments and packages of hot dog and hamburger buns. A graying, middle-aged man trailed after her, one hand clutching a supersized bag of chips. Ned Voight.

"Your mother brought a date." Nancy spoke in a whisper.

"Are you sure he's her date?" Jenna whispered back. "She told me she and Mr. Voight are only friends."

"Then they're *very* friendly. He can't stop touching her." Nancy nodded toward the couple. Mr. Voight's free hand rested on her mother's back. "I think it's cute."

Jenna did, too.

"Jenna, I'm glad you made it." Her mother set down the buns and condiments on the eight-sided picnic table and turned to Mr. Voight. "You remember Ned, don't you?"

"Wonderful to see you again, Jenna." He came forward with his hand outstretched, insisting she call him by his first name. He reminded Jenna of Clay, tall and handsome, filled with life and charm.

As the afternoon wore on Jenna noticed the

accuracy of Nancy's observation. Ned found reasons to touch her mother, whether to rub her shoulder while he sat beside her or to brush her hand when he passed her a burger.

Burgers and hot dogs were the feature fare. Despite the apron imprinted with "Super Dad," obviously a Father's Day gift from the boys, Jeff's expertise didn't extend past a typical cookout menu but nobody seemed to mind.

"Can I have another dog, Dad?" Kevin asked.

"May I have another dog, please?" Nancy corrected.

Kevin screwed up his freckled face. "*You* want another dog, too, Mom? You don't usually eat more than one."

They all laughed. The afternoon continued in that vein, with everybody seeming to talk at once about their lives and jobs. Jenna discovered that Jeff had been promoted, Nancy had taken a volunteer position on a literacy council and her mother had been named employee of the month at the health club.

Jenna settled into her family's easy rhythm, the tension that had paralyzed her at the gate disappearing like the food. She couldn't reveal her connection to Darcy and Clay today, not with Ned Voight present.

"I wish I could stay longer but my daughter's

taking me out for dinner," Ned suddenly announced and patted his stomach. "I'm going to try my best to pretend I haven't already eaten too much."

Jeff offered to drive their mother home later, and the boys ran into the house to change out of their wet clothes. Suddenly Jenna was alone with her brother, mother and a sister-in-law who was in a playful, prying mood.

"What's going on, Lorraine?" Nancy asked Jenna's mother, eyes twinkling. "Was that love I smelled in the air along with the charcoal?"

Jenna's mother actually blushed, unwittingly lending credibility to Nancy's observation. "Oh, stop it. Ned's a nice man whose company I enjoy. End of story."

Nancy bugged out her eyes in an obvious show of skepticism, and her mother laughed. "Pick on somebody else, why don't you?"

"Okay," Nancy readily agreed, turning to Jenna. "How about you, Jenna. Have a new man in your life?"

Jenna couldn't speak. How did Nancy know? Had her sister-in-law seen the happiness shining in Jenna's eyes? Read it on her face?

Nancy didn't wait for an answer. "If not, we can fix you up with the hot new guy at Jeff's office."

"You think Peter Denardo is hot?" Jeff asked.

"Exceedingly." Nancy moved to the deck chair her husband occupied, sat on his lap and kissed him on the mouth. "But not as hot as you, dear."

Jeff laughed even while settling her more securely on his lap. "You are such a fraud."

Nancy didn't deny it. "What do you say, Jenna? It'd give me an excuse to ogle Peter."

"I appreciate the offer but I'm going to pass. I'm…" *Involved,* she thought. "Busy," she said.

"That's right." Nancy patted her husband on the knee and got up from his lap to snag a potato chip from the half-full bowl on the picnic table. "The gig in Memphis."

Jenna drew in a breath, hoping to fill herself with courage, as well as her lungs with air. "There's something I need to tell you about that gig."

"You're not singing in a strip joint, are you?" Nancy asked. Jeff and her mother chuckled, and Jenna silently thanked her sister-in-law for presenting the worst-case scenario. What she had to say wasn't as bad as that.

"Ha, ha. Very funny. I'm singing at a little bar on Beale Street called Peyton's Place. It's quite charming, really."

"Then what is it?" The levity on Jeff's face was

gone, and he answered his own question. "It's the guy who owns the bar, isn't it? I meant to check him out but you never did tell me his name."

Jenna swallowed, the time of reckoning upon her. "Clay Dillon."

Jenna could tell the name didn't resonate with Jeff but her mother stiffened, pain appearing on her face as clearly as though written in ink.

"Who's Clay Dillon, Mom?" Jeff asked her.

"Margo's son," her mother said in a flat voice.

"You've got to be kidding me," Jeff exclaimed.

"Now, Jeff. Calm down." Nancy crossed the deck to lay a hand on his shoulder. "I'm sure Jenna has her reasons for accepting the gig."

Jeff didn't give Jenna a chance to supply them. "I'll tell you why. Clay Dillon didn't tell her who his mother was. Isn't that right, Jenna?"

Jenna hated to reveal Clay's duplicity, but she'd discussed the gig with Jeff before she discovered the truth. "That's right."

"Why would he keep something like that from you?" Her mother sounded both outraged and confused. "What could he possibly want from you?"

"To get to know his sister." Jenna watched the pain on her mother's face intensify. Her mother's reaction to any mention of Margo, and, by extension, her daughter, still hadn't changed.

"Her name's Darcy," Jenna continued. "She's twenty-two, and she just finished her junior year at the University of Tennessee."

"Does she look like Margo?" Her mother's voice was so thick with emotion her question was barely decipherable.

"Yes." Jenna rubbed the back of her neck, mentally considering and rejecting ways to get her family to understand that Darcy had become a part of her life. "I know neither of you want to hear this, but you'd like Darcy. I like her."

Jeff got out of his chair and stood behind their mother, as though this were a battle and he'd chosen his side. "You can't have anything more to do with her."

"Why shouldn't she, Jeff?" The question came not from Jenna, but from Nancy. "I know neither you nor Jenna had a good relationship with your father, but he was still your father. That makes Darcy your half sister."

"You have another sister, Dad?" Chad stood at the foot of the deck, fully dressed with his hair damp from swimming in the pool. Nobody had heard him emerge from the house.

Jeff slanted his wife an annoyed look. "No, son. Jenna's my only sister."

"But I heard—"

"Listen to me, Chad," Jeff interrupted. "Your

grandmother and grandfather had two children together. Me and Jenna. That's it."

Confusion clouded Chad's features, but he nodded before asking permission to watch television and going back in the house. Jenna waited until her nephew was gone to glare at Jeff. "How could you mislead him like that?"

"Would you rather your brother tell Chad your father replaced us with a new family?" her mother asked, still in the same quiet, hurt voice.

"All three of your grandsons know you're divorced, Mom," Jenna said.

"That's all they need to know for now," Jeff interjected. "When they're older, I'll tell them more."

"What if the subject of Darcy comes up again?" Jenna asked.

"Why should it?" Jeff asked. "No good can come of you associating with Margo's children, and you know it."

She accepted that arguing further wouldn't change Jeff's opinion. But now that Jenna had met Darcy, cutting ties with her half sister would be like carving out a piece of her own heart. She couldn't do it, but she could ensure Darcy never crossed paths with her family. It would be easy. Once Jenna stopped spending weekends in Memphis, she could phone Darcy and make the occasional trip to visit without involving her family.

Figuring out her future with Clay was tougher. They'd only slept together once and already she craved him. If she let things progress, she could envision building a life with him.

Jenna's mother couldn't bear that, which would prevent Jenna from enjoying true happiness with Clay. Better to make absolutely sure he know their time together was up when she left Memphis.

"Don't look like that, Jenna," Jeff said. "We're all the family you need."

The words were similar to the ones her mother had repeatedly spoken to her and Jeff over the years, especially when times got tough.

The difference was, Jenna no longer believed them.

DARCY SLOUCHED IN FRONT of the high-definition television set in the family room Tuesday night, watching a rerun of the Simpsons while she picked at the plate of food her mother had cooked for her.

Basil chicken, glazed carrots and plain couscous might have come highly recommended by the transplant center's dietitian, but Darcy couldn't work up an appetite for it.

Truth be told, her eyelids felt so heavy it was a struggle to keep her eyes open.

Because high-quality protein was good for her, she shoveled more chicken into her mouth and chewed unenthusiastically while on television Homer stuffed his face with custard-filled donuts.

Darcy licked her lips, nearly salivating as she imagined the sugary taste of yet another forbidden food. The phone rang, giving her a welcome reason to switch off the television and push aside her meal. She reached for the cordless receiver on the coffee table, recognizing the number as belonging to Peyton's Place.

"Hello, Clay," she said.

A pause. "It's Mike Puffenbarger. The battery on my cell's dead so I'm calling from Clay's office."

She sat up straighter. "Is Clay all right?"

"He's fine. It's slow tonight so he took off early." Another pause. "I called to see if you wanted to talk about anything."

Mike Puffenbarger, Darcy decided, was quickly developing into a good friend. An intuitive friend, too. He hadn't asked the dreaded how-are-you-feeling question, which could be why she felt like answering it.

"You mean about Kenny breaking up with me or about how dialysis went today?" she asked.

"Either, both, neither," he said. "I'm easy."

She smiled into the phone, wondering if Mike

realized she could interpret his comment sexually, wondering why she had. He was a friend, she reminded herself. A friend in whom she couldn't resist confiding. She'd persuaded her mother to keep her dinner date by insisting she was doing fine but couldn't keep up the same fiction with Mike.

"I feel like somebody punched me when I was down," she said.

"Dialysis was that tough today?"

"It's always tough, but that's not what I meant." She arranged her jumbled thoughts. "I have to stop working at Peyton's Place Saturday nights. I feel fine Fridays, when I'm only one day removed from dialysis. But Saturdays are tougher, especially the later it gets."

"I noticed you barely got out of your chair last night and wondered if your feet were swollen."

Swollen hands and feet were usually Darcy's first indication of a problem. Some dialysis patients gained as much as twelve or thirteen pounds between treatments, but Darcy strived to limit her weight gain to three or four pounds, not always successfully.

"That Internet site must have been a good one."

"I looked at more than one site," he confessed. "But it's common sense you'd retain more fluid than usual on Saturdays when it's the only time all week you go two straight days without dialysis."

The irony was that Darcy felt even worse on dialysis days.

"It's partly my fault," she said. "I've been eating too many meals out lately. It's been so hot I've been drinking too much water, too."

"You're supposed to freeze juice into ice cubes, then eat them like popsicles so it fools your brain into thinking you're getting more liquid than you are."

"Thank you, Dr. Puffenbarger. I'll try that one." She smiled again, the second time in as many minutes. She heard the front door open and moments later Clay walked into the family room. Darcy held up a finger to indicate she'd be with him in a moment, thanked Mike for the call and hung up.

Clay's eyebrows rose when she told him who she'd been talking to. "My bartender sure is sweet on you."

"He's a friend, Clay." She pushed her now-cold plate of food farther away from her. "Guys don't get sweet on girls who need kidney transplants."

"Hey," he protested. "Where'd that come from?"

"Nowhere." She leaned back against the sofa

cushion. "I'm tired today, is all." She made herself smile. "What did I do to deserve a visit?"

"I didn't know I needed a reason to visit my sister."

"You don't need a reason, but you have one. I can tell."

"Guilty as charged." He sat down on the russet-colored leather recliner positioned at an angle from the sofa, perching on the edge of the seat. "I want your permission to tell Jenna you need a kidney transplant."

Her heart seized, a brief preview of what it must feel like to have a heart attack. "No."

"But Darcy, your health's at stake. You can't stay on dialysis indefinitely."

"I can stay on dialysis until I can get a cadaver organ."

"That could take years."

She tried to shut out the ramifications if that time frame proved true, but the images came anyway. Years of having so little energy she spent as much time in bed as out of it. She shut out the mental pictures. "I'll manage."

"How can you expect me to keep quiet when Jenna's kidney might be a match?"

"You'll keep quiet because you promised," she said fiercely. "We talked about this, Clay. This affects me more than you."

"Maybe that was true once, but not anymore," he said softly. "I'm falling for her, Darcy."

"Well, that's…" She paused, trying to decide how she felt about her half sister and half brother starting a relationship. "…great," she finished. "Absolutely great."

"Then you understand why I need to tell her. I never meant to keep your condition a secret. It's already gone too far."

"No," Darcy repeated, her heart beating harder, faster. "You can't tell. You promised you wouldn't."

He rubbed a hand over his lower face. "Why not, Darce? Don't you think she deserves to know? To figure out for herself if she wants to give you a kidney?"

"And what if she doesn't? What then, Clay?"

"It wouldn't come to that. I know Jenna. She'd volunteer to get tested."

"Because she'd feel obligated to help me."

"She might *want* to help you."

Darcy wouldn't let herself believe a pipe dream. She knew from talking to other patients at the center that sometimes even the most loving family member balked at giving up a kidney. "I can't take that chance."

"You can't keep this from Jenna forever, either." His voice sounded passionate. "She's in my life, Darcy. She's in yours."

"She's only under contract to Peyton's Place for a few more weeks."

"Maybe so, but I won't end my personal relationship with her when our business arrangement is over. You won't, either."

"Jenna doesn't live in Memphis, Clay. If I don't tell her, she won't know. Period. So, yes. I think I can keep it from her until I get a transplant."

He got up from the chair and paced to the television set and back, his frustration obvious. "What if I asked you to let me tell Jenna as a favor to me, Darcy? What would you say then?"

She'd never seen his strong, handsome face more serious or his eyes more grave. A wave of love washed over her so powerful she nearly swayed.

"I'd say that I'd do just about anything for you." She got up from the sofa to stand in front of him, then reached up to touch his face, her next words paining her as much as they would him. "But not that."

She couldn't bring herself to offer him more of an explanation, because he still wouldn't understand. He hadn't been inside her skin when Kenny broke up with her because she was sick.

Darcy wasn't stupid. She'd taken some psychology courses in college that taught her something about human nature.

If Jenna didn't offer to get tested, that would be the end of their friendship. Guilt would drive Jenna back to Little Rock and away from Darcy. Then Darcy would be even worse off than before.

She'd still need a kidney, but she'd be without something even more valuable. A sister.

CHAPTER ELEVEN

THE FLOWERS ARRIVED IN Jenna's office Monday morning. A dozen long-stemmed red roses that made it clear she needed to talk to Clay about keeping things casual. Soon.

The phone call came soon afterward.

"Hey, Jenna. It's Clay," he said, as though he needed to identify himself when the sound of his voice had instantly transported her to the Memphis hotel room where they'd made love. "Am I calling at a bad time?"

"There's really no good time around here." She turned away from the computer and the report she'd been working on, trying not to sound too glad to hear from him.

"I won't keep you long then." A pause. "Did you get my flowers?"

She touched one of the petals, pleasure filling her as she breathed in the flowery scent. "Yes. Thank you. But you shouldn't have."

"I wanted you to know I was thinking about

you," he said. "Especially since I couldn't get you on the phone yesterday."

That was a tactful way of saying she hadn't returned the messages he'd left on her cell and home phones.

"How did things go at the cookout?" he asked.

She should tell him her family's reaction had convinced her she couldn't let things between them get serious, but choked on the words. "Not well."

"Do you want to talk about it?"

She swallowed. "Not really."

"I'm not much for talking on the phone anyway," Clay said. "So why don't I take a night off and come to Little Rock?"

Jenna clamped her teeth together so she wouldn't suggest he drive down tonight.

"Jenna," he prodded after a few moments of silence, "are you still there?"

"Could you hold a minute, Clay?" She got up from her desk, then walked across her office to shut the door even though none of her coworkers were paying attention to her phone call. Feeling marginally more composed, she got back on the line. "I don't have anything else to say about my family."

"Okay, then. Why don't I come to Little Rock anyway?" His voice softened. "I can't stop thinking about you, Jenna. I don't want to wait until the weekend to see you."

While she thought about how to dissuade him, he asked, "How does Wednesday sound? I can time it so I arrive when you get off work."

Jenna shook her head, then realized that of course he couldn't see her. "I'm having dinner with some clients Wednesday night."

"Then tell me what day's best for you."

Anyday, anytime. She could switch her Wednesday night obligation to another time. Jenna shored her resolve. That kind of answer wouldn't get across the message that they needed to slow things down.

"I'm swamped this week, Clay," she said. "I usually work some on weekends. Since I've been going to Memphis, I have to put in extra hours to catch up."

Silence filled the phone line, stretching for uncomfortable seconds.

"Okay," he said finally. "Then I guess I'll have to wait until this weekend."

After they ended the phone call, she sat staring at her computer, the words on the screen not registering.

Because if she hadn't been able to tell Clay over the phone they needed to keep things casual, how much harder would it be to do it in person?

JEFF DIDN'T REALIZE WHAT a creature of suburbia he'd become until he stepped into Peyton's Place Friday night.

The noise. The crowd. The smell of beer. They all hit him at once, overloading his senses and making him wish he was back in Little Rock with Nancy and their three sons. The way Nancy wanted him to be.

"I can't stop you from going to Memphis, but don't expect me to support you," she'd said when he told her where he was headed. "Seriously, Jeff, what do you possibly hope to accomplish?"

"I want to see where Jenna's singing and make sure Clay Dillon isn't taking advantage of her," he said, a course of action he'd decided on last weekend during the Father's Day cookout.

"If you think for one minute your sister is letting someone use her, you don't know her very well." Nancy hardly took a breath before continuing. "I'll tell you another thing. Jenna will not appreciate you checking up on her."

Nancy had a point. Although Jeff was Jenna's big brother, he'd never fought her battles. Their mother had made sure Jenna had the tools to fight her own.

The conversation with Nancy flashed through Jeff's mind as his eyes adjusted to the dim light. Considering Nancy's objections, he couldn't stay long and risk sleeping through the alarm clock tomorrow morning. There'd be hell to pay if he didn't have the family to Magic Springs by park opening for the all-day outing they had planned.

Jeff had promised to accompany Chad on every roller coaster and that little daredevil Kevin insisted he was coming along. Ben, his least rambunctious middle child, hadn't chimed in. If Ben didn't go on the coasters, Jeff intended to praise him for resisting peer pressure.

But that was a task for tomorrow. Today, Jeff had a different mission.

"Welcome to Peyton's Place." A fresh-faced young blonde sitting on a high stool off to the side of the door greeted him with a sunny smile. Jeff didn't particularly feel like smiling, but couldn't hold one back.

"I haven't seen you in here before," she continued. "Is this your first time?"

"That's right."

"Then you're in for a treat. We have a duo performing on Friday and Saturday nights you'll absolutely love."

He couldn't help but be charmed by her exuberance. She reminded him of an older, more mature female version of his son Kevin. "How do you know I'll love them?"

"Besides my ESP, you mean?" Her wide-set

eyes sparkled. "I know because they're both fabulously talented. So talented, in fact, that I'll personally refund the cover if you don't love them."

There was a cover? Jeff must have missed the sign. He dug in his pocket for his wallet, pulled out a bill and handed it to her. "How do you know I won't claim I didn't like them so I can get my money back?"

"You have an honest face." She playfully pointed a finger at him. "You don't think I make that guarantee to just anyone, do you?"

He laughed, something he never dreamed he'd be doing inside Clay Dillon's bar. "I suppose not."

A number of other customers arrived, preventing him from asking the appealing young woman where he could find the owner. No matter. Jeff would track down Clay Dillon soon enough.

He took a seat at the bar and ordered tonic water, already planning his trip back to Little Rock. If he left after the first set, he'd get home about midnight and be asleep by one. Then he'd be plenty rested for tomorrow.

"Here you go." A bartender with a mop of hair who was too young to be Margo's thirty-one year old son set the tonic water in front of Jeff. Clay Dillon had been eight, four years younger than

Jeff, when his mother married Jeff's father. Jeff used to picture Clay in the backyard of the house in Memphis playing catch with Jeff's father. After Jeff made the high-school football team, he imagined his father sitting in the stands at Clay's games.

Jeff shook off the images. He had no way of knowing if Clay had played football or if his father had done either of those things. He only knew Donald Wright hadn't done them with him.

A soft spotlight flashed on, drawing his attention to Corrine and Jenna on the stage. He focused on his sister. The light illuminated the rich auburn of her hair and the silky texture of her complexion. She wore a sleeveless black shirt over tight-fitting blue jeans and short black boots. He blinked. She looked different than he'd ever seen her. More animated. More alive. Before she sang a note, the entire place applauded.

"Wow," she said when the applause died down. "After that welcome, Corrine and I better deliver."

She laughed. Most of the people in the bar— who'd obviously heard her before if she could command this kind of regard—joined in the laughter. He'd taken a seat at the very end of the bar, not in her direct sight line, and settled back to listen as she poured herself into a song about

Bobby McGee that Janis Joplin had made famous.

Why hadn't he known Jenna could sing like this? He'd heard her before, of course, but that had been years ago, before her voice had developed this raw sensuality, this mature texture.

A typical set lasted forty-five minutes, he knew. But the time passed so quickly he tabled his mission to find Clay Dillon until she sang the last stanza of her final song, a bluesy piece about love coming along at last. Applause filled the bar, with Jeff clapping perhaps most enthusiastically.

He half rose to meet her, to tell her how amazing she'd been. A tall, dark-haired man intercepted her first, putting a hand on her arm and leaning close to address her. They didn't kiss, but the intimacy between them was unmistakable. They seemed as though on the verge of becoming lovers if they weren't already.

Jeff motioned over the young bartender, then nodded toward the pair. "Who's that with the singer?"

"Clay Dillon. He owns the bar."

Jeff had anticipated the answer but could scarcely believe what he was seeing. Jenna knew how much their mother had been hurt by Margo Wright, how much the appearance of the other woman had impacted all their lives.

After everything their mother had been through—hell, after everything they all had been through—how could Jenna allow herself to get involved with Margo's son?

POSITIONING HIMSELF at the foot of the stage, Clay waylaid Jenna before she could pull off another of her magic tricks. It certainly seemed as though she'd developed David Copperfield's knack of disappearing whenever he was nearby.

He put a hand on her arm, ridiculously glad she didn't shake it off. Their gazes locked, and he felt the chemistry between them reignite. He briefly wondered if he'd imagined her trying to put distance between them. But, no, he had evidence to back that up.

He leaned close to ask, "Are you avoiding me?"

Her eyes slid away from his, although it seemed to him that she leaned toward him. More puzzling behavior. "Why would you think that?"

He touched her cheek, not able to stop himself. "Because you're not looking me in the eye. Because you're evading the question. Because we've barely spoken since we slept together."

Her eyes fastened on his for the space of a few seconds before darting away again. "We talked on Monday after you sent me the flowers."

The red roses best conveyed what was in his heart, but he'd stopped short of mentioning love in the card. He intended to tell her that in person.

"I couldn't get anything but your voice mail the rest of the week."

"I already told you. I have to cram a lot into my week so I can have my weekends free," she said.

"I know when a woman's—"

"Hey, Jenna." A man Clay hadn't seen approach stood at his elbow, a tight-lipped expression on his face. The shade of his hair was an exact match for Jenna's, leading Clay to search for other similar features. He found them in the oval shape of the man's face and the fullness of his mouth. "Surprise."

Jenna sprang apart from Clay as if he had a contagious disease, her guilty look alerting Clay that this must be her brother.

"Jeff," she said, confirming he'd guessed right about the man's identity. "What are you doing here?"

"I came to hear you sing." He leveled a hard look at Clay. "A better question would be, what are you doing with him?"

Clay stuck out a hand. "I'm Clay Dillon."

"I know who you are," Jeff told Clay, ignoring his offered hand. "I also know what you did to get my sister to Memphis."

His condemnation blindsided Clay. Clay hadn't anticipated that Jenna would tell her family he'd manipulated her into singing at his bar, not after what they'd shared last weekend.

Clay dropped his hand. "I don't expect us to be friends, but there's no reason we can't be civil."

"Here's a reason. If Jenna wanted to meet your sister, she would have arranged it herself," Jeff said. "But she didn't because she knew how much it would hurt our mother. So stay away from her."

Jenna positioned herself between them and placed a hand on her brother's chest. "Stop it, Jeff. You don't know what you're talking about."

"I know something is going on between you and him."

"You're right," Jenna said, causing Clay to relax a little. He thought she'd been about to deny it. "But it's nothing serious so you can stop harassing him."

The disbelief hit Clay first, closely followed by pain. Jenna thought making love to him was *nothing serious?*

She wasn't through dressing down her brother. "I don't appreciate you showing up in Memphis like this and ordering me around."

"I'm looking out for our family's best interests," he shot back.

"It would be in your best interest to get back to your wife and sons in Little Rock." She took him by the elbow, barely sparing a glance at Clay.

He watched brother and sister walk out the door, within a few paces of where Darcy sat collecting a cover charge from three laughing young women. Jenna kept herself positioned between Jeff and Darcy, obviously having no intention of introducing the half siblings. Darcy seemed not to notice them pass.

Nothing serious.

Jenna's phrase stuck in Clay's mind like the lyrics of an exasperating song. His feet moved toward the exit even while he tried to convince himself to stay put, following the path Jenna and her brother had taken into the balmy night.

The two Wright siblings stood in the middle of the street, not fifteen feet from the bar. Clay's steps slowed as he planned his approach, but before he reached them Jenna kissed Jeff on the cheek. Jeff said something to her, then headed in the opposite direction of the bar.

Jenna turned back and spotted Clay. She didn't pull a disappearing act this time but walked straight up to him. "I'm sorry about that. Believe it or not, Jeff's actually a good guy. You didn't see him at his best."

"I knew things didn't go well when you told

your family about Darcy and me," he said, "but I hadn't guessed they went that badly."

"My mother got really upset. Jeff takes his cue from her, so he did, too." She pursed her lips. "You've got to understand, your mother is still a sore spot with my family."

"I'm not my mother. Neither is Darcy."

Her head bowed before it rose again. "My mother doesn't seem to be able to make that distinction."

"Can you?"

"Yes," she said. "You know how I feel about Darcy."

"What about me, Jenna? How do you feel about me?"

As it had in the bar when he confronted her, her gaze slid away from his. "That's more complicated."

"So you're going to let your mother and your brother tell you who to date?" He didn't wait for her response. "Are you going to let them tell you not to associate with Darcy, as well?"

"Absolutely not," she retorted, sounding insulted. "Once I'm back in Little Rock for good, I'll talk to Darcy on the phone, maybe see her a few times a year."

"On the sly?" He let out a harsh breath. "Like it's something to be ashamed of?"

"It's not something I need to broadcast." Around them on the street, bar goers laughed and talked, traveling from one establishment to the other, the party atmosphere in stark contrast to the mood between Clay and Jenna. Her eyes pleaded with him. "Don't look at me like that. I already told you I'm not cutting ties with Darcy."

"But you are cutting them with me?"

"It's a moot point. In a few weeks I'll be in Little Rock while you'll still be here in Memphis."

The first vestiges of panic grabbed him by the throat. Jenna stood in front of him but it already seemed as though she was slipping away. "Memphis and Little Rock are only two hours apart."

"That's a good distance when two people have busy careers."

Clay disagreed. He'd find the time to go to Little Rock, if that's what it took to be with Jenna. But he needed more time with Jenna to convince her they should be together. "What if I offered to extend your contract past six weeks?"

Clay spotted what he thought was yearning flash in Jenna's eyes before it vanished. She looked more hurt than happy. "You already know I won't agree to that. I'm an accountant, not a singer."

"I thought you might change your mind." He drew in a breath, then went with his heart. "Not only about singing, but about staying in Memphis."

"I won't. I'm going back to Little Rock and my accounting job, just like I told you."

"Is that why you told your brother what we have going on isn't serious?"

"One night hardly constitutes a serious relationship. We can enjoy each other while I'm in Memphis, but I can't see us committing. How could we, considering what's between our families?"

She seemed to think they could easily turn off the attraction between them.

"So let me make sure I understand this. You want to go on like we have been?" he asked. "Sleeping together but not getting too involved?"

"That's right."

He was hardly aware of reaching for her, but suddenly his hands were on her shoulders. He dipped his head, not giving her the chance to avoid his lips. They came crashing down on hers, demanding a response.

Her resistance, if there was any, was slight. She put her arms around his neck, tangled her tongue with his and kissed him back as though she'd never denied the significance of what was between them.

The kiss could have lasted a minute, or an hour.

Clay's senses were so scrambled, he didn't know how much time had passed when he finally lifted his head. He tipped up her chin so she had to look at him, the fingers of one of his hands still buried in her glorious hair.

"I love kissing you." She stroked his face, her expression a bit dazed, her lips dewy and slightly swollen. "So I'm glad you can keep it casual."

She thought that kiss was keeping it casual? His heart felt so full of her, so weighted by his emotions, he couldn't bring himself to speak.

"You *can* keep it casual, can't you?" She continued to stare at him, waiting for him to agree with her ridiculous request.

But, really, since he couldn't give Jenna up, there was only one answer he could give.

"Sure can," he said.

EARLY THAT SATURDAY morning Corrine pulled her serviceable Honda over to the curb on the quiet, shady Little Rock street a half block from the split-level she called home.

She shut off the ignition, remembering how excited she'd been nearly two years before that she and Maurice were starting their married life in such a darling house. Recalling, too, how Maurice had whispered in her ear that he'd make love to her in every room, a promise he'd kept.

Corrine hadn't known then that a woman with designs on her husband would move in down the block.

She didn't know for certain that Maurice was having an affair with Imelda Santos but it was time to quiet her doubts.

Those suspicions had caused her nothing but heartache. If she'd whole-heartedly trusted Maurice, she wouldn't have lashed out at Jenna for relaying he'd been seen with another woman. Neither would she have assigned Maurice motives for buying her that extravagant pearl bracelet.

She wouldn't have awakened at six and driven one hundred twenty miles despite not getting back from Peyton's Place until the wee hours of the morning, either.

The clock on the dashboard showed barely a quarter past eight, much too early for the late-sleeping Maurice to be up and around. She reached for the styrofoam cup in the built-in holder and drained the rest of her second helping of coffee of the morning.

"Here we go," she said, her voice sounding inordinately loud in the quiet vehicle.

She got out of the car, careful to shut the door as quietly as possible. If any of the neighbors were awake, she'd claim to be taking a walk. But, no, the street was deserted, with nobody between her and the house.

She started down the sidewalk. Her breathing quickly turned ragged as though she were jogging toward the proof she didn't want to find. *Please let Maurice's car be in the garage,* she prayed. Six parallel windows lined the top of the garage door, but she had to get close to see inside. Closer. Even closer.

The color red imprinted itself on her consciousness, and her knees went weak with relief. Maurice drove a red Trans Am convertible. Maurice was upstairs asleep.

Except he might not be alone, a nasty voice nagged. *He might not even be there. Imelda only lives a few houses away. Go inside. See for yourself.*

"No," Corrine said aloud. "I can't do this."

If her marriage to Maurice stood a chance, she needed to have a modicum of faith. At least that's what she told herself as she walked swiftly up the driveway toward the sidewalk.

What sounded like the squeak of a door hinge broke the quiet on the street. Corrine froze, her eyes flying to the front door of Imelda's house. She heard birds singing and leaves rustling, but Imelda's house was as quiet as the rest of the homes on the avenue.

Silly girl, she mentally chided herself. She was jumping at shadows, searching for clues where none were to be found. She was about to return to her car when she heard the clank of metal, as though somebody had opened a gate.

A man emerged from the yard behind Imelda's house, walking quickly and silently on soft grass damp with dew. A fine, handsome man wearing the same pair of faded jeans in which Corrine had found the pink paper with the telephone number.

As though sensing someone watching, he looked up. His step faltered. Even from this distance, Corrine identified the guilt that descended over his face.

"Corrine, wait," he yelled.

But she'd already turned and run back to her car, tears streaming down her face. The knowledge that she'd been right to suspect him of cheating doing nothing to stem their flow.

CHAPTER TWELVE

JENNA WOKE UP Saturday morning regretting the decision she'd made the night before.

She stared at the hotel room ceiling, reliving the moments before the bar was about to close, hearing herself turn down Clay's invitation to spend the night at his house.

"I'm beat, Clay," she'd said. "Can we take a rain check?"

She'd actually said that. A rain check. As though they were discussing nothing more serious than, say, a day in the park once a storm had passed and the sun came out.

As though she didn't want to go back to his house.

Then she'd succumbed to temptation and invited him to her hotel room tonight.

She turned over and punched the empty pillow beside her. As though she'd be any more in control of her emotions tonight than she'd been yesterday.

She hadn't been overly tired last night. Though she'd been so affected by Clay's passionate kiss she couldn't take a chance on making love to him.

So far, her demand that she and Clay keep things casual wasn't going so well. But not because of Clay. She hadn't trusted *herself* not to get too deeply involved.

To keep her mind off what she couldn't stop thinking about, she dressed, ran on the treadmill in the exercise room and swam a few laps in the hotel pool before she showered.

She was wondering how to occupy herself—and, in the process, keep her mind off Clay—for the rest of the day when Darcy called and invited her shopping.

A few hours later, as she and Darcy walked through a busy downtown mall, she held up a bag containing a sexy red dress that left almost nothing to the imagination. "I don't know how I let you talk me into this. I probably won't have the nerve to wear it on stage."

"Then wear it for my brother." Darcy's eyebrows danced. "Just think how he'll react when he sees you in it."

As far as leading comments went, this one was way ahead of the pack. Jenna made a noncommittal sound. "Hmm."

"I'm fishing for information and all you can say is hmm?" Darcy even did exasperation cheerfully. "Help me out here, Jenna. Clay told me you two were seeing each other so I paid attention last night. I could tell something was wrong."

"Nothing's wrong," Jenna denied. "Things between us aren't serious, anyway. Not like they were between him and Peyton."

Darcy visibly started. "Why do you think he was involved with Peyton?"

And why, Jenna thought, was she fishing for information about Clay even while denying she was interested in him? Jenna was giving off mixed signals even she couldn't understand. "He named his bar after her."

"Yes, he did," Darcy said slowly. "But we weren't talking about her, we were talking about you."

It registered with Jenna that Darcy wasn't going to tell her about Peyton, either. *Who was she?* She thought about pressing Darcy for the answer but that would hardly lend credence to her denials about Clay.

"Clay and I are enjoying each other's company while I'm in Memphis. That's as far as it goes," Jenna said, willing her explanation to be true.

"Really?" With one word, Darcy conveyed her doubt. "Whatever was happening last night seemed pretty serious to me."

"We had a disagreement, but we worked it out," Jenna said. They were on the second floor of the mall, closer to the skylights that should have bathed the place in light, but outside the day was gray and rainy, no doubt contributing to the size of the crowd.

"About me?" A wealth of vulnerability laced Darcy's question.

"Not about you," Jenna refuted quickly.

"Then about what?"

Darcy, it seemed, could be as persistent as her brother. Jenna debated how to answer, deciding not to tell her about Jeff's appearance at Peyton's Place. Mentioning Jeff would serve no purpose.

"Partly about Clay wanting to extend the Two Gals contract."

Twin lines appeared between Darcy's eyebrows. "Why would you be angry about that?"

"Because Clay can't get it through his head that I'm through performing after the six weeks are up." Tears tapped at the backs of Jenna's eyes at the prospect of never singing again, but she didn't let them get close to falling. "Juggling singing and my job isn't easy."

"I'm sure it isn't," Darcy agreed. "But what about Corrine? She won't stop playing, right? How will she find somebody as good as you?"

Tendrils of guilt clutched at Jenna, the same as

they always did when someone mentioned the other half of her duo. "Corrine knows our arrangement is temporary. She'll catch on with another band, the way she always does."

"She hasn't tried to talk you into making it permanent?"

"She knows better than that."

"Well, I don't. I just might start pestering you about it. So don't be too hard on Clay for trying to keep you in Memphis. I'd like that, too. Very much."

When Darcy stated her case that way, Jenna could hardly take offense. Neither could she confide that a silly, giddy part of her envisioned singing in Memphis indefinitely while pursuing happily ever after with Clay. Jenna shut out the images, reminding herself she was an accountant who dealt in facts and figures. Not dreams.

The downtown mall's large skylight created the impression of an enclosed town square complete with fountains and greenery. Shops competed for retail space with restaurants, many of them offering "outdoor" seating areas featuring umbrella-topped tables.

"You know what we should do after we finish shopping?" Darcy answered her own question. "We should play miniature golf. There's a place upstairs that has the coolest…"

Darcy's voice trailed off abruptly and her steps

slowed. Her gaze fixated on an attractive blond woman walking toward them. The yellow sundress the woman wore with high-heeled sandals showed off her excellent figure.

Could this be Margo Wright? Jenna speculated. No. Although she generally resembled the photo of Margo on Clay's desk, this woman wasn't much older than Jenna. Thirty-five, tops. Margo Wright was in her late forties.

"Darcy, darling. How wonderful to see you." The woman, whoever she was, had no reservations about running into Darcy.

"Hello, Pam," Darcy said, the usual sparkle missing from her manner.

The sparkle certainly wasn't missing from the diamonds adorning Pam's fingers.

Pam kissed the air on either side of Darcy's cheeks, then turned to Jenna, her painted lips forming a ready smile. She seemed to be waiting for an introduction, but the normally polite Darcy didn't provide one. "I'm Pam Meier," the woman finally said.

"Jenna Wright."

"Wright? Then you must be Donald's other daughter."

"That's correct," Jenna said.

Pam laid a beautifully manicured hand over

her breast while her expression turned sad. "He was a wonderful man who is dearly missed."

A man Pam Meier had obviously known well.

"That woman has a lot of nerve," Darcy said after Pam left them. Darcy held herself stiffly, her dislike of Pam Meier evident.

She and Darcy resumed walking, but Darcy no longer noticed what was on display in the windows of the stores they passed.

"You know Dad had a heart attack, right?" Darcy continued. "It happened while he was at a hotel with Pam. It was pretty awful for my mom."

The revelation that their father had been unfaithful to Margo didn't bring Jenna any pleasure. She could only think about how the news must have hurt Darcy.

"My mother didn't know he was cheating until he asked for a divorce." Jenna pressed her lips together, irritated at herself for speaking before thinking. As much as she disliked Margo Wright, the woman was Darcy's mother. "I'm sorry. I shouldn't have said that."

"That's okay. Your mother hates mine so much I figured it had to be something like that." Darcy's voice gentled. "That must have been hard on you."

"I was only seven, too young to understand about cheating. I did know my mother was unhappy and your mother had a lot to do with that. But I didn't put it all together until much later."

The conversation had gotten so intense that sometime during the exchange they'd stopped walking and now stood in the atrium. Next to them was a fountain where people threw coins hoping their wishes came true. Jenna wished Donald Wright hadn't cheated on either of his wives.

"I don't expect you to believe this, but she's a good mother," Darcy said. "She loves Clay and me. Whenever we've needed her, she's been there."

Jenna nodded, her impression of Margo Wright shifting. Margo would always be the woman who'd stolen Jenna's father but now she also became a wronged wife and a caring mother.

"I'm glad she's been a good mother, Darcy. You deserve nothing but the best." Jenna squeezed her half sister's hand and was rewarded with a smile that broke the somber mood.

"Hey, why don't we ditch the shopping and play minigolf right now?" Darcy suggested. "The mall's course is wild. It glows in the dark. We can even call Corrine and ask her to meet us."

Jenna hesitated. "Corrine and I haven't been on the best terms lately."

"That's why you should call her."

Jenna widened her eyes. "So now you're into fixing broken friendships?"

"It's the least I can do. You helped me through a bad breakup."

"How exactly did I do that?" Jenna asked. "You didn't mention Kenny once all day."

"You took him off my mind. A bad boyfriend can't compete with a good sister. So dial."

"Since you're being that bossy, I will." Jenna took her cell phone out of her handbag and pressed in Corrine's number, secretly relieved to have an excuse to contact her. The phone rang three times before Corrine answered.

"Hello."

From that single muffled word, Jenna knew Corrine had been crying. "Corrine, it's Jenna. Are you okay?"

"Yes. No. I don't know." A pause. "Maurice is cheating on me."

Jenna's stomach turned over. "Are you in your hotel room?"

"Yes."

"I'll be right there." Jenna hung up, then laid her hand on Darcy's arm. "You know how much I want to spend the afternoon with you, but I've got to go."

"Is it Maurice?"

Jenna tilted her head. "How did you know?"

"It seemed like something wasn't right when Corrine talked about him."

Jenna threw her arms around Darcy and hugged her tight. "You're the greatest. Don't let anyone tell you differently."

"Back at you," Darcy said.

Glad she and Darcy had chosen a downtown venue for their shopping, Jenna got to Corrine's hotel room in minutes. Corrine answered the door, looking like a shell of her usual self. Her eyes were red rimmed, her hair askew, her clothes wrinkled. Their recent friction forgotten, Jenna took both of her friend's cold hands in hers.

"You're right about Maurice." Corrine's lips trembled visibly when she spoke. "I went to Little Rock this morning and saw him sneaking out of the neighbor's house. She's divorced, blond, beautiful."

Jenna rubbed her friend's arms in a comforting gesture. "Oh, honey, I'm so sorry."

Corrine sat down heavily on the bed and Jenna positioned herself next to her.

"I'm sorry I was such a bitch. I figured out he was cheating a while ago," she said in a low, miserable voice. "I just couldn't admit it to myself."

"You don't need to apologize to me, Corrine."

"Sure, I do. I know the value of an apology.

Probably because I won't be getting one from Maurice."

"You talked to him?"

"Not in Little Rock, no. I ran. I half hoped he'd follow me and beg my forgiveness. When I got back to the hotel, I came up to the room and waited. He never showed." She sniffed. "He called, though. About an hour ago."

"What did he say?" Jenna prompted when Corrine grew silent.

"He said that I knew about his weakness for women when we got hitched. He made it sound like it was my fault for not seeing this coming. He said it was just a fling, that it didn't mean anything. He said that he still loved me. That nothing between us had to change."

Jenna stayed silent, wanting to give Corrine time to put her thoughts together.

"I think this has been going on for a while now. I doubt it's even the woman he started with. When I look back on it, it's really kind of obvious. The late nights. The hang-up calls. The excuses. I don't even think he feels bad about it. The only thing he regrets is getting caught."

"What are you going to do?" Jenna asked.

"What should I do?"

"I can't make the decision for you, Corrine. You know that. But I heard some advice once that made a lot of sense. Ask yourself whether you're better off with him or without him."

Corrine's shoulders slumped. "I've been so down lately. I think…" She sniffed, then started again. "I think I'm better off without him."

Jenna hugged her friend, feeling Corrine's pain as though it were her own. Maybe that was because once upon a time, Jenna had witnessed her mother experience a similar type of heartache.

But her mother had thrived in the ensuing years. She'd gone back to school, passed the exam enabling her to become a licensed massage therapist and volunteered for causes in which she believed. She'd recently added the final piece of the puzzle, resurrecting her love life by dating Ned Voight.

Because of what her mother had gone through, Jenna had no trouble believing Corrine would be better off without Maurice.

So why had it taken Jenna so long to understand that her mother hadn't needed Donald Wright in her life to be happy?

And that Jenna had let her mother's skewed view of the past affect Jenna's chance for happiness in the present?

CLAY LEANED THE BACK of his head against the padded wall of the elevator and closed his eyes.

Fatigue washed over him, unsurprising considering he'd put in a long Saturday night at Peyton's Place that had only just ended.

What stunned him was the decision he'd reached. Jenna would be surprised, too, but not in a good way. No woman who invited a man to her hotel room expected him to show up and do what Clay was about to do.

The elevator doors parted. He straightened and walked slowly down the deserted hallway, thinking about how complicated the situation had gotten with Jenna. When he'd watched her singing in that bar in Little Rock, he had every intention of telling her about Darcy's need for a kidney transplant. He had no plans to fall for her. Yet he didn't even have to close his eyes to envision how sexy she looked on stage tonight.

She'd worn red, a color that caused her skin to glow and brought out the fiery highlights in her hair. Like a moth, Clay had been drawn to her. And now, he was about to get burned.

She answered the door at the first light knock, took his hand and drew him inside the room. Before he could tell her what he'd decided, she pulled down his head and kissed him.

The scent of her surrounded him, pulling him into the kiss like he was sinking in quicksand. He responded like a man with no strength, his body making a mockery of his decision.

She ended the kiss, then smiled up at him. "I've been wanting to do that all night." Her eyes sparkled. "In fact, I've been wanting to do a lot more than that."

She wanted them to have a fling, he reminded himself. A short-lived affair, after which they parted ways and didn't look back. The thought gave him the energy to step back until he no longer touched her. The corners of her eyes crinkled in confusion.

"You probably already know I can't look at you without wanting to make love to you," he said. "But I'm not going to."

The lips he'd just kissed—the lips he'd just devoured—molded into a frown. "Then you're giving off some very mixed signals."

He ran a hand over his lower face, feeling the stubble of his beard and the wealth of his weakness for her. "This is going to sounds nuts. Hell, it sounds crazy to me. But here it is. I can't make love to you. Not on the terms you outlined last night."

He was halfway to the door when she said, "I didn't ask you up to my room for sex."

He stopped, turned. She looked like one of his fantasies come alive, standing there in the sexy outfit she'd worn on stage, her bare feet with her toenails painted red somehow making her seem even more desirable. "Talk about giving off mixed signals."

"Talking is what I want to do. I need to tell you about some things that happened today. Some things I figured out."

"You want to talk?"

She nodded. He didn't trust himself to get any closer than he already was, so stayed put. "About what?"

"Pam Meier, to begin with. I met her today while I was at the mall with Darcy."

"Did Darcy...?" He couldn't think of how to tactfully finish the question.

"She told me our father was at a hotel with Pam when he had the heart attack," Jenna said.

He shifted his weight, sorry the information had come out. "And how do you feel about that?"

"At first I was shocked. I had this image of your mother as this calculating blond bombshell who lured my father away from my mother."

"And now?"

"Now I can put most of the blame on my father, where it belongs. He was the one who broke the vows he made to my mother. Who didn't bother to exercise his visitation rights. Who cared more about himself than anyone else."

Despite his resolve to stay away from her, her words drew him to her. He took her hand.

"I'm sorry, Jenna. Your father wasn't a bad man, but he was a self-centered one. It's like I told you before when we talked about him and Darcy. Just because Darcy lived in his house doesn't mean he paid attention to her."

"I don't understand something," Jenna said. "If your mother knew my father was unfaithful, why did she stay married to him?"

"I'm not sure she did know he was cheating until after he died. None of us did. But the simple answer is she loved him."

"And the complicated one?"

"You'd have to know my mother to understand. Don't get me wrong, she's a great mother. Loving. Caring. Involved. But when it comes to her relationships with men, she's…" He searched for a word. "Dependent. My mother, she doesn't do alone well."

"My mother does," Jenna said. "That's another thing I figured out today. That after my father left, she learned to take care of herself. She even thrives on it. When we first moved into the house in Little Rock, the grass was brown. But you should see her yard now. There are flowers and plants everywhere, like a small piece of paradise."

"She sounds self-sufficient."

"I didn't realize how self-sufficient until today." She shook her head. "She's complained for years about your mother wrecking her life. And Jeff and me, we bought into it. By agreeing, we enabled her to keep on believing it. But her life isn't in ruins. The life she built for herself is pretty great."

"I haven't met her, but I do know one thing about her," Clay said. "She managed to raise a re-markable daughter."

"She raised me to be independent enough to make my own decisions, even though she might not agree with them." She touched his cheek with the hand he wasn't holding. "In fact, I've already made a decision she won't agree with."

She wet her lips, seeming to have difficulty phrasing her next words. "It was stupid of me to insist things couldn't get serious between us. When you kissed me last night, I knew I didn't want us to end when my contract is up. But I couldn't admit it."

The fatigue that had dragged him down disap-peared. "And now?"

She looped both of her arms around his neck and gazed into his eyes. "And now I want more from you than a fling."

"Then I should apologize in advance."

"Apologize for what?"

"The all-out campaigning I'll wage to keep you in Memphis."

Her eyes clouded. "I haven't changed my mind about my singing."

"Why can't you be an accountant and a singer? The last I heard, there are accounting jobs in Memphis."

"But—"

"Don't say anything yet." He placed one of his hands at her nape, then ran it down her back, pulling her to him. "Not until I embark on my campaign."

"I like the sound of that."

"I hope you'll like the sound of this better." He took her face in his hands and gazed deeply into her eyes. "I love you."

Her gaze softened and she pulled him to her, kissing him deeply and thoroughly. But all through the long night and the next morning as they made love over and over again, Clay was aware of one thing.

Jenna never said she loved him back.

CHAPTER THIRTEEN

CLAY LOVED HER.

He'd only said it once, but the words consumed Jenna during the work week in Memphis. So, too, did thoughts of their lovemaking.

They'd stayed in bed until noon on Sunday, even phoning the front desk to extend the checkout time. Clay hadn't tried to verbally persuade her to stay in Memphis long-term, but his lovemaking spoke volumes. That had been extremely persuasive.

She wouldn't give up her accounting career to take a chance on singing, of course. But if things progressed the way she hoped they would with Clay, she could see herself finding an accounting job in Memphis.

In the meantime, she could swing a long-distance relationship if she worked forty hours a week instead of fifty or sixty. She phoned her boss early Tuesday morning to road test her theory.

"You're what?" Frank Gorham exclaimed in his unnaturally high voice. She pictured him at his mahogany executive desk, his reading glasses pushed down his nose, his large hands tightening around the phone. Frank did not react well to anything deviating outside the norm, which could be why he and Jenna got along so well.

"I'm taking today off as a comp day," Jenna repeated. "The hours really add up when you work ten-hour days."

"But…but," he sputtered, "you've never taken a comp day before."

"I'd come in if I thought I needed to, but the things I have to do can wait until tomorrow. I'll see you then," Jenna said firmly and disconnected.

She had no intention of waiting until this weekend to be with Clay, not when she could be in Memphis in two hours. But halfway into her trip, she couldn't be sure when she'd actually see Clay. She tried his cell phone unsuccessfully for the third time, then dialed Darcy.

"You don't know where Clay is, do you?" she asked after explaining her impulsive decision to take the day off.

"As a matter of fact, I do," Darcy said. "He mentioned he was attending an all-day seminar for small-business owners. Seems to me he said it won't be over until five."

"That explains why he's not answering his cell." The disappointment that coursed through Jenna didn't last long. "Hey, if you're free why don't we spend the day together? Sort of a rain check for last Saturday when we cut our shopping short. We could go to Graceland. Believe it or not, I've never been there."

Darcy didn't say anything for so long Jenna thought she might have lost the connection. "Darcy? Are you still there?"

"I'm here. It's just that I have an…appointment at eleven o'clock."

"What kind of an appointment?"

"A, um, doctor's appointment." Before Jenna could ask for details, she added, "But it's routine."

"Then I'll pick you up when I get to Memphis, take you to your appointment and wait until you're through."

"Oh, no. I couldn't ask you to do that."

"I want to. It doesn't matter what we do as long as we're together, even if it's only driving to and from your doctor's appointment." Jenna kept her eyes on the flat, straight stretch of highway, thinking it symbolic that the distance between her and Darcy was closing. "I'm making good time so I should be there in, say, forty-five minutes."

It took her forty. Since she'd only seen the backs of the houses from the Riverbluff Walkway, she had to crane her neck to pick out the house number once she got to the road running in front of the elegant dwellings.

Almost as soon as she pulled into the two-car driveway, Darcy exited the house, but without her usual pep. Her skin looked sallow even in the bright sun, and she appeared to have gained weight. Jenna frowned. She'd seen Darcy only six days ago. It must be an optical illusion, brought on by the shapeless orange shirt Darcy wore over summer-weight pants.

Darcy let herself into the passenger side of the car, smiling in her usual good-humored way. "Are you ready for Graceland?"

"Graceland? I thought we were going to your doctor's appointment first."

"I rescheduled."

"Should you have done that?"

"How often does my sister skip work to have fun? Having fun is Graceland. It's not waiting for me at a doctor's office."

"You're sure about this?"

"As sure as I am that you are absolutely going to flip when you see the Jungle Room at Graceland."

"Flip?" Jenna cut her eyes at her. "Is that college-girl talk?"

"You laugh now," Darcy said. "But wait until you step into the jungle."

Getting to the jungle was no easy matter, especially on a day the temperature was in the high eighties and rising. After driving to a commercial neighborhood on the outskirts of Memphis that featured all things Elvis, including the Heartbreak Hotel, they stood in line. For tickets, for the shuttle bus that ferried them to the mansion and then for their turn inside the two-story home with the white pillars and the Tennessee limestone exterior.

Sweat dripped down Jenna's brow by the time Elvis Presley's incomparable voice musically welcomed them to his world, courtesy of the MP3 player issued to each ticket holder for the length of the self-guided tour.

The other tourists crowded to the right of the foyer to get a look at the black baby grand piano and white custom sofa in the elegant living room, but Jenna's eyes stayed on Darcy. She'd gotten quieter with each moment they spent waiting in the heat, and Jenna could tell she was breathing hard.

Jenna took off her headphones and touched Darcy on the arm to get her attention. "You okay, Darcy?"

Darcy gave a thumbs up, causing Jenna to worry that her labored breathing made talking difficult. Unconvinced but unsure how to get to the truth, Jenna put the headphones back on.

The voice in her ear directed them past a dining room with a crystal chandelier, a rather pedestrian kitchen and eventually to the jungle room. The decorations were almost too much to take in at once. Lime-green shag carpeting lining the floor and ceiling. An indoor waterfall dripping from one stone wall. Carved wooden sofas and chairs covered in faux fur. Overflowing artificial greenery. Ceramic tigers. A mirror framed in pheasant feathers.

"Wow. You weren't kidding." Jenna turned around to address Darcy, only to see two girls in their early teens, silver braces flashing as they pointed and laughed at a Chinese dragon on the armrest of one of the chairs.

Jenna stood on tiptoes, fruitlessly trying to locate Darcy over the line of people behind her.

"Excuse me," she told the girls. They didn't move, undoubtedly because the commentary on the MP3 player drowned out Jenna's voice. Unable to come up with an alternative, Jenna shouldered past the two startled girls.

"Hey, you're going the wrong way." The admonition came from a scowling bearded man wearing madras shorts and tennis shoes, a camera hanging from his neck.

"Sorry," Jenna said absently, trying to remember the color of Darcy's shirt. Orange. She scanned the vicinity, spotting a flash of the color in her peripheral vision. Lowering her gaze, she saw Darcy slumped against a far wall, her face deathly white. Elvis was singing on the MP3 player, adding to the surreal experience. Jenna whipped off her headphones, shoving through the line of protesting, oblivious tourists.

"Darcy!" She got down on her knees in front of her sister, her pulse racing, her panic building. "What happened?"

"It's…nothing." Darcy's face was damp, her complexion waxy, the blond hair around her brow darkened with sweat. "I'm just having…trouble catching…my breath."

They'd spent the better part of an hour in the heat before entering the mansion, but the air-conditioning inside the house felt blessedly cool. A woman as young as Darcy should not be having trouble breathing.

"I'm calling 9-1-1," Jenna said.

Darcy clutched at her arm with a surprisingly firm grip. "No, Jenna."

"But I—"

"I don't…need an ambulance."

The resolve on Darcy's face and the steeliness in her voice alerted Jenna that her sister knew the reason for her collapse. Jenna would wager it had something to do with the missed appointment.

"Okay," she said. "But I'm asking somebody to stay with you until I find a tour guide who'll get us out of here."

Jenna flagged down a motherly woman regarding them with concern, then moved counterclockwise through the house until she encountered a Graceland employee who instantly transformed from teenage boy to crises solver.

Darcy was standing and protesting that she was fine when they returned to the jungle room, but neither Jenna nor the tour guide took her word for it. They flanked her, each taking one of her arms, and helped the still-protesting Darcy to the shuttle bus that transported guests back to the ticket hub.

"The king has made many women faint," the teenage tour monitor told Darcy when they were on the bus. "You're not the first, honey."

He offered to wait with Darcy until Jenna pulled her car around to the front of the ticket hub, then sent them off with a wave. Darcy leaned back against the headrest, looking wan and exhausted.

"Should I drive you to a hospital?" Jenna raised her voice to be heard above the air conditioner she'd turned on full blast.

"Not the hospital." Darcy still spoke haltingly

but seemed to be having an easier time breathing. "They can't do anything for me there."

A shaft of fear pierced Jenna. "Then where? To the doctor's office where you were supposed to have that appointment?"

"I wasn't going to see a doctor." Darcy closed her eyes. "I was going to dialysis. That's where you should take me."

Dialysis? Jenna knew the procedure had something to do with the kidneys but was too upset to think clearly. "I don't understand."

Darcy's voice sounded weary. "That appointment I missed this morning, it was for one of my three weekly dialysis sessions. I thought it would be no big deal to go for treatment later this afternoon, especially because my last session was two days ago. It might not have been a problem if it wasn't so hot today."

A dozen questions ran through Jenna's mind, the two most paramount being how sick was Darcy and why hadn't she told Jenna about her condition before now?

Even as the questions formed, Jenna noticed the dark circles under Darcy's eyes. Jenna had a dim memory of a coworker explaining dialysis because an elderly relative was undergoing the procedure.

"Tell me where the dialysis center is and I'll take you there," Jenna instructed.

Now was not the time to give Darcy the third degree, but sometime soon Jenna meant to get her answers.

DARCY DUTIFULLY WENT through the postdialysis motions, trying not to wince when the attendant removed the needles. Or to faint during the standing blood pressure and dry weight measurements, even though her knees shook and holding up her head required an effort. But trying, most of all, not to feel like too much of a fool.

"It's a mystery to me why you thought you could skip a treatment." Her attendant Regina stood glaring at her, hands on rounded hips, eyes narrowed, like a mother who'd caught her child sneaking in after curfew.

"Postpone a treatment," Darcy corrected. "I was coming in later this afternoon."

"You know better than that, child. We schedule these machines. You're lucky one was available when you got here."

"I'm sorry, Regina." Darcy really was dismayed that she'd upset the normally unflappable attendant, who'd been scolding and fussing over her since she arrived.

"Don't you pull something like this ever again," Regina ordered.

"I won't," Darcy promised, duly chastised.

"All right, then." Regina's expression softened. "I didn't see your mom out there waiting for you. How you gonna get home?"

"My sister."

"That woman asking Mary Dee all those questions is your sister?" Regina referred to the grandmotherly social worker assigned to the center. "I didn't know you had a sister."

"Jenna's my half sister. We just started getting to know each other."

"That explains all her questions, but doesn't explain how you thought you could keep something like this from somebody who cares about you."

Darcy sighed. "I guess I thought wrong."

"You sure did. You need to tell her what's going on because we can't."

Darcy nodded, weariness settling over her.

"You take better care, you hear me?" Regina lowered her voice. "I don't want anything bad happening to my favorite patient."

Jenna was waiting in the reception room, some pamphlets about dialysis on her lap. She jumped to her feet as soon as she spotted Darcy, concern etching her features.

"I'm okay," Darcy said before Jenna could ask, aware she was still unsteady on her feet, still pale. People unfamiliar with dialysis often mistakenly believed patients walked out of the center feeling terrific. Darcy felt an odd combination of nausea, energy and exhaustion. Exhaustion usually won. "I just need to go home and take it easy for the rest of the day."

"I'll drive you," Jenna said.

"That'd be great, but I feel terrible about this," Darcy said. "We were supposed to have fun today and instead you've been waiting hours for me to finish up dialysis."

"Don't worry about that," Jenna said. "The only frustrating part was I couldn't find out what was going on with you. Nobody here would tell me and I couldn't get Clay on the phone."

"I'll tell you." Darcy's knees quivered, and nausea closely followed. "But could we go to the lobby and sit down first?"

The love seat they settled on in the corner of the lobby had a view onto a courtyard resplendent with summer blooms, but Darcy could hardly focus on them. She leaned back against the sofa, fighting fatigue.

"Maybe I should get you home before we talk," Jenna said.

"My mom might be there so I'd rather talk here, where we have privacy." Darcy blew out a breath, then provided Jenna a rundown of her medical history, including her previous transplant and ending with her current predicament.

Jenna remained silent while Darcy talked, but her sister's expressive eyes grew more pained, reminding Darcy of the way Clay sometimes looked at her.

"I don't understand why you didn't tell me about this before," Jenna said.

"A lot of reasons, but I guess mainly because I didn't want you to treat me differently because I have kidney disease."

"Why would I do that?"

"People do." Darcy affected a shrug, as though what she was about to say didn't matter. But it did. Very much. "I didn't tell you the whole story about why Kenny broke up with me. He said he wasn't cut out to be around somebody who was sick."

"I'm not like Kenny," Jenna retorted. "And once you have another kidney transplant, you won't be sick."

"That might be a while."

"Not if my kidney's a match, it won't. I'm getting tested as soon as possible."

Tears sprang to Darcy's eyes at her sister's offer, but she blinked them back. She could hardly believe she was about to argue against the chance to have an operation she desperately needed. "I appreciate that. So much. But you can't already have decided you'd give me your kidney."

"The pamphlets say a live donor is the best option. The transplants have a higher success rate and the organs have a longer life span," Jenna continued. "That's right, isn't it?"

"Yes, but…" Darcy's voice trailed off, her eyes falling on the Band-Aid covering the gauze pad on her arm where the dialysis needle had been. She straightened her backbone. She couldn't let her dislike of being chained to a machine sway her. "This is exactly why I didn't tell you."

Jenna put a hand on Darcy's knee. "I'm sorry, but you're not making sense."

"I don't think you've thought it through." Darcy leaned toward Jenna, hoping to make her understand. "If our blood and tissue types match, you'd have to go though more tests. You'd be hospitalized and you'd have to take time off work. You'd only have one kidney left. If anything happened to that one, you're out of luck."

"From what I read, complications from the surgery are rare," Jenna said.

"Rare, but not impossible. And have you thought about how your mother would react? Your brother?"

"It sounds like you're trying to talk me out of it."

"Maybe I am." Darcy sighed. "You've barely had time to get used to us being sisters, let alone take in I need a transplant. I couldn't stand it if you felt obligated."

"Of course I'm obligated, but not in the way you mean. It's not my brain or my conscience telling me to get tested." Jenna put a hand over her chest. "It's my heart."

Darcy's own heart skipped a beat, but the moisture leaked from her eyes. She dabbed at her tears. "Now you've gone and made me cry."

"I was trying to make you happy."

"These are happy tears," Darcy admitted. "I can hardly believe you'd do this for me."

Jenna took both of Darcy's hands in hers and pressed. "Absolutely. You're my sister. I just pray I'm a match."

"Our blood types don't only have to match. Our tissue types do, too, and mine's uncommon," Darcy said. "Tissue type has been the sticking point when other family members got tested."

"Has everyone besides me and Jeff been tested?"

Darcy nodded. She thought she read regret on Jenna's face but her eyelids were growing heavier by the second. "Can you drive me home now? I think I need to rest."

"Sure, sweetie," Jenna said.

Darcy must have fallen asleep in the car because when she awoke they were in her driveway and Jenna was opening the car door. Darcy blinked, in that groggy state between consciousness and sleep.

"I'll come inside with you," Jenna offered.

Darcy had enough of her wits about her to note the absence of her mother's Jag, erasing one argument against Jenna coming inside. The other was less complicated. At twenty-two years old, Darcy was well able to take care of herself. She meant to go straight to sleep, anyway. But instead of trying to dissuade Jenna, she found herself nodding. "Thanks."

Darcy staggered inside the house, her steps heavy but her heart light because her sister accompanied her. A sister willing to sacrifice a part of herself to help Darcy lead a healthier life.

Jenna hovered nearby while Darcy changed into her usual sleeping attire of a T-shirt and boxer shorts, then turned back the lacey comforter on her queen-size bed. She sat down.

If she and Jenna had grown up together, this could have been a repeat of a scene from the past. The older sister babysitting the younger, assuring that she went to bed at a reasonable hour.

"I wish we hadn't missed so much time together," Darcy said, her voice choking on regret.

"We can't do anything about the past, but we can make up for lost time." Jenna bent down and hugged Darcy. "I'm not going to lose you now that I've found you."

Darcy hugged her back, unshed tears dampening her eyes. She blinked them away, because with Jenna in her life there was even less reason to cry.

"I love you, Jenna." Darcy felt the emotion swell like a balloon that had lain dormant inside her, waiting to be inflated.

"I love you, too." Jenna's eyes glistened with unshed tears when she straightened. She swiped at them. "We're such a couple of girls."

"The Wright kind of girls." Darcy giggled, swung her legs into the bed and got under the sheets. "Did you know I get silly when I get tired?"

Jenna sounded amused. "I do now."

"Clay used to call me the Giggler." Darcy felt her eyelids growing heavier. "I'm so glad you and Clay are together. Try not to be mad at him, 'kay?"

"He should have told me you needed a kidney transplant."

"Made him promise not to." Darcy yawned. "So angry with him."

"Why were you angry?" Jenna's voice seemed to come from a distance.

Darcy was tired. So very tired. She tried to focus. Clay. They were talking about Clay. "Never should have done what he did."

She settled deeper beneath the cool, white sheets, something elusive dancing at the corners of her mind. It had to do with the promise she'd demanded of Clay, but she couldn't quite grasp why it was important.

The information still maddeningly out of reach, Darcy drifted into a deep, dreamless sleep.

JENNA PULLED THE DOOR TO Darcy's room shut and descended the stairs to the first floor, the heels of her shoes sinking into the plush carpeting as her hand gripped the railing.

While pouring over pamphlets at the transplant center, Jenna had thought of nothing besides Darcy's health. Now her mind turned toward Darcy's insinuation that Jenna had cause to be angry at Clay.

Before she could solve the puzzle of why Clay hadn't told her about Darcy's illness, she heard the front door open and shut, then a woman's voice calling, "Darcy, I'm home. Do you have company? I don't recognize the car in the driveway."

Jenna stood stock still at the bottom of the stairs as the tap tap of heels against terrazzo floor grew louder, squashing a childish instinct to dash back up the stairs to the safety of Darcy's bedroom. Within seconds she found herself face-to-face with Margo Wright.

Despite the passage of time, Margo was as beautiful as Jenna remembered, her face devoid of all but the finest lines, her blond hair salon-perfect, her white summer dress elegant in its simplicity. The other woman had been a larger-than-life figure for so long that Jenna was surprised to realize Margo was no taller than five feet two.

"Are you a friend of Darcy's?" Margo tilted her head questioningly, her expression puzzled.

Jenna didn't seem capable of doing anything more than nodding.

Margo's breathing changed, becoming harsher, her mushrooming panic easy to read. "Is my daughter okay? Where is she?"

Jenna cleared her throat and found her voice. "Darcy's sleeping." She wasn't familiar enough with Darcy's health problem to keep what had happened from her mother. She filled in Margo about Graceland, watching the older woman's expression switch from panic to relief to worry.

"I'm going to check on her." Margo moved past her and rushed up the steps with surprising speed for someone wearing three-inch heels.

Get out of here, Jenna's mind screamed as soon as Margo was out of sight. Jenna had done her duty by telling Margo about Darcy's health scare. No other reason existed to subject herself to more of the other woman's company—except it seemed wrong to slink away. When Margo slowly descended the stairs, Jenna hadn't budged.

From a distance Margo resembled one of those beautiful, pampered women who thought of nothing but their own pleasure. But the closer she got, the more Jenna could identify the anxiety radiating from her.

"Darcy knows how important those dialysis treatments are," Margo said, almost as though she were speaking to herself. "I don't understand why she'd skip one."

She sounded so distraught that Jenna felt compelled to provide an answer. "I asked her to spend the day with me. I gather she didn't want me to find out she needed a kidney transplant."

Bewilderment marred Margo's features. "Why wouldn't Darcy want you to know about her kidney?"

"So I wouldn't feel obligated to get tested to see if I could be her donor." The statement seemed to confuse Margo further, leaving Jenna no choice but to tell her the rest. "I'm Jenna Wright."

Margo's beautiful blue eyes widened as she made the connection. "Oh, yes. I should have recognized you from Donald's photos. But I still don't understand. When did you and Darcy meet?"

"When I started singing in your son's bar."

"You're the singer Darcy keeps raving about?" Margo shook her head, and a lock of honey-blond hair fell artfully across her forehead. "But none of this adds up. Why didn't Darcy tell me about you? And why didn't you know about her condition?"

"Because Darcy made Clay promise not to tell me."

"Clay?" Margo's brows drew together but the line between them was almost too faint to be visible. "Oh, I get it. He went to Little Rock to find you, didn't he? I should have guessed, especially because of what happened the first time."

Jenna's head spun as she tried to comprehend Margo's words. "What first time?"

"The first time Darcy needed a transplant. Clay wanted to contact you and your brother Jeff when nobody else in the family matched."

"Why didn't you?"

Margo shrugged her dainty shoulders. "I tried, but your mother hung up on me before I could say anything. The same way she did when I called to tell her your father had died."

"You called?" Jenna's mother had never mentioned it.

"Twice. She hung up both times. I was so devastated by Donald's death I didn't have the energy to try again."

Jenna's back stiffened. She could well imagine her mother reacting poorly to a phone call from Margo, but this wasn't just any phone call. "That's no excuse. You should have got the message to us some other way."

"You're right. I've always been sorry about that. I wanted to apologize, but I didn't know how. Your mother's never made a secret of the way she feels about me. A part of me doesn't even blame her. I've done some things I'm not proud of."

"You mean like never having Jeff and me visit our father in Memphis?"

"That wasn't my doing. Your father didn't want you and your brother around me because of how your mother felt. That's the same reason he wouldn't ask you to get tested. We argued about it but he put his foot down, especially after he found out Darcy could get a cadaver organ. He said neither of you would have agreed to the testing, anyway."

Had her father been right? Would Jenna have let her mother's hatred of Margo cause her to refuse to try to help? The possibility shamed her.

"I can't say what I would have done, but I know what I'm going to do now," Jenna said. "I'm getting tested."

Margo brought a hand to her mouth to cover her gasp. Her voice trembled when she spoke. "That's wonderful. Oh, you're an angel to do this."

"I'm no angel," Jenna refuted firmly. "I'm just a woman who wants to help her sister."

Margo hugged Jenna tightly. Not like a woman who'd stolen another woman's husband or neglected to notify his children of their father's death in a timely manner, but like a mother who loved her child with all her heart. "Thank you."

Margo kept hugging her and thanking her while it occurred to Jenna that, although they'd never be friends, she wouldn't be able to think of Margo in quite the same way again. Jenna's body slowly relaxed and she patted the other woman on the back, realizing that in this, at least, they were allies.

Margo finally drew back, dabbing at eyes that looked lovely even when she cried, like a sea of blue tears. "Clay was right to bring you to Memphis, especially if you're a match."

Her declaration reverberated through Jenna. The cloud of confusion that had hung over her since she discovered Darcy needed a kidney transplant dispersed. The air thickened with something else: betrayal.

"Clay intended all along for me to volunteer to get tested," she said aloud, her voice almost robotic.

"He did," Margo confirmed. "Clay's not the kind of man who stands by and does nothing when he has the means to make a difference."

The means to an end, Jenna thought. Was that what his romancing of her had been?

"Are you okay, Jenna? You look pale."

"I'm fine," she lied, the blood pumping with such force through her veins that she thought a vessel might burst. "I'm just thinking I should get over to the transplant center as soon as possible. I'm only in town for the day so maybe I can persuade them to take my blood samples."

"You're a good person, Jenna. My daughter is lucky to have you in her life." Margo's sincerity was hard to miss. "I'll call Darcy's transplant co-ordinator as soon as you leave and tell her you're coming. That should speed things up."

They moved toward the back door in tandem, with Margo still talking, still expressing her gratitude. Jenna checked her watch, already knowing where she'd head after she left the transplant center.

The Marriott, where Darcy had told her Clay's seminar was being held. Jenna no longer wanted to surprise him, as she'd planned when she set out from Little Rock this morning.

She wanted the truth.

CHAPTER FOURTEEN

"SO WHAT DID YOU THINK of the seminar?" The tall, attractive brunette who'd been vying for Clay's attention all day fell in step beside him as he exited the conference room.

He remembered her name was Brielle but couldn't recall the type of business she owned. A boutique, maybe? A spa? Or was it a hair salon? "Well, Brielle, I'm an optimist so I think small-business owners shouldn't pay attention to those one-in-ten failure odds."

She beamed at him with straight teeth so white they must have been professionally bleached. Her A-line skirt prohibited her from taking long strides, so he had to slow his gait to match hers.

"We survivors have to stick together." She stepped onto the escalator beside him, occupying the same wide step although there was hardly room for both of them. "I'd love to talk to you in more detail about beating the odds." She peered at him from under long, dark eyelashes. "Or about anything else."

If a woman as stunning as Brielle had propositioned Clay as recently as five weeks ago, he would have leapt at the suggestion. But five weeks ago, he hadn't met Jenna.

"I appreciate that, Brielle, I really do. But I'm involved with someone."

"Are you gay?" she asked.

"As a matter of fact, I'm not." He failed to comprehend how his sexual preference fit into the equation.

The scent of her musky perfume enveloped him as her shoulder brushed his. "Then I don't mind you being involved with another woman as long as you give me your full attention when we're alone."

The escalator reached the top of its climb, preventing Clay from immediately telling her that *he* minded. He stepped onto the lobby floor and looked straight at Jenna. Jenna, who was supposed to be in Little Rock.

The pleasure that filled him was short-lived. She held herself so rigidly, he couldn't tell whether she was angry or upset. He envisioned the guilty picture he and Brielle must present, considered how Jenna could view the tableau as déjà vu. Like mother, like son.

"Oh, no," he muttered under his breath.

"Are you turning me down?" Incredulity spiked Brielle's voice before she followed his gaze. "Oh, I get it. That's your girlfriend."

His eyes still fastened on Jenna, Clay said, "Just so we're clear, I never intended to take you up on your offer."

"Yeah, sure. If you change your mind, give me a call." Brielle walked away, blowing him a kiss as she went.

Clay quickly crossed the lobby to where Jenna stood, seemingly frozen in place, looking as vibrant as she did on stage in floral print capri pants and a turquoise camisole. Splotches of red stained her cheeks.

"I know how it looks, but I can explain," Clay began.

"You think I'm upset because that woman was coming on to you?" She sounded incredulous, possibly not even realizing she'd admitted she trusted him.

"You're upset about something." He nodded toward the lobby coffee shop, aware that some of the people who'd been in the seminar were regarding them curiously. "Let's go over there. I see a lot of empty tables."

She shrugged off his hand when he tried to take her arm, proceeding to the coffee shop ahead of him, distress evident in her every step.

She knows why I really brought her to Memphis, Clay thought. Nothing else would have this effect on her.

Guilt churning inside him, he held out a chair for her at a table away from other customers. Before he settled into his own seat, a waitress came by. He ordered two decafs to get rid of her.

"How could you not tell me Darcy needed a kidney transplant?" Jenna spoke in a low, hurt voice as soon as the waitress was gone.

He sighed heavily. "I wanted to, but I promised Darcy I wouldn't."

"Darcy didn't know about you coming to Little Rock to find me," she accused.

He stared down at his hands, which were linked together, as though in prayer for a better explanation than he had.

"Let me take a stab at it," she continued before he could attempt to explain. "You thought the odds of me volunteering to get tested would rise once I got to Memphis and met Darcy."

"Yes."

"Was making me fall for you part of the plan?" Her voice wobbled. "If I didn't get sufficiently attached to Darcy, did you think I'd get tested to please you?"

"That's ridiculous." He released a harsh breath

and shook his head, shaken by the suggestion. "You know me better than that."

"Do I?" She let out a humorless laugh. "The man I thought I knew, the man I was actually stupid enough to fall for, wouldn't have deceived me like you did."

He balanced his forearms on the table and leaned forward, desperate to make her understand. "It wasn't like that, Jenna. When I first met you, yes, I was only thinking about how sick Darcy was. But everything changed when I fell in love with you."

"The fact that you were lying to me didn't change."

"My hands were tied. I couldn't break the promise I made to Darcy. Surely you can see that."

"That would never have been an issue if you'd told me up front who you were and what you wanted." Her voice vibrated with what sounded like unspilled tears. If she blasted him, that would have been easier to take.

Pain claimed his gut, but he couldn't think only of himself no matter how much he was hurting. "Darcy still needs a kidney donor. Don't let what I've done stop you from helping her."

The waitress came by and set the two cups of coffee on the table, preventing Jenna from immediately answering. She wouldn't meet his eyes, as though it sickened her to look at him.

"Darcy's my sister," she finally said. "If the blood tests come back positive, I'll be her donor."

"You already had the tests?" It seemed almost too incredible to digest. "When?"

"I just came from the center."

He resisted an urge to pick her up and twirl her around, so great was his gratitude. "Thank you."

Now she did look at him. "I didn't have the tests for you. I did it for Darcy." She sucked in some air before she continued. "Two Gals is contracted to Peyton's Place for two more weeks, but I'm breaking the agreement. Corrine will understand I don't want to have to see you again."

Everything inside him rebelled at letting her go, but he couldn't dredge up a convincing argument to get her to stay. He watched the steam from their untouched coffees rise and dissipate into the air.

"Okay," he said, the agreement stabbing at him. "Just don't let what happened between us make you stop singing."

"Leave my singing out of it."

He leaned closer. Maybe in this, at least, he could do something for her. "How can I? You come alive when you sing, Jenna. Being a singer is who you are. It's what you were born to do."

"Because you say so?" She shook her head, seemingly in disgust. "You have a lot of nerve presuming you know what's right for everybody else."

"I don't do that."

"Oh, please. Did I ask you if I should keep singing? Did Darcy ask you to track me down? And that bartender who worked for you for like two minutes, did he ask you for a job?"

Clay's shoulders squared. He couldn't defend himself on the first two counts so addressed the third. "Nick as good as asked by saying nobody else would hire him."

Jenna rolled her eyes, dismissing his explanation, and kept talking. "How about your mother? You said she has money trouble. I bet you help her out."

"She's my mother. Of course I help her."

"By giving her money so she doesn't have to get a job? Aren't you perpetuating her idea that she can only get along with a man's help?"

Clay frowned. Could Jenna have a valid point? He'd repeatedly urged his mother to look for a job but had never threatened to stop helping her pay the bills if she didn't.

"You're always charging to the rescue, not even realizing some people don't need rescuing." She stood up. "I don't need rescuing."

"Where are you going?"

"Back to Little Rock."

Clay couldn't let her leave, not until he attempted to get her to see reason. "I'll walk you to your car."

"Weren't you listening, Clay? I'm perfectly capable of walking myself to the car. I don't need your help."

She walked quickly away from him. He shot to his feet, the hand he braced on the table knocking over one of the coffee cups. The now-warm liquid splashed over his hand and onto his slacks before dripping to the floor. Like spilled dreams.

Jenna kept walking without a backward glance. Out of the coffee shop, out of the hotel and out of his life.

"COME ON, BABY. ROLL for me now. Yes. Yes. A little farther. And it's in!" Darcy pumped her fist in an imitation of victorious athletes everywhere. "Count it."

Mike Puffenbarger glanced up from the scorecard, Darcy noted what she thought was amusement on his face. It was kind of hard to tell considering his face was in darkness and his white shirt glowed like the moon even though it was Wednesday afternoon.

"By my count, you had a four on that hole, which would give you fifty-nine total." Mike spoke loudly to be heard over the squeals of young children and the techno beat of the blaring music. "That's, let's see, twenty-three over par."

"What did you finish with?"

"Sixty-one."

Darcy did a little dance on the velvety black surface of the eighteenth hole, right between the scowling lime-green monster and the sprawling lemon-yellow sunflower. "Call me the queen of glow-in-the-dark miniature golf."

Mike laughed. "That you are."

Darcy was still grinning when she walked with Mike back into the relative quiet of the mall. "That was a lot of fun. I'm glad you suggested it."

Mike had called that morning to "touch base," another of the ambiguous phrases he used when calling to check up on her.

He'd barely said hello when she blurted, "Jenna got tested yesterday to see if she could be my donor. The results are supposed to come in today, and I'm so nervous I can hardly stand it."

Mike, good friend that he was, had immediately offered to distract her. He'd first taken her to a horror movie so stupid they'd laughed as green-faced zombies moving in ultra slow motion managed to chase down terrified citizens. Then he'd suggested glow-in-the-dark minigolf.

"I've been wanting to try that course but

couldn't get anybody to go with me," Darcy said. "Kenny said it was for kids."

"Kenny's an ass."

Usually thoughts of Kenny made Darcy feel like weeping, but Mike's comment had been so instantaneous that she laughed. "You really think so?"

"I know so."

Now Darcy had an inkling of why she kept confiding in Mike. He was 100 percent on her side. He hadn't said so but she suspected he'd finagled time off from his second job of delivering flowers to spend the day with her.

"What do you want to do next?" he asked.

"You'll laugh," Darcy said. Kenny always did when she suggested it. "Bowling."

Mike didn't hesitate. "Then let's go. Isn't there a bowling alley inside the mall?"

"Not far from the minigolf. It's—" The ring of Darcy's cell phone, which she'd been waiting to hear all morning, coincided with the spike in her heart rate. She pulled the phone from a side pocket in her purse and checked the number. Her eyes locked on Mike's, her fingers wrapped tightly around the phone. "It's the transplant center."

"Answer it," he urged gently.

She took a deep breath, established the connection and said hello.

"Darcy. It's Melinda," her transplant coordinator said. "I'm afraid I have disappointing news. The results of the blood test are back, and your sister's not a match."

Air whooshed out Darcy's lungs and her legs threatened to give way. She spied a bench nearby, peripherally aware that Mike held her arm as she sank into it. Melinda talked a while longer, with Darcy making the appropriate noises, but she'd stopped processing anything other than the pertinent nugget of information.

Jenna wasn't a match.

Darcy's smile muscles seemed weighted by gravity but she forced herself to lift them after Melinda hung up. "Jenna can't be my donor."

"I'm sorry, Darcy."

She didn't grasp that Mike was holding her hand until he squeezed it. "It's okay."

He touched one side of her mouth, smoothing the fake smile. "You don't have to pretend with me. It's okay to be disappointed."

"I didn't realize how much hope I'd invested until just now. I kept telling myself it was enough Jenna offered to get tested. And it should be enough." She dabbed at her eyes, disappointed that she couldn't keep tears from forming, and released a shaky breath. "But somehow it's not."

Mike put a finger under her chin and turned her to face him. Shoppers went about their business, conversation and mall music buzzing around them, but Darcy's entire focus was on Mike's face. "Listen to me, Darcy. Nothing's wrong with hoping for the best."

"But things could be so much worse," she argued. "Some people on dialysis have diabetes and high blood pressure. I should be thankful for what I have instead of focusing on what I don't." She rolled her eyes. "Like a boyfriend."

"Why can't you have a boyfriend?"

"I'm hardly the picture of health."

"Who put that crap in your head?" His eyes narrowed. "Kenny?"

"You've got to admit Kenny has a point. Who wants to get involved with a sick girl who needs a kidney transplant?"

"Me. I'd give you my kidney if I could. But I asked Clay your blood type so I already know I can't be your donor."

"You're a good friend to say that, even if you're only trying to make me feel better." She laid a hand on the thigh nearest her own.

He covered her hand with his. "It's the truth, Darcy. Here's another truth. With a little encouragement, I could fall in love with you."

She started to make another flippant comment before it registered that Mike wasn't joking. "You're serious."

He lifted his hand, breaking the connection between them. A deep blush crept up his neck and stained his cheeks. "I'm also an idiot. Forget I said it, okay?"

"So you didn't mean it?"

"I didn't mean to make you uncomfortable. Let's go back to being friends, just like before." His cheeks got redder, and he didn't seem to know what to do with his hands, making him look adorably flustered.

A sort of peace settled over her. "What if I can't?"

He sighed heavily. "Then I'll kick myself for the rest of my life for opening my big mouth."

She reached out with her forefinger, tracing the softness of his lips. "The more you talk, the more I realize I like your mouth."

A spark of hope flashed in his eyes. "Are you saying what I think you're saying?"

"I'm repeating your advice," she said softly. "There's nothing wrong with hoping for the best."

That mouth she recently realized she liked creased into a wide smile. And just like that, one of the most disappointing days of Darcy's life got a whole lot better.

JENNA TOOK THE JAR FROM the lazy Susan in her kitchen, ripped off the plastic covering and brought a heaping teaspoon of chocolate fudge icing to her mouth.

Even though she'd found out her kidney wasn't a match for Darcy's the day before, she'd been almost frantic while searching her townhouse for her favorite comfort food. The rich taste of the icing did nothing to assuage her lingering sadness.

Her craving for chocolate gone, Jenna capped the icing and was shoving the jar to the very back of a refrigerator shelf when the doorbell rang. Strange. The doorbell of Jenna's brick townhouse never sounded after nine at night. Especially on a Thursday. It hardly ever rang, period, unless FedEx or UPS was delivering a purchase Jenna had made over the Internet.

That suited Jenna fine. She usually wasn't in the mood for visitors after spending her workday meeting with clients and interacting with coworkers. She was even less inclined for company tonight.

She certainly didn't feel like dealing with her surprise visitors: her mother, in the navy blue scrub pants and polo shirt she usually wore to work, and her brother. A head taller than their mother, Jeff stood slightly behind her, his manner protective.

"Can we come in?" Her mother's face was

pinched, her expression troubled, alerting Jenna this wasn't a social visit. "We need to talk to you about Clay Dillon."

Jenna gazed from her mother to her brother, instantly recognizing they wouldn't have anything good to say. Surrendering to the inevitable, she stepped back to admit them.

A few moments later, at her mother's request for a glass of wine, she uncorked a forgotten bottle of merlot she found on the wine rack built into one of the kitchen cabinets. She poured her mother a glass and started on one for her brother.

"Nothing for me, thanks," Jeff said. "I'm driving."

The wheels in Jenna's brain turned. If Jeff had driven to her place, that probably meant their mother had swung by Jeff's house to instigate the visit.

"Maybe you should have a drink, too, Jenna," her mother said after she had a swig of the wine. "You won't like what I have to say."

Jenna joined her mother and brother at one of the four tall stools that surrounded the breakfast bar in the kitchen. "I don't need a drink. I need to know what this is about."

Her mother got straight to the point, the way she usually did. "Remember Stephen Edwards, you father's former law partner? I called him today to find out what he knew about Margo Wright's children, and I think I figured out why Clay Dillon was so anxious for you to meet his sister."

After the breakup with Clay and the devastating news that her kidney wasn't a match for Darcy, Jenna had believed things couldn't get worse. Now she knew she was wrong.

"Darcy Wright needs a kidney transplant," her mother announced.

"Darcy needs *another* kidney transplant," Jenna clarified, noting the widening of her mother's eyes. "She had her first six years ago but that kidney's failing. Now, at twenty-two, she's on dialysis three times a week. That's why I took a blood test to see if I could give her one of mine."

Her mother's face went nearly as white as the laminated surface of the kitchen counter. "Why would you do such a thing?"

"I can take a stab at that," Jeff said while Jenna was formulating her response. He peered at her the way he used to when they were kids and he suspected she was holding something back. "There's more going on between you and Clay Dillon than you let on."

"Oh, my gosh." Her mother got up from the stool, anchoring one hand on the counter as though she needed support to stand. Her eyes filled with hurt. "Is it true? Is something going on between you and Margo's son?"

"Not anymore." Jenna's voice caught, her heart clutching at the finality of her answer. Even though the split had been her decision, she felt as though it had cut her in two. "And Clay isn't the reason I tried to help Darcy. I got tested because she's my sister, and I love her."

"She's Margo's daughter! And Clay Dillon is Margo's son," Jeff interjected. "How could you let yourself get involved with either of them when you know how much Margo hurt Mom?"

The two people Jenna had always thought of as the only family she'd ever need stared incredulously at her, hurt emanating from them. Jenna was sorry for their pain, but it was time for all of them to face some harsh truths.

"I know how you feel about Margo, Mom, but it's time you let go of your hatred," Jenna said gently. "In fact, I think Margo did you a favor."

"A favor?" Her mother's voice sounded strangled. "How do you figure that?"

"Do you know what Margo got after she married Dad?" Jenna answered her own question. "A cheating husband. Look at what you got: A career, your independence and a darn good life. Now that you're dating Ned Voight, I've never seen you happier."

"But I had to struggle every step of the way to get where I am," her mother cried.

"Aren't you the one who always told us anything worth having is worth the struggle? And even though things weren't easy for you, you made sure Jeff and I had a happy childhood. You did that for us, Mom."

"Then you can do something for me." Her mother drew to her full height, her back ramrod straight, her expression unflinching. "Don't give Margo's daughter your kidney."

"It's a moot point," Jenna said. "It turns out I don't even have the same blood type as Darcy so I'm not a match."

"Thank God," her mother said, her body relaxing.

"But Jeff might be." Jenna voiced the possibility swirling around in her head since she'd gotten her results. "I didn't remember my blood type, Jeff, but I recall you saying you were registered at the Red Cross as a universal donor. That means you have type-O blood, the same as Darcy."

Her mother pounded the kitchen counter with the palm of one hand. "Stop it, Jenna. Jeff has a wife and three boys who depend on him. He won't jeopardize his health by giving his kidney to a stranger."

"Darcy's not a stranger. She's your sister," Jenna said, speaking directly to Jeff. "She got lucky the first time and only had to wait nine months for a cadaver kidney. She'll probably have to wait much longer this time because she has an uncommon combination of blood and tissue type. She wouldn't have to wait at all if your tissue matches hers."

"I don't think of her as a sister, Jenna," Jeff protested, although not as vociferously as their mother. "I've never even met her."

"I think you have. She was the blonde collecting the cover at the door last Friday at Peyton's Place."

From the recognition that dawned on his face, Jenna could tell that Jeff remembered Darcy.

"This is ridiculous," her mother said. "What does it matter if he met the girl once?"

"Mom's right," Jeff said slowly, emotions Jenna couldn't read flitting across his face. "She's still a stranger."

"She wouldn't be if you got to know her, the way I have."

"I can't believe what I'm hearing." Her mother's posture turned rigid, echoing her resistance. "I have sympathy for the young woman. I do. Nobody that young should have to deal with that kind of health problem. But Jeff's main responsibility is to his wife and sons. He shouldn't take any unnecessary risks with his health."

"Any surgery has risks, but complications to living kidney donors are very rare," Jenna argued.

Her mother anchored both arms on the counter. "Just because you let Clay Dillon manipulate you into getting tested doesn't mean you should do the same thing to your brother."

"Clay did not manipulate me," Jenna denied hotly.

"Okay, then, he *used* you." Her mother emphasized the word.

"If he did, it was only because he can't stand to see Darcy suffer," Jenna said. "You can't blame him for exploring every option to help his sister secure a kidney."

Yet Jenna had. She blamed Clay even though she'd have done the same thing in his place. By trying to convince Jeff to get tested, she was doing the same thing.

"He lied to you, Jenna," Jeff pointed out.

"He lied because he wanted me to find out for myself what a terrific person Darcy is," Jenna explained. "He did what he did out of love for his sister. Only a good man is capable of that kind of love."

Clay Dillon was a good man. Jenna had known that in her heart all along. Why hadn't she seen it with her eyes?

Was it because she'd been so focused on

creating a safe, stable life for herself after what her mother had gone through that she was afraid to take a chance on Clay? A chance on them?

"You sound like you're in love with him," her mother accused.

"What if I am?"

"That's crazy," her mother said.

"What's crazy is I let the grudge you have against Margo become my grudge. I can't do that anymore, Mom. I have to do what my heart tells me is right. Weren't you the one who raised me to be independent?"

"You do whatever you have to," her mother announced, "but don't expect me to endorse it."

"I don't," Jenna said quietly, "but I do expect you to accept that I'm in love with Clay."

It wasn't only the first time Jenna let herself say the words aloud. It was the first time she let herself think them.

Her mother said nothing. Neither did Jeff. But even without their acceptance, Jenna's next step was as clear as the glass holding the merlot her mother had barely touched.

She needed to tell Clay she loved him—and pray he hadn't stopped loving her for the mistakes she'd made.

CHAPTER FIFTEEN

CLAY'S MOTHER HUGGED him tightly late on Friday afternoon, her signature perfume tickling his nostrils so it was a struggle not to sneeze. She beamed up at him without the smile lines that had bracketed her mouth before the face-lift she'd had the year before her husband died.

"I'm glad you stopped by. It saves me a phone call." She clasped her hands together. "Simon and I want you and Darcy to have dinner with us tonight at that fabulous new downtown restaurant everybody's talking about."

Which one of his mother's men, Clay wondered, was Simon? The plastic surgeon? The engineer? The financial planner?

"It's Friday, Mom," he said. "I have to work in a few hours."

"You have to work every night. Can't you come in late just this one time? I so want you and Darcy to meet Simon. I've already called the restaurant and got the chef to agree to make something that would fit Darcy's diet."

Although his mother was needy in other ways, she seldom made demands on Clay's time. Since his stepfather had died, she'd never suggested he or Darcy meet any of the men she was dating.

"What's going on?" he asked. "Why is it so important Darcy and I meet this guy?"

"I swore I wouldn't tell you until tonight, but I never could keep a secret." She clapped her hands like a child with big news. "Simon asked me to marry him."

He took a moment to digest the news, concluding he'd always known his mother would remarry. "What was your answer?"

"I'm not giving Simon an answer until you and Darcy meet him." She dug into her leather designer handbag as she talked, pulled out a small black velvet box and opened it. A diamond that must have been over a karat winked up at him. "But I'm holding on to this for safekeeping."

"It's…" Ostentatious, flamboyant, gaudy. "…Impressive."

"Isn't it gorgeous? I told Simon it was too much, but he said not to worry, that the commission from some stock or bond had already paid for it."

Ah. So Simon was the financial planner.

"Do you love him?" Clay asked.

"I do, I do. He's rich, gainfully employed and crazy about me and only me. He's not as good-looking as Donald was, another plus. This is not a man who'll be fighting off other women."

Jenna's claim that Clay had unwittingly reinforced his mother's idea that she could only get along with a man's help echoed in his head. "What about the job you told me you'd look for?"

"I don't need a job now."

"I don't agree, Mom. Even if things work out with Simon, and I have no reason to think they won't, it'd be good for you to get out in the workforce. To find something that makes you happy. Something you're good at."

She patted him on the cheek. "You're a dear to worry about me, but I already found a job that made me happy. Taking care of you, Darcy and Donald. And now I'll be happy taking care of Simon."

Now that his eyes had been opened, Clay's instinct was to try to get his mother to see things his way. How had Jenna put it? To come to her rescue. But Jenna was right about another thing. Some people didn't need rescuing.

"Then if you're happy," Clay said, "I'm happy for you, Mom."

"I'd love to stay and chat, but my favorite boutique gets in new shipments on Fridays. I thought I'd look for a wedding dress sooner rather than later."

"Have a good time with that."

"Believe me, I will." She kissed him on the cheek, probably leaving an imprint of her pink lipstick. "Darcy's in the office. Tell her I'm going out for a few hours, but don't tell her about Simon's proposal. I want it to be a surprise."

When his mother was gone, he moved over the terrazzo floor to the office that had once been Donald Wright's and stood unseen at the open door. Darcy sat at the office chair in front of a flat-screen monitor, her fingers poised over the computer keys, her brow knitted in concentration.

The sunlight streaming into the room washed over her, causing her hair to look lighter and her skin paler, like she was some fragile creature who needed to be rescued. Despite Jenna's criticism, Clay still wanted to rescue her.

He straightened from the doorjamb. "Hey, Darce."

She turned, bestowing upon him a smile as bright as the sun that filled the room. "Hey, Clay."

His step faltered. Although the verdict that Jenna couldn't donate her kidney had come down two days before, he'd yet to see Darcy show any disappointment. "Mom said to tell you she was going shopping."

"Did she ask you to dinner with this guy she's dating?"

"Yeah. She was pretty insistent about it, too. So I told her I'd go into the bar late."

"Me, too. If that's okay."

"I hired another waitress so it should be fine. If not, the customers who get there early don't have to pay a cover. It's no big deal. Mom made it sound like dinner was."

"I think she's stuck on this new guy."

"How do you feel about that? It's only been two years since your father died."

"Let's face it, my parents didn't have the strongest marriage. If this new guy makes her happy, then I'm happy."

He moved deeper into the room as they talked and looked over her shoulder at a computer screen filled with coding. "What are you doing?"

"Remember the day care center where I was going to work this summer?" She pressed a key and an eye-popping web page decorated in primary colors appeared. The focal point was a photo of a young boy and girl flashing identical missing-tooth smiles. "I got the assignment to do the center's Web page. What do you think?"

He kissed the top of her head, smelling the

same fruity shampoo their mother used, proud of his sister for her fortitude. "I think you're talented at very many things."

"And I think you're good for my ego." She smiled, as though it wasn't killing her to be stuck designing Web pages when she really wanted to be teaching elementary school children. "What brings you here?"

"A surprise." He took from his pocket the purchase he'd just made at the Orpheum Theater box office. "Two tickets for *Phantom of the Opera.*"

Her face filled with pleasure as she took the tickets from him. "Oh, cool. Thanks. Are you going with me?"

"You know I love you, Darcy. But there are some things I just won't do. Going to a musical is one of them."

"Then maybe Jenna would like to go…or Mike."

"Mike." He repeated the name she used for Puff. "I wondered if you two were dating."

She nodded, the thought obviously bringing her pleasure. "We're going to take it slow, see how it goes."

"Puff's a good guy. If Jenna won't go see *Phantom,* he will. Even if musicals make him break out in hives."

"Oh, stop. It's supposed to be a terrific production. I've been wanting to see it for ages."

"That's why I bought you the tickets."

She sobered, her eyes narrowing. "Is it really, Clay? Or did you get me the tickets because you feel sorry for me?"

"I wouldn't put it that way. It's pretty hard to feel sorry for someone as upbeat as you. But I know you were disappointed about Jenna."

"How disappointed could I be? I've gained a sister."

He nodded, regret over his own fractured relationship with Jenna spilling over into his gladness for Darcy. "Then you're not still mad at me for tricking Jenna into coming to Memphis?"

"How could I be, considering the result?"

The tension in his shoulders didn't abate. "Jenna broke up with me because of what I did."

"I'm sorry, Clay."

He wiped a hand across his mouth, still feeling the pain. "She says I stick my nose into other people's business even when they don't want it there."

"That's kind of cold, but you have been known to do that."

"That's why I'm here, for permission to stick my nose into your business." Clay moved to the window, took in the view of the meandering Mississippi before turning back to her. "I want to try to talk Jeff Wright into getting tested."

"No," Darcy said.

Clay sighed heavily. "He's the only family member we haven't contacted."

"I'd be surprised if Jenna hasn't already said something to him," Darcy said. "It's obvious Jeff Wright doesn't think of me as part of his family. How could I ask him to sacrifice a kidney for me?"

Frustration flowed through Clay. "We don't know what kind of man he is, Darcy. If you let me talk to him, I might be able to get—"

The ringing of the telephone interrupted the rest of his argument. Darcy picked up the phone. He turned back to the view of the river, watching a tugboat in the distance chug past and cars stream over the bridge that linked Tennessee to Arkansas.

A gasp interrupted the quiet. Clay turned to see Darcy covering her mouth with a hand. Her head bobbed, but he couldn't hear the other side of the conversation. She hadn't greeted the caller by name, so he couldn't even guess who she was talking to. Finally, her stunned expression still in place, she put down the phone.

He moved swiftly across the room. "Darcy, what is it?"

Her hand dropped from her mouth. "Tell me

the truth, Clay. Did you already talk to Jeff Wright?"

"No. Why?"

"Because that was Melanie." She named her transplant coordinator. "Jeff came into the center this morning for blood tests. He asked Melanie not to tell me anything until she had the results so I wouldn't get my hopes up."

"Are the results in?" Clay asked, his heart beating hard.

"Melanie pulled some strings so she could do a rush on them." Darcy's voice filled with wonder—and hope. "Jeff's a match."

CLAY WASN'T AT THE BAR.

The rapid beats of Jenna's heart slowed considerably, the adrenaline ebbing from her body. She'd been so sure he'd be here. She supposed she should have phoned to let him know she was coming but she was afraid. Fear was the same reason she hadn't driven hell-bent to Memphis last night after realizing what a fool she'd been.

Getting up the nerve to tell a man you loved him took some time. Especially when you might already have killed his love for you.

"Just like a man," Corrine quipped. "Never around when you need him."

Corrine had insisted on accompanying Jenna to Memphis for moral support, although Jenna couldn't be sure who needed the support more. Maurice had moved out but suggested marriage counseling, an offer Corrine was considering.

"If you're including Maurice in that comment, you don't need him," Jenna said. "You're supposed to decide whether you still want him."

"I know that," Corrine said. "But this is about you. And right now you need to talk to Clay. So let's find out where he is."

Corrine headed directly to the bar, where she flagged down Puff. He met them at the less-crowded end. "Hey, I thought you two weren't going to be here tonight."

"Change of plans," Corrine said. "Jenna has some unfinished business with Clay."

"He should be here soon. Darcy left a message on my cell that she and Clay are having dinner with their mom. She also said she has news. Any idea what it is?"

"No clue," Jenna said.

Somebody called for a bartender. Puff put up a finger, then said, "I've got to go. But before I do, there was a man in here earlier asking about you. Had something to do with a concert. His name was Mason something or other."

"Guerard?" Corrine asked.

Puff snapped his fingers. "That's it," he said, then left them to wait on his customer.

"How'd you know that?" Jenna asked Corrine.

Her friend looked guilty. "He talked to me last Saturday after one of our sets."

"Who is he?"

"Don't be mad," Corrine said, then explained Guerard was the manager of the city's most popular blues group. "He said Rhapsody in Blues was looking for an opening act for the concert they're doing next month."

"And he's considering us?"

"Maybe. I didn't hear from him all week so that's why I didn't mention it. But Guerard showing up tonight's a good sign."

Through the sea of people between herself and the door, Jenna spotted the top of a familiar head of dark brown hair. Clay. The rapid thumps of her heart started again.

Corrine kept talking. "I can tell Mr. Guerard that singing is just a temporary thing for you. I'm not trying—"

"If he asks, we should do it," Jenna interrupted, her eyes fastened on Clay. Darcy was with him, but she immediately veered off to head toward the bar. Probably to talk to Puff.

"What?" The hope in Corrine's voice blended with disbelief. "You heard me say this was next month, right? What happened to you giving up singing? You said performing and accounting didn't mix."

"Then maybe I'll quit my accounting job," Jenna said. Clay stopped to talk to a couple customers, looking as though he was interested in what they had to say. He truly cared about the people around him, Jenna finally understood.

"Well, that's…awesome," Corrine said. "That's exactly what you should have done a long time ago. But did you swap places with an evil twin I don't know about?"

Jenna smiled, her eyes still on Clay. "I'm the new, smarter version. It finally got through my thick skull that only people who take big risks get big rewards. But I can't talk about this right now."

"Why not? Something bigger pressing?" Corrine was clearly puzzled. Until she followed the direction of Jenna's gaze. "Why didn't you tell me Clay was here instead of letting me yak? Go get him."

Jenna went, aware she was about to take the biggest risk of her life. As she moved toward Clay, he spotted her. Her eyes locked with his, her pulse fluttering wildly. The distance between them closed until they stood between two tables, just inches and the angry words they'd spoken to each other separating them.

He spoke first, bending close so she could hear him above the typical bar noise. "I know how you feel about me, but today of all days I thought we could put the past behind us and—"

She covered his lips with three fingers, effectively silencing him. "Don't talk. Just listen or I won't have the courage to get through this."

Even though customers jammed the place, her entire world narrowed to his strong, handsome face. The high cheekbones, heavy brows, dark eyes and long nose all combined for an arresting picture. How could she ever have thought he wasn't her type? "This isn't the best place for this, but I can't wait any longer to tell you how wrong I was."

His brows drew together. "Wrong about what?"

"About everything. Blaming you for luring me to Memphis, resenting the way you kept your promise to Darcy, even getting angry when you told me not to give up singing." She shook her head. "No. Don't say anything yet. Because of you, I realized I've been afraid to take chances. So I'm not even upset about you arranging to have Mason Guerard listen to Corrine and me."

"I know I'm not supposed to interrupt, but who's Mason Guerard?"

"The manager for Rhapsody in Blues." Her

voice trailed off at the incomprehension on his face. "You didn't have anything to do with Mason Guerard being here last weekend, did you?"

"Not a thing," he confirmed. "I listened when you told me not to stick my nose where you didn't want it. So you can't blame me for Mason Guerard."

"But I said yes, Clay." She put her hand on his chest, not far from his heart. "I decided to give singing a shot, even if it means doing part-time accounting, or…quitting my job. That's what I've been trying to tell you. It's time I started taking chances." She took a deep breath and looked directly into his eyes. "So here goes. If you still want me, I'm yours."

His hands rose to lightly grip her shoulders as his face filled with hope and something she didn't understand. "I can't believe I'm going to ask this, but are you sure? What about your mother?"

"She'll never be friends with your mother, but she took the news about how I feel about you better than I expected." She touched his face. "I love you, Clay."

"That's music to my ears." He drew her fully into his arms, as though he'd never let her go, but something obviously still bothered him. "I have to confess something. I tried not interfering in the lives of people I love but I'm not very good at it."

"As long as you don't go overboard," she

quipped. "I can see now that your willingness to interfere is part of what makes you special."

"Said the woman who's been known to do some interfering herself," Clay said. "One of these days, you'll have to tell me how you convinced your brother to get tested."

She drew back in his arms. "Jeff got tested?"

"This morning. The results already came in, and he's a match."

Jenna's heart, which seemed to have stopped beating at the news of her brother's about-face, kick-started with a vengeance. "That's fantastic. But I wonder what made him change his mind."

"After Darcy called to thank him, she said he didn't want to be a hypocrite. Seems like he was scolding one of his sons for not sticking up for his brother. He told his son family members need to have each other's back."

"That makes sense," Jenna said. "Jeff tries very hard to be a good role model for his sons."

"Your brother's become my role model, too," Clay agreed. "If I wasn't so grateful to Peyton Smith and her family for the years Darcy got out of her last kidney, I'd think about renaming the bar Jeff's Joint."

"That's why you call the bar Peyton's Place?" Jenna asked. "Because Peyton was the name of Darcy's first kidney donor?"

"It was my way of honoring her for the gift she gave Darcy."

Jenna's smile grew at his touching gesture. She threw her arms around his neck and kissed him, right in the middle of the bar in front of anyone who happened to be watching. Including the half sister they shared.

She wanted everyone to know how she truly felt about Clay—especially Clay. She planned to make up for lost time with Clay and with Darcy, because being able to spend time with the people she loved was perhaps the greatest gift of all.

EPILOGUE

THE BREEZE BLEW OFF the Mississippi River and over Jenna's heated skin, the same way it had that day Clay had taken her to Tom Lee Park and she'd tossed the Frisbee around.

If she threw a Frisbee today, she'd never get it back. People jammed the park, clustering around the outdoor stages where performers entertained the crowd.

Just in case anybody didn't know about the annual event that took place each May, a banner visible from Riverside Drive announced the Beale Street Music Festival.

"I can't believe how many people are here," Jenna remarked to Clay, a comment he wouldn't have heard if the rock 'n' roll band hadn't just finished its set.

"Then come over here so we don't get separated." He pulled her to him with one long arm and kissed her briefly and thrillingly on the mouth.

She laughed up at him. "You don't need an excuse to do that. Any old time's fine with me."

The sun glinted off the diamond engagement ring that adorned the hand resting on his shoulder. It was a fitting sign because, after nearly a year of dating, the passion between them burned as brightly as ever.

"If you two don't quit the mushy stuff, you'll give the kids ideas." Corrine indicated Darcy and Mike Puffenbarger with a nod. The two stood facing each other, their hands linked, Puff's head bent to listen to what Darcy was saying.

"The kids already have their own ideas," Jenna said, having no intention of moving out of the circle of Clay's arm.

"Jeff is coming, right?" Corrine stood on tiptoes, scanning the crowd. "Shame he's happily married with kids. I've got to get used to being the single one again."

Corrine's divorce from Maurice was nearly final, a process that hadn't been as painful for Corrine as Jenna thought it might. Maurice had unwittingly made the entire ordeal easier, showing his lack of character by blaming Corrine for his cheating because of her frequent trips out of town.

"I'd take your poor-little-me act more seriously

if men didn't hit on you everywhere we went," Jenna said. "If you wanted a man, you'd have one."

"And one of these days, I'll get one," Corrine said. "But not now. Before Maurice, I'd been with one guy or another since I was thirteen. It's nice to be on my own for once."

"When you find the right guy, you'll know." Jenna nestled more fully against Clay, still amazed that the son of her father's second wife was the right man for her.

"There's Jeff," Clay said in a loud voice. "I'm impressed he found us in this crowd."

"Jeff's here?" Darcy emerged from her Puff-induced stupor, dropping her boyfriend's hands and spinning around. As soon as she spotted her half brother, she ran to him and launched herself into his arms.

"Hey, Bro," she cried, laughing.

"Hey, Sis." He caught her and spun her around, a neat trick considering the tight confines. "You're looking beautiful, as usual."

Jenna blinked away happy tears. Anybody could see how strong the bond between her two siblings was. But only those who knew them knew the bond went further than skin deep, with

Jeff's kidney functioning flawlessly inside Darcy's body.

Jeff approached Jenna and Clay, Darcy at his side. He shook Clay's hand and kissed Jenna's cheek.

"Where's Mom?" Jenna asked.

"She cancelled at the last minute but it's a good sign that she considered coming at all," he said. "She knew everybody would be here."

Jenna nodded. For now she'd have to be satisfied with that. "Well, you got here just in time. Corrine, are you ready?"

"I'm always ready," Corrine said before linking her elbow through Jenna's and walking away from their tight-knit group.

A short time later, Jenna gazed down into a sea of faces from her vantage point atop the stage by the river. She spotted Clay immediately, then picked out Jeff, Darcy and Puff.

"Have we got a treat for you," one of the festival hosts said into the microphone. "This duo about to perform is a Memphis treasure. So let's give a big Tennessee welcome to Jenna Wright and Corrine Sweetland, the talented ladies who make up Two Gals."

The crowd applauded, and the familiar butterflies fluttered inside Jenna's stomach before

settling into an excited dance. Then she grabbed
the microphone and launched into a song about
love, her eyes on Clay as the lyrics resonated
soundly and sweetly in her heart.

* * * * *

Every Life Has More
Than One Chapter

Award-winning author Stevi Mittman delivers another hysterical mystery, featuring Teddi Bayer, an irrepressible heroine, and her to-die-for hero, Detective Drew Scoones. After all, life on Long Island can be murder!

Turn the page for a sneak peek at the warm and funny fourth book,
WHOSE NUMBER IS UP, ANYWAY?,
in the Teddi Bayer series,
by STEVI MITTMAN.
On sale August 7.

"Before redecorating a room, I always advise my clients to empty it of everything but one chair. Then I suggest they move that chair from place to place, sitting in it, until the placement feels right. Trust your instincts when deciding on furniture placement. Your room should 'feel right'."

—TipsFromTeddi.com

Gut feelings. You know, that gnawing in the pit of your stomach that warns you that you are about to do the absolute stupidest thing you could do? Something that will ruin life as you know it?

I've got one now, standing at the butcher counter in King Kullen, the grocery store in the same strip mall as L.I. Lanes, the bowling alley cum billiard parlor I'm in the process of redecorating for its "Grand Opening."

I realize being in the wrong supermarket probably doesn't sound exactly dire to you, but you aren't the one buying your father a brisket at a store your mother will somehow know isn't Waldbaum's.

And then, June Bayer isn't your mother.

The woman behind the counter has agreed to go into the freezer to find a brisket for me, since there aren't any in the case. There are packages of pork tenderloin, piles of spare ribs and rolls of sausage, but no briskets.

Warning Number Two, right? I should be so out of here.

But no, I'm still in the same spot when she comes back out, brisketless, her face ashen. She opens her mouth as if she is going to scream, but only a gurgle comes out.

And then she pinballs out from behind the counter, knocking bottles of Peter Luger Steak Sauce to the floor on her way, now hitting the tower of cans at the end of the prepared foods aisle and sending them sprawling, now making her way down the aisle, careening from side to side as she goes.

Finally, from a distance, I hear her shout, "He's deeeeeeaaaad! Joey's deeeeeeaaaad."

My first thought is *You should always trust your gut.*

My second thought is that now, somehow, my mother will know I was in King Kullen. For weeks I will have to hear "What did you expect?" as though whenever you go to King Kullen someone turns up dead. And if the detective investigating the case turns out to be Detective Drew Scoones…well, I'll never hear the end of that from her, either.

She still suspects I murdered the guy who was found dead on my doorstep last Halloween just to get Drew back into my life.

Several people head for the butcher's freezer and I position myself to block them. If there's one thing I've learned from finding people dead—and the guy on my doorstep wasn't the first one—it's that the police get very testy when you mess with their murder scenes.

"You can't go in there until the police get here," I say, stationing myself at the end of the butcher's counter and in front of the Employees Only door, acting as if I'm some sort of authority. "You'll contaminate the evidence if it turns out to be murder."

Shouts and chaos. You'd think I'd know better than to throw the word *murder* around. Cell phones are flipping open and tongues are wagging.

I amend my statement quickly. "Which, of course, it probably isn't. Murder, I mean. People

die all the time, and it's not always in hospitals or
their own beds, or…" I babble when I'm nervous,
and the idea of someone dead on the other side of
the freezer door makes me very nervous.

So does the idea of seeing Drew Scoones
again. Drew and I have this on-again, off-again
sort of thing…that I kind of turned off.

Who knew he'd take it so personally when he
tried to get serious and I responded by saying we
could talk about *us* tomorrow—and then caught
a plane to my parents' condo in Boca the next
day? In July. In the middle of a job.

For some crazy reason, he took that to mean
that I was avoiding him and the subject of *us*.

That was three months ago. I haven't seen him
since.

The manager, who identifies himself and points
to his nameplate in case I don't believe him, says
he has to go into *his cooler*. "Maybe Joey's not
dead," he says. "Maybe he can be saved, and
you're letting him die in there. Did you ever think
of that?"

In fact, I hadn't. But I had thought that the
murderer might try to go back in to make sure
his tracks were covered, so I say that I will go
in and check.

Which means that the manager and I couple up
and go in together while everyone pushes against

the doorway to peer in, erasing any chance of finding clean prints on that Employee Only door.

I expect to find carcasses of dead animals hanging from hooks, and maybe Joey hanging from one, too. I think it's going to be very creepy and I steel myself, only to find a rather benign series of shelves with large slabs of meat laid out carefully on them, along with boxes and boxes marked simply Chicken.

Nothing scary here, unless you count the body of a middle-aged man with graying hair sprawled faceup on the floor. His eyes are wide open and unblinking. His shirt is stiff. His pants are stiff. His body is stiff. And his expression, you should forgive the pun—is frozen. Bill-the-manager crosses himself and stands mute while I pronounce the guy dead in a sort of *happy now?* tone.

"We should not be in here," I say, and he nods his head emphatically and helps me push people out of the doorway just in time to hear the police sirens and see the cop cars pull up outside the big store windows.

Bobbie Lyons, my partner in Teddi Bayer Interior Designs (and also my neighbor, my best friend and my private fashion police), and Mark, our carpenter (and my dogsitter, confidant, and ego booster), rush in from next door. They beat the cops by a half step and shout out my name. People point in my direction.

After all the publicity that followed the unfortunate incident during which I shot my ex-husband, Rio Gallo, and then the subsequent murder of my first client—which I solved, I might add—it seems like the whole world, or at least all of Long Island, knows who I am.

Mark asks if I'm all right. (Did I remember to mention that the man is drop-dead-gorgeous-but-a-decade-too-young-for-me-yet-too-old-for-my-daughter-thank-god?) I don't get a chance to answer him because the police are quickly closing in on the store manager and me.

"The woman—" I begin telling the police. Then I have to pause for the manager to fill in her name, which he does: *Fran.*

I continue. "Right. Fran. Fran went into the freezer to get a brisket. A moment later she came out and screamed that Joey was dead. So I'd say she was the one who discovered the body."

"And you are…?" the cop asks me. It comes out a bit like who do I *think* I am, rather than who am I really?

"An innocent bystander," Bobbie, hair perfect, makeup just right, says, carefully placing her body between the cop and me.

"And she was just leaving," Mark adds. They each take one of my arms.

Fran comes into the inner circle surrounding the cops. In case it isn't obvious from the hairnet and bloodstained white apron with Fran embroidered on it, I explain that she was the butcher who was going for the brisket. Mark and Bobbie take that as a signal that I've done my job and they can now get me out of there. They twist around, with me in the middle, as if we're a Rockettes line, until we are facing away from the butcher counter. They've managed to propel me a few steps toward the exit when disaster—in the form of a Mazda RX7 pulling up at the loading curb—strikes.

Mark's grip on my arm tightens like a vise. "Too late," he says.

Bobbie's expletive is unprintable. "Maybe there's a back door," she suggests, but Mark is right. It's too late.

I've laid my eyes on Detective Scoones. And while my gut is trying to warn me that my heart shouldn't go there, regions farther south are melting at just the sight of him.

"Walk," Bobbie orders me.

And I try to. Really.

Walk, I tell my feet. *Just put one foot in front of the other.*

I can do this because I know, in my heart of

hearts, that if Drew Scoones was still interested in me, he'd have gotten in touch with me after I returned from Boca. And he didn't.

Since he's a detective, Drew doesn't have to wear one of those dark blue Nassau County Police uniforms. Instead, he's got on jeans, a tight-fitting T-shirt and a tweedy sports jacket. If you think that sounds good, you should see him. Chiseled features, cleft chin, brown hair that's naturally a little sandy in the front, a smile that…well, that doesn't matter. He isn't smiling now.

He walks up to me, tucks his sunglasses into his breast pocket and looks me over from head to toe.

"Well, if it isn't Miss Cut and Run," he says. "Aren't you supposed to be somewhere in Florida or something?" He looks at Mark accusingly, as if he was covering for me when he told Drew I was gone.

"Detective Scoones?" one of the uniforms says. "The stiff's in the cooler and the woman who found him is over there." He jerks his head in Fran's direction.

Drew continues to stare at me.

You know how when you were young, your mother always told you to wear clean underwear in case you were in an accident? And how, a little farther on, she told you not to go out in hair rollers because you never knew who you might see—or who might see you? And how now your best friend says she wouldn't be caught dead without makeup and suggests you shouldn't either?

Okay, today, *finally,* in my overalls and Converse sneakers, I get it.

I brush my hair out of my eyes. "Well, I'm back," I say. As if he hasn't known my exact whereabouts. The man is a detective, for heaven's sake. "Been back awhile."

Bobbie has watched the exchange and apparently decided she's given Drew all the time he deserves. "And we've got work to do, so…" she says, grabbing my arm and giving Drew a little two-fingered wave goodbye.

As I back up a foot or two, the store manager sees his chance and places himself in front of Drew, trying to get his attention. Maybe what makes Drew such a good detective is his ability to focus.

Only what he's focusing on is me.

"Phone broken? Carrier pigeon died?" he asks me, taking in Fran, the manager, the meat counter and that Employees Only door, all without taking his eyes off me.

Mark tries to break the spell. "We've got work to do there, you've got work to do here, Scoones," Mark says to him, gesturing toward next door. "So it's back to the alley for us."

Drew's lip twitches. "You working the alley now?" he says.

"If you'd like to follow me," Bill-the-manager, clearly exasperated, says to Drew—who doesn't respond. It's as if waiting for my answer is all he has to do.

So, fine. "You knew I was back," I say.

The man has known my whereabouts every hour of the day for as long as I've known him. And my mother's not the only one who won't buy that he "just happened" to answer this particular call. In fact, I'm willing to bet my children's lunch money that he's taken every call within ten miles of my home since the day I got back.

And now he's gotten lucky.

"*You* could have called *me*," I say.

"You're the one who said *tomorrow* for our talk and then flew the coop, chickie," he says. "I figured the ball was in your court."

"Detective?" the uniform says. "There's something you ought to see in here."

Drew gives me a look that amounts to *in or out?*

He could be talking about the investigation, or about our relationship.

Bobbie tries to steer me away. Mark's fists are balled. Drew waits me out, knowing I won't be able to resist what might be a murder investigation.

Finally he turns and heads for the cooler.

And, like a puppy dog, I follow.

Bobbie grabs the back of my shirt and pulls me to a halt.

"I'm just going to show him something," I say, yanking away.

"Yeah," Bobbie says, pointedly looking at the buttons on my blouse. The two at breast level have popped. "That's what I'm afraid of."

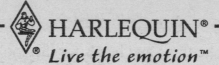

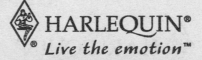

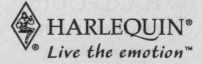